They Survived Darkness

ISBN: 978-1-946886-28-6

Library of Congress Control Number: 2021914779

Cover Design by Bruce Borich

Middle River Press
1498 NE 30th Ct
Oakland Park, FL 33334
www.middleriverpress.com

First Printing

They Survived Darkness

Will they find the light again?

Y.M. Masson

MIDDLE
RIVER
PRESS

To my beloved wife, Lucy, whose support,
advice, and wisdom guided me through the
long process of creating this novel.

Chapter 1

El Boussaid, Algeria

February 1960

Sitting in his jeep in the middle of the large central plaza of El Boussaid, Lieutenant Lucas was talking with Mustapha, the elder of the small village, when he saw a pretty little girl with all-messed-up black hair walk up to where he was parked.

Intrigued, he asked the old man, "Who is this?"

"Her name is Hana," Mustapha said, "She's an orphan. Her dad was killed sometime last year and her mom died a few days ago."

Holding what looked like a much-loved raggedy doll close to her left cheek, Hana approached the jeep, looked up at the lieutenant, and then swiftly lowered her eyes to the ground.

Lieutenant Lucas got out of his seat and looked down at Mustapha, who was only five-foot-two, and pointed at her. "How old is Hana?"

"She must be about five or six. I'm not sure."

The lieutenant frowned. The little one looked up at him again, and turned her eyes back to stare at her bare feet, but she stayed where she stood. The officer bent down and picked her up. Hana showed him a little smile.

"Who's taking care of her now?" Lieutenant Lucas asked Mustapha.

Mustapha shrugged. "Who knows? Some people gave her food, I guess."

The lieutenant glared at him. "Is that all you have to say? You guess some people gave her food? She is a child; she needs to be taken care of. Where does she live?"

Mustapha shrugged again. He had no answer.

The lieutenant looked at Hana's delicate face graced with charming greenish-blue eyes. She was adorable in spite of her chin spotted with patches of dried food remnants and her dirty hands and feet. "You're beautiful, Hana," he said, but she only spoke Arabic and did not understand French. Standing next to Mustapha was Ahmed, an Algerian farmer whose property was on the western edge of the hamlet. He translated for her. Her smile got a little bit warmer.

Mustapha finally spoke. "Look, Lieutenant. She is only a girl, and she's not like us. She even has blue eyes. Nobody wants her."

Lieutenant Lucas could not believe his ears. He understood that in the local culture, boys were more important and esteemed than girls, but he never thought it would go that far.

The lieutenant thought about his own childhood, when at age five, as he fled the Nazi invasion on crowded French country roads, German dive bomber planes strafed him. He survived the machine guns and the bombs and returned with his mom to his home in Paris, only to be reunited with his irritable father who never showed any interest in him. His mother became too busy looking for food to have any time for her son. He had felt very much alone at the time and in the midst of the German occupation of the French capital, he had treasured the support of any adult who paid attention to him. It was nothing like what this poor little girl had suffered, but Hana reminded him of that period of his life. He knew what war was like for children, and he understood her isolation and her fears; he felt for her.

Seeing the scared little girl reminded him of the faces of Isaac and Sarah, the seven-year-old twins who, with ashen faces and trembling lips, were dragged out of Lucas' classroom by armed German soldiers and French police officers. Isaac and Sarah were never seen again. They were Jewish. Like them, Hana was another victim of war and of prejudice.

Lucas had been drafted in the French army to fight the Algerian rebels who fought for regaining control of their country. His job was to protect civilians from the insurgents. He had seen many little boys and girls, French and Algerian, scared, maimed, even killed, in a war they could not understand but which terrified them. Rescuing children in trouble had become his personal crusade.

Before he could say anything to the elder, a loud detonation came from the other end of the plaza. The explosion happened close to one of the white houses that surrounded the public square. The loud noise startled Hana, who frantically clung to the neck of the lieutenant, her head pressed against his, the wrinkled doll on the other side of her face. The hot wind of the blast hit them, and then the acrid smell of powder enveloped the jeep.

"What happened?" The lieutenant asked the soldier who manned the machine gun on the back of the jeep.

"I saw a boy walk toward us at the end of the plaza. I didn't know why or what he held in his hands. I did not want to have to shoot such a young child, but I watched him," the soldier said. "Then the little guy dropped the grenade he carried and it exploded when he tried to pick it up. I guess he had been sent to make it go off near us. A man and a woman took the boy inside the house. He must have died."

His eyebrows up, the lieutenant stared at Mustapha. "What was that all about?"

Mustapha shook his head. "No idea, sir."

Algerian rebels were trying to throw the French out of their country, but Ahmed did not support their side. Because of that, his farm had been attacked a couple of times by his countrymen. The lieutenant's platoon had rescued him both times, also saving his wife Basira and his daughter, little Aisha, who now adored the lieutenant.

Ahmed turned to Mustapha. "Where's Hana going to go now?"

Mustapha opened his arms, the palms of his hands open toward Ahmed. "Who knows?"

Lucas' face reddened. "How can you...?"

Ahmed interrupted him. "What if I take her with me? We'll keep her at the farm. My daughter can use a sister."

Mustapha's face brightened up. "It's okay with me, and nobody else cares."

Ahmed said something in Arabic to the little girl, who smiled. She did not say anything, but she closed her eyes and hugged the lieutenant's neck as strongly as she could.

Irritated at Mustapha, irritated at the villagers who abandoned an innocent child and sent a young boy to kill him and his soldiers, and irritated at the wretched war of insurgency of the Algerian nationalists, Lieutenant Lucas got back in the jeep, took Hana on his lap and told Ahmed, "Hop in. I'll take you home."

He drove away from the depressing square barely shaded by water-deprived palm trees. When they arrived at the farm surrounded by low walls to keep the animals from roaming outside, Ahmed's wife Basira and his daughter Aisha were getting out of their neighbor Tom's truck. Short and of darkish complexion, Basira had hair hidden by a head covering but she wore European type clothes that were more suited to farm work than the Arab long dresses and veils. She did not speak French as well as Ahmed, but she could communicate. Aisha was back from her French language lesson with Tom's wife Francine. The little girl was about five or six, petite, cute, with auburn hair, a gentle smile, and a birth mark on the corner of her left eye. When she saw the lieutenant get out of the jeep carrying Hana, she ran to him, and grabbed his hand. Basira pointed to Hana and asked, "Who is this?"

Ahmed responded, "This is Hana," and he explained to her what happened to the little girl. "I thought we could take her in. She has no place to go, no family, and no one in the village wants her. What do you think?"

Basira smiled. "This little girl sure needs help." She took a quick glance at her and added, "And she needs shoes and a good scrubbing."

They had spoken in French. Aisha was not yet fluent in the language, so Basira had to explain to her in Arabic she was going to have a sister. Hana understood they were talking about her. Then Aisha, who still held the lieutenant's hand, touched Hana's leg and spoke to her. Hana looked at the lieutenant, and wiggled to get down. He put her on the ground and Aisha took her hand. Still clutching her doll, Hana just stood there.

Basira approached Hana and then looked at the little girl more closely. "She must have slept with goats; she's full of goat hair and straw," she said to no one in particular. Then she wrinkled her nose. "And she smells like them too."

The lieutenant had no idea how many days Hana had been on her own, but he guessed then that she had found a way to hide and not be alone. Unlike humans, animals don't care what one looks like, and animal mothers take care of the young ones, sometimes even if they are not theirs. Hana had found refuge with the goats, and saved herself. She had been resourceful when she needed to be. She impressed Lucas by her resilience. She had given him a chance to rescue her, and thanks to Ahmed, he had been able to do it. He loved helping kids.

Tom had observed the scene develop. He watched the six-foot, red-haired lieutenant, the five-foot, dark haired Ahmed and his even short-er wife save a young girl, a total stranger to all of them. He crossed his arms, not believing what he had seen. He looked at Ahmed and Basira.

"You guys are special."

"How could we say no to her?" Basira replied.

Tom nodded, then said to her, "Bring Hana with Aisha to Francine next time you come for her French lesson; she'll teach her too." He turned to Lieutenant Lucas. "You did a good deed, Lieutenant."

Lieutenant Lucas hugged Hana. "You'll be safe here, little one. I'll be back." She did not know what he had said, but returned his smile. He sat back in the jeep. Basira came to pick up Hana, who clung to her neck as she had done with the lieutenant and had another little smile for him when she waved good-bye.

"I have to get back to the war," Lieutenant Lucas said to Ahmed. "Take care of my girls." He nodded to the three adults and left.

The lieutenant had been posted in Mascara, a small town on the lower slopes of the Atlas Mountains of Algeria, a few miles west of El Boussaid. He would run his platoon until he was discharged, maybe for another couple of years; that is if he made it that long.

Chapter 2

Paris

February 1962

Sitting at her desk, a beautiful mahogany Louis the Fifteenth secretaire, Madame de Sèvres, the Comtesse de Berry, a strikingly elegant woman, remembered sitting on the very same chair about a year ago, the day she received the phone call that changed everything. She had put the receiver down, leaned back, and sighed, trying to slow her heart down. Her lawyer had just confirmed to her that she had won her suit against the family of her late husband the Comte de Berry. She had felt an intense sense of accomplishment; she would be able to use their former country residence as she saw fit.

The count, one of the few wealthy survivors of the former French nobility, had been gravely wounded in the late nineteen-forties, at the beginning of the Indochina war when he led his company in the hills of North Laos. He had been nursed back to Paris on a hospital ship, lingered a short time in a military hospital, but did not recover from his wounds. The countess, thirty-four years old at the time, had seen him pass away shortly after his return. After his death, she had inherited their Paris sumptuous residence, the hotel particulier, a mansion, on Boulevard Malesherbes, and the manor in Maligny, north of the town of Chablis in Burgundy.

The Countess enjoyed her social life in the French capital where she could dedicate herself to her favorite causes. She had refined features and graceful hands. She usually wore a hint of Chanel No. 5 perfume, and certainly was no hunter. She hardly visited the country place, and never had any intention or desire to spend much time in the hunting haven hidden in the middle of the vast forest which made up much of the property.

When she had told the Berry family that she intended to use the manor for worthwhile social causes, they absolutely refused. But a few years later, when Charles de Gaulle became the new president of France and escalated the Algerian insurrection into a full-fledged conflict, the countess expected that military casualties would again swell the ranks of those maimed by wars which she felt were unjustified. She thought the Maligny Domain would be a suitable place to be used as a center for rehabilitation for the wounded soldiers who needed help to re-enter civilian life. She believed her husband might still be alive if there had been such a facility at the time of his final days. Again, the aristocrats of the Berry family balked at the idea, and sued her to regain control of the property. That day a year ago, she learned that, after the three-year-long litigation, she had won the legal challenge and retained custody of the domain.

ᴄᴚ

But although she had been pleased with the legal decision, her excitement had not been solely due to winning the legal battle. She had closed her eyes and thought fondly about Raimond, the man she had met a few years after her husband's death, the man she loved but could not marry, the man who had devastated her when he died of cancer. He was a common man, so she could not formalize their relationship lest her and her husband's aristocratic family disinherited her.

Raimond had raised his nephew Lucas because his sister's husband, an angry, selfish man, had little interest in his own son. The countess had gotten close to the young Lucas after Raimond's death. When he became an infantry lieutenant in that useless and costly Algerian war, she had prayed that the young man would not be hurt, but she now knew that if he did, she could help him recover. That made her heart beat faster and her cause even more important. But she could not waste any time.

ᴄᴚ

She had asked her assistant to call the Ministère des Armées and request an appointment with the official in charge of the veterans' affairs, and also called Colonel Dubois, an old friend of her husband with whom she had kept in touch over the years. She had asked the colonel to call her back on an important subject.

Later that February morning, the phone rang again.

"Madame la Comtesse, how nice to hear from you. I trust you are well." The warm, strong, familiar voice filled her ears.

"Indeed, Colonel; I am and I hope you can help me." She told him about her plan for the Maligny property.

"What I am looking for," she told him, "is a retired superior officer who can help me deal with the Veterans' Affairs bureaucracy and make sure they implement my plan. I need someone of high enough rank to have status with the government, someone energetic, not afraid of taking on slow bureaucrats, and who won't be intimidated by high-ranking politicians, or by army brass."

The colonel laughed. "There are indeed quite a few bureaucrats and politicians in that administration, but I have your man. He is retired General de Vangarde. I used to work for him. He might remember your husband. He's quite a guy, and I'm sure he'll be excited by the opportunity. I'll contact him and have him call you."

"I am so grateful. I'm glad you're back from Germany, Colonel; we need good men here to lead the army. I'm afraid that Algerian mess might turn out to be a catastrophe."

"I would not want to be quoted on that, but I agree," the colonel replied. "We've been rushing into this without being prepared, and it's going to cost more lives, actually much too many."

༄

The afternoon of that fateful day, the general had called. After listening to Madame de Sèvres' plan, he exclaimed, "Madame, I am honored that you asked me to help in this most important project. The need for such a facility is dire, but government after government could not find the wherewithal to even begin to investigate the feasibility of establishing an agency to perform that function. May I ask what exactly you want me to help with?"

"I have requested to meet with the Veterans' Affairs leadership. I want them to assign a person to lead the effort and get it done. I would like you to come with me to that meeting, and make sure the plan gets executed."

"I will be happy to do that. It is a subject dear to my heart. I believe any soldier of any rank who fights and sees soldiers injured and killed would want to know such a facility exists. Then they'll know that if they are hurt, not only would they be treated in the military hospital, but also that they would be rehabilitated so they could function as normally as possible."

The countess agreed.

The general continued, "Once the meeting is scheduled, I'm sure I'll know the person who has been selected to work on your project. May I suggest that we meet then and outline a plan for dealing with the government representative."

"Thank you for accepting the challenge. I will contact you as soon as I know anything."

For the following few months, General de Vangarde worked tirelessly with the ministry of the army and the military medical corps. The manor, actually a gigantic hunting lodge which could accommodate up to seventy guests, became a convalescent hospital with patients' bedrooms, medical support labs, and rehabilitation facilities and equipment. Temporary staff housing for the medical personnel had to be secured. That did not prove difficult because the property was not far from good-size towns: fifteen miles from Auxerre, forty from Troyes, and ninety from Dijon, a city with its substantial military infrastructure.

The countess worked out a budget. She contributed her property and its maintenance cost; the administration funded the staffing and the care of the soldiers. The first wounded warriors received treatments there a little over a half-year later. The tall oaks and dark green bushes of the large forest combined with the silence and the sweet smell of the damp moss to make the atmosphere of the facility bucolic and peaceful. It played a significant role in helping the recovering warriors relax and get the most benefits from their re-education treatments. It had become an instant success. Madame de Sèvres had felt wounded warriors needed help. Now it had become available.

On that day of reminiscence in February 1962, sitting at her same secretaire, she had learned that Lucas was to be discharged in a short time. She thanked God that he would not have to be a patient of the facility. Just a few more days, and he would be home safe.

Chapter 3

Paris

March 5, 1962

After fighting Algerian rebels in North Africa for three years, First Lieutenant Lucas stepped out of the train which had pulled into la Gare de Lyon at 6:30 in the morning. He was back in Paris. Wearing the black beret of elite infantry troops and proudly displaying on his chest the hard-earned unit citations his platoon had been awarded, he walked briskly out of the train station onto the Rue de Lyon.

He bought the daily, *Le Figaro*, and went to one of the several cafes surrounding the train station, sat down at a table on the sidewalk terrace, and ordered a croissant and an express, the strong black coffee the locals favored. None of these Parisian staples had he been able to enjoy in a long while. The newspaper listed ads for furnished rentals. He noted a couple of studios in areas he liked and planned to call later to find out more about them. He had to have a place to stay.

He felt good, soaking in the cool and grey March morning, the damp air, and the familiar smell of warm coffee mixed with that of car exhaust fumes. He had made it back home after the long months spent in North Africa. Yet he was not quite comfortable. There he was in Paris, the city he loved where he had spent his childhood, gone to school, had memorable, and not, love encounters, the city where he grew up to be a man. But the passersby and the café's customers looked at him as if he were an oddity, a pariah.

The day before, he had left in Algeria close friends whose lives were in danger, and children he had saved, but could not protect anymore. He had left soldiers he trusted with his life and who entrusted theirs to his leadership. He had also said his good-byes to his superior officers who respected him as much as he did them. The day before, he had left a country where Arabs and Europeans tried to survive the mayhem of what had become a civil war. The French and the Algerians who were on the French side, looked at him as their protector and their friend. They trusted him, and knew he and his soldiers would help them. And he had left little Hana who had made him look at the war from the side of the children. She had made him compassionate toward the young Algerian girls, victims of the war and scorned by the cultural heritage around them. She had captured his heart. She had changed him.

But here in Paris, on a bleak Monday morning, absorbed in their drab existence, folks hurried to work with their head down. Here, General De Gaulle, who had escalated the Algerian conflict four years ago to gain support of the military in his successful bid to run France, had changed his mind. He had decided to surrender Algeria to the Arabs who lived there first. People were confused. Passions ran high between those who embraced the new policy, and those who wanted to keep Algeria French, De Gaulle's chant when he seized power. Lucas had no conviction as to the wisdom of France keeping the former colony as a part of its territory or not. He had been there to do the job he had been drafted for. But he felt that if the general meant to abandon the French families who had lived there over a century, he should not have waited that long to do it. Why waste so many lives? But the general had done it and never apologized for the tens of thousands of casualties among the Algerian people. To justify his late decision, he had distorted and belittled the contribution and the sacrifice of the twenty-six thousand soldiers who gave their lives in that war and the countless ones who went home maimed. For Lucas some of these dead and wounded had names and faces etched in his mind.

Lucas glanced at the paper's headlines. The misleading reports on what was actually happening in Algeria, now that France was on her way out, astonished him. That made him mad. Had the writer been there? Obviously not! He decided to ignore the rag and went to call Nicole, his best friend Thierry's sister whom he looked at as his own sister too.

She picked up the phone right away.

"I hope I didn't wake you. It's Lucas."

She paused for an instant, then, she shouted, "Lucas? Is that you? Where are you?"

"In Paris. I just got off the train."

"Thank God you're alive. Come and see us. I'll wake Thierry up. We can't wait to hug you."

"I'll be there in a half-hour."

 споро

In the metro, Lucas had to ignore the looks of the commuters staring with scorn at the elite officer he had become. He got off at the Raspail station, and still carrying his army canvas bag, walked up the six stories of dark narrow stairs to the apartment Nicole and Thierry shared, two levels above that of their parents, and rang the bell.

Nicole opened the door. He instantly recognized the strange familiar smell he had never been able to identify, but he also saw the shock that jolted her backwards.

Her eyes dilated; her lips trembled. "Lucas?" She mumbled, and stared.

Surprised at her reaction, Lucas managed to say, "Hi Nicole."

Her eyes riveted at him, her face froze. She stuttered.

"You stand so tall…You… look so strong…so tough… You're… tan, and your eyes… your eyes… are so dark; they drill into me. My God, you have changed so much."

Trying to smile, he teased her. "Nicole. It's me, Lucas."

She took his hands in hers. "I know." She caressed the fingers. "And your hands are so rugged! You almost scare me."

Her eyes went up and down, searching for the familiar Lucas she had trouble finding. She shivered, then she drew Lucas to her, and gave him a kiss.

"I'm sorry. I'm confused." She led him into the apartment. "Welcome back. Come in. Can I get you some coffee?"

Lucas's throat went dry. Did he look that bad? But he managed to say, "That'd be great. I may look different because of the past three years, but I'm still the old Lucas."

"You may be, but we need to dress you like the civilian you are now, and put that wonderful smile of yours back on your face. We still have the clothes you left with us when you went to Algeria." She hesitated a second, grinned, and said, "But I'm not sure your old smile is in that box."

❧

Thierry came in. He had not changed one bit, still a baby face and curly brown hair. He stopped and stared at his old friend, his mouth open.

"Lucas?" He managed to say.

"Hi Thierry."

He shook his I-don't-believe-it reaction away and almost whispered, "How's the seasoned infantry leader? It's so nice to see you in one piece. You look... wonderful, healthy, in great shape, and... ominous."

"It's me, no matter who you see." Lucas became more convinced he had really changed.

"It may be, but you look so strong, so powerful, and so full of energy." Thierry suddenly lightened up. He tried to laugh. "I would not want to be on the wrong side of you, or meet you at night in a dark alley."

"I have seen combat month after month, I have become a fighter. I carried a gun every minute of the past three years. I used it on human beings. Good soldiers, nice young men who followed my orders died, or were maimed for life."

"It must have been hard," Thierry ventured to say.

"I have seen terrible harm done to innocent people, even children. But I don't have a gun anymore and never will carry or use one ever again. You two have to help me forget those times. I am still Lucas, or at least want to be him again."

"You will and we'll make sure of it." Nicole replied. "Let's sit and have coffee."

"It'll take some time. I know I can do it with your help. But let's talk about you," Lucas reached for Thierry's wrist. "What's going on in your lives?"

Nicole answered first, "I'm finishing dental school this spring and I'm getting married in June to a professor of mathematics. He teaches at Lycée Condorcet, but he will transfer to the Lycée de Lille in the north of France this September to become the head of the calculus department. I'll work first in my uncle's dental office in Paris near the Madeleine church, then in Lille in the dental office of a friend of my uncle."

Lucas clapped. "That's wonderful news. Congratulations to you, and to?"

"Gilbert is his name."

Lucas raised his cup. "To you and to Gilbert." He turned to Thierry. "What about you?"

"I got discharged last week. My war didn't resemble yours. You were so courageous; you put your life on the line while I sat behind a desk and spent most of my time in Paris or Algiers. I have no concept of what fighting is. I'm ashamed I didn't do my part. I feel terrible."

With a pat on the back, Lucas said, "Don't. You did not miss anything. I wouldn't recommend infantry life to anyone."

Thierry went on. "Anyway, my plan is to go to work in my dad's firm. They manufacture aircraft engine parts. And you? Do you have any plans?"

"I have to re-enter civilian life, forget the infantry and the world of combat. I need to get a job, find a place to live, and maybe meet a woman and start a family. But Nicole told me I had to get rid of my uniform first."

Thierry chuckled. "Are you going to try to stay at your parents'?"

"No I won't. When I left home a year before I went to Algeria after one too many fights with my dad, it was for good. I have not changed my mind, but there have been some developments. My mother has left my father and took my brother with her."

"Did they divorce?" Nicole asked, her hand over her mouth.

"I don't know. She just dropped me a note a couple of months ago to give me the news about her leaving my dad. I'm not sure where she is. I'll have to go to my dad's pharmacy to find out."

They could not catch up on two-and-a-half years of war, but they chatted, remembering old happier times.

"Is Josette happily married to that guy; what was his name? Gérard?" Lucas asked Nicole.

She shook her head. "You remember him. As a matter of fact, she is not. Your former lover did not marry Gérard."

Lucas raised his eyebrows "What happened? I thought that was her plan."

"He signed up for a residency at a hospital in Nantes in the west of France, without consulting her. Incensed, she told him she was shocked he had not asked her if she would agree to move and go work in a provincial city. She had not even finished medical school yet. He replied that she did not need to work because she would stay home and raise their children."

Lucas laughed. "Really? I bet she loved that."

Nicole shrugged. "You know Josette; she was beside herself. She exploded, called the wedding off, and stormed out of the relationship. That was two years ago."

"I didn't know Gérard well, but I'm surprised he thought Josette would go along with not practicing her pediatric career that everyone knew was her passion," Lucas commented. "What is she doing now?"

"She lives in Paris, in her same apartment. She works in a hospital nearby. She's not finished with her residency. I don't know what her plans are after that. Actually, she spent a semester in a London clinic as an exchange student and enjoyed it a lot."

Nicole pondered for a moment and with a sly smile added, "I don't believe she's seeing anybody."

Lucas put his hand on his chin. "Maybe I'll give her a call. What do you think?"

Nicole peered at Lucas, squinting her eyes, then she said, "I have a better idea. You're the only guy from our group of friends who fought in North Africa for so long. We'll have a party to celebrate your service and your return; you'll meet my fiancé Gilbert and I'll invite Josette. We need to reset your mind."

"Thanks," he nodded and then got up. "I better go see about the rentals I have found in the paper. I need a place to live. Can I leave my bag here for the day?"

"Sure," Nicole nodded, "As long as you need, Lucas. It was good to see you."

✂

Later that morning, Lucas rented a furnished studio near the opera and was told he could take possession later that day. A trip to the bank to secure the money for the rent and a visit back to Nicole to get his stuff got him a place for the night and for the foreseeable future. The next few days were busy getting settled. He stopped by the Vincennes fort, where he had spent his first day in uniform months ago. There, he signed his final discharge papers, hoping that by doing so he'd close the war chapter of his life. But he knew that the signing did not erase the heavy baggage of memories of his Algerian episode. It might take a while for them to disappear from his soul.

Chapter 4

Paris

March 8

Curious to find out what had happened between his mother and his father, Lucas went to his dad's pharmacy. His father saw him walk in and did a double take. With no word of welcome, or greeting — not that any were expected — he snapped, "Are you already discharged from the army?"

What does he mean, 'already'? Three years not long enough? Lucas's chest tightened. I really can't stand him.

"Yes, I'm a civilian. I received a letter from Mom saying she had left you. Is that true?"

"Yes. She took your brother with her and she's now living with my friend Fernand." He shrugged, and blew air from the side of his mouth. He had always done that. He wanted us to believe it meant *I don't care* but I knew better. It meant *I am annoyed.* "They apparently had been lovers for years," he added. Another blow came out of his mouth. He was really annoyed!

"Do you know where they are now?" Lucas asked him.

"No I don't. I can give you her lawyer's phone number if you'd like."

"That'd be great. But where do you live, now?"

"Same old apartment. When your mom left, my sister, your Aunt Madeleine, moved in to take care of me."

"So you're well looked after of, I see. Well, I'll be seeing you. I'll try to talk to Mom."

With these empty words, Lucas left him. His dad did not look utterly distraught about his wife leaving him. His pride was hurt, but he should not have been surprised, not with the way he had treated her over the years. Lucas decided to go see his aunt at the old apartment where he used to live to get the real scoop. He called her to make sure she could see him. Glad to hear from him, she agreed.

❧

Lucas walked up the dark and damp staircase he ran up and down a million times when he was a kid, and rang the bell. His Aunt Madeleine opened the door and greeted him warmly. "It's good to see you back from the war. You look great. Come in. You are okay, aren't you?"

Lucas entered the apartment where he lived until he was twenty-one. It still smelled musty.

"Yes, I am fine," Lucas replied. "I have to re-adjust to normal life, whatever that is." Then he asked her, "What happened? Dad told me that Mom and my brother now live with his friend Fernand?"

"It all came out after your grandfather's death. She inherited quite a bit of money and therefore could afford to live without your dad. The legal proceedings were complicated because although your uncle died a couple of years before, his money and assets were mixed up with your granddad's, and his estate had not been settled because her sister contested that will. But it's all over and done now."

"When did she leave him?"

"A few months ago. But you must call her lawyer. I believe your uncle left you some money. It's part of the settlement."

"Thanks. Do you know how I can get in touch with my mom?"

"I have her phone number. They are still at Fernand's place."

"What about Fernand's wife? Aunt Odette, I called her."

"I don't know where she is."

"She was such a lovely person. That's too bad."

"Also," Aunt Madeleine chuckled. "I believe your mom plans to move to the south of France."

"Really? The south of France? Mom is leaving Paris?" Lucas was stunned. "That's unbelievable."

"That's what I heard, but also, your dad is going to sell his business and move back to Troyes where we were born and where our brother lives. I'll move there too."

All that amounted to a lot to absorb. Lucas thanked her and went home to digest the news.

✌

Lucas went out and had dinner in a local restaurant near his new studio. The owner greeted him warmly, and asked if he was just back from Algeria.

A bit defensive, Lucas stared at him. "What makes you think that?"

"You're tan, you look fit, and you stand and sit like a military man."

"Good guess. Actually I got back a couple of days ago."

His face lit up. "I knew it. Where were you?"

"The Atlas Mountains and the Northern Sahara."

"That's beautiful country, there," he reminisced, "Colors, endless horizons, hot as hell. I used to have a restaurant in Sidi Bel Abbès a few years ago."

"That was my last stop before I left the country. The city is a mess these days: bombs, kidnappings, riots, etc."

"What a shame. What branch of the army were you in?"

"Special Forces Lieutenant, infantry. I feel like I patrolled the whole Atlas Range on foot, and you're right. It's a beautiful place. A shame what happened to it with the war."

Lucas enjoyed his meal and felt good. He had finally met a Parisian who respected what he did in North Africa.

✌

But being alone in his new home that night proved to be difficult for Lucas. He did not quite know what to do with himself. He felt nostalgic about the country he just left and would never see again. Then he thought of Ahmed, of his wife Basira, their daughter Aisha, and mostly, little Hana. He had felt something special for Hana when he took her in his arms the day he found her, recently orphaned, with no one to go to. Since the day she had been traumatized by the loss of her parents, she had tried to adjust to the loving care of Ahmed and Basira, but seemed to always be scared and sad.

The bond between him and the little girl had become stronger over the months. Anytime he returned from a routine patrol, he had his driver stop the jeep at Ahmed's farm so he could hug Hana. Tom's wife, Francine, taught her, and Aisha, French and how to read. Hana became more fluent every time he stopped by. She loved to talk to him in her new language and he adored her. She was inside the farm most times when Lucas came. He suspected she was afraid of the villagers and was hiding. She loved it when he took her in his arms and she put her head on his neck. Almost every time she saw him, she thanked him for having taken her out of the village.

He missed them all, and felt like he had abandoned them. His soldiers were there with another lieutenant to protect them, but what would happen when the troops left the country? That worried him, but tonight, he decided he did not want to think any more about the war traumas that encumbered his mind. He left the apartment and walked aimlessly for a while, and tried to focus on Josette. Thinking of her helped his mood. He looked forward to seeing her again. Maybe she could be the key to his healing. He finally went home and fell asleep with many questions on his mind about who he would turn out to be. He had found out he could no longer be the Lucas who left Paris for Algeria, and was not anymore the soldier who fought there.

✿

The next morning, he called his mom and told her he was back from Algeria. Then he asked her, "Are you divorced from Dad?"

She hesitated and then blurted out, "The judgment is not final but it'll be in a couple of weeks."

"Wow. That's something. I'm assuming you are happy. Right?"

She replied with joy in her voice, "Indeed. Fernand and I have been seeing each other for a long time."

Lucas nodded to himself. "I remember you going to see him for physical training a couple of times a week during the German occupation. You were always cheerful when you returned from your visits, but I had no understanding at that time of the real purpose of these outings. But it made sense later."

There was a long silence, then she murmured, "Amazing. And you never said anything. Also, you need to know that Fernand is the father of your brother."

Lucas laughed. "I had figured that out too. Is my brother with you?"

"Yes, sort of. He has been drafted and will be going for basic training in three weeks."

"The good news is that he'll go to Germany, and he won't have to go to Algeria now that the war is over." Lucas stated.

Lucas' mother replied, "He would not have to go to North Africa because you were there. They don't send two brothers to the same war."

Lucas replied. "That does not always work. But Germany won't be a bad posting. Anyway, I'm happy for you. Dad was awful to you, as he was to me. I'm glad you're rid of him."

"I had been longing for that for a long time. But are you back from the military?"

"Yes, I am. Could I come and say hello?"

"Sure. You know Fernand's place, Rue de Bucharest."

"I'll be there after lunch if that works."

"I'll see you then," she hung up the phone.

Not having seen her in over three years, Lucas wondered if he would feel any emotion seeing her in person, but she just gave him her usual peck on the cheek, and they commented on how good they both looked. They sat in the living room and then he asked her how all the changes happened.

She fidgeted on her chair. "Your granddad and I had plotted that before he passed away, about four years ago. He knew I would be able to leave your dad once I inherited his money, and he encouraged me to do so. He also is the one who made sure you got your uncle's assets because he knew that was what Uncle Raimond wanted. He also added some of his own money to what your uncle left you because he thought highly of you. I'm not sure how much there is, but the lawyer will tell you. I believe it's quite a bit."

"Granddad was always nice to me," he said to her as he stood up. "And thank you for telling me what happened."

Then Lucas' mom seemed to look at him for the first time. "You look to be in great shape. Back from the war? Are you okay?"

"Yes, I am. All I need to do is to figure out what's next for me. I understand you are moving to the south of France."

"That's the plan. Fernand has an opportunity to run an athletic training facility in Antibes. The move is imminent."

"Great! Here's my phone number and my address. Let me know when you have settled. I might drop in some day."

She opened her arms. "I guess I paid more attention to your brother than to you. I am sorry." She offered a timid smile.

"Not to worry. I knew you were struggling with dad. Say hello to Fernand, and good luck with the move."

With that, the conversation was over. They never had a close and warm relationship.

The next day, he called his mom's lawyer who confirmed that he had indeed been awarded a substantial inheritance. When he met the lawyer, Lucas found out about the astounding amount of money that had been set aside for him. He was not sure how to deal with it, but he realized that he was financially secure for a while. He did not have to rush and get a job.

❧

Most importantly, Lucas had to stop at Madame de Sèvres' residence. She was the beautiful woman his uncle had a relationship with at the time he died. After his uncle's death, Lucas had become close to her. She wrote to him regularly while he fought in Algeria, and helped with her support and encouragement.

He went to pay her a visit.

He went through the huge double-door street entrance, the porte cochère, and crossed the large courtyard to the steps leading up to the doorway to the mansion. He rang the bell. The butler, who had been very protective of the countess when Lucas first came to see her, opened the door and welcomed him warmly. "Monsieur Lucas," he opened his arms and hugged him in a very plebeian way, shunning the usual aloofness his aristocrat masters expected of him, "You are back from the war. It is comforting to have you back visiting. I'll get Madame right away."

He came back a few minutes later to take Lucas to her parlor.

Lucas loved the exquisitely furnished and decorated room with its floor-to-ceiling windows, pastel drapes, and chair coverings. He found the countess as beautiful as he remembered her: trim, well groomed, eloquent eyes, a welcoming smile, and a regal posture. A touch of grey in her hair, and as usual dressed to the nines, still wearing that hint of the same perfume he had learned to love. She fussed over having him back. They sat and the countess offered him tea.

He shook his head. "I'm fine, thank you."

"After all the battles you were in, the hero you are is back in one piece. Your Uncle Raimond would have been proud of you. From what you wrote to me, I know you earned even more decorations than he did."

"Well, the decorations I have are those my platoon earned."

She smiled. "You are so modest. I have enough officers in my family to know that the platoon's awards are that of the platoon leader. Anyway, I am proud of you. Now how are you? Do you have plans? Do you know where you'll work?"

"Not yet. I just got back yesterday."

"Your uncle and I often talked about you, even before I knew you; you were so important to him. He had told me that when you started looking for a job, he would help you find the one which would give you the best prospect for career growth. I'm not him, but I know many executives and I could help you."

Lucas wrinkled his nose. "To be frank, I'm not quite ready for work yet. I need to settle back down in civilian life. I'm no longer in the military, but my mind seems to still be there. But I appreciate your offer, and I will welcome your guidance when I enter the job market."

"Anytime, Lucas. And you know that if you need financial help, I am here for that too."

"Thank you, but you probably know that Uncle Raimond left me his money so I am quite set for the time being."

"Take your time, Lucas. There's nothing you have to do right away. I know from our letters that, although not harmed by bullets or shrapnel, you have suffered psychological trauma that you have to heal. That process, whichever it will be, will lead you into the life that you will feel comfortable to live. Just relax and be patient."

As in her letters, her well-thought-out advice had always helped Lucas get through tough moments in his life. Today had proved to be the same.

Chapter 5

Paris

March 10

Lucas felt a bit awkward at Nicole's party. He enjoyed being with his friends he knew so well, but unlike him they had not changed at all since they had graduated from engineering school. Some had never left Paris during the Algerian war; a couple served in the artillery, but never fired a salvo; one served in the Air Force; most sat behind military desks in France or in the northern cities of Algeria. They all knew the conflict from a spectator's point of view. They had not participated in the fight itself. They were never shot at, nor did they ever aim a rifle at a human being. None ever witnessed the atrocities and the killings, let alone the suffering of innocent children who were maimed, orphaned, or abused. But the occasion gave him a good opportunity to initiate his healing process.

One of Lucas' closest friend asked him, "How was the fighting, old buddy?"

Looking at his feet, Lucas responded, "It was rough, I had casualties, young guys maimed, a few killed."

"But how was it to fight?"

Lucas' face reddened. "Combat is impossible to explain." He realized it was an abrupt answer, and went on, "And for sure it cannot be talked about in a peaceful environment with a glass of wine in one's hand. I'm sorry."

Another guy joined them and said, "Were you hurt?"

"Minor injuries. Listen, I don't really want to talk about Algeria if you don't mind."

"Sorry. We look at you as our hero."

"Well, I'm no such thing. I did the job, the dirty job."

But his pal would not let go. "One last question. Did you fire your weapon often?"

Lucas looked at his friends in amazement. "Are you for real? I carried a rifle or a submachine gun every minute of the day, and I slept with it for months."

"Did you see any civilians hurt?"

"Yes. Children too."

Lucas looked up and saw Josette come in. His heart skipped a few beats when he saw her after over three years, as beautiful as ever, almost as tall as him, flowing blond hair, and dark eyes that could mesmerize, the biggest smile, and the most contagious laugh.

"Excuse me," he told his friends, and went to greet Josette.

The two of them hugged, and could not stop talking. So much had happened to both in the past years.

"Nicole told me you were a changed man, stronger and tougher than the nice, kind, smiling young man I was in love with. I can see she's right," she said.

"The truth is, I'm the same man, maybe physically more fit, and more confident in my ability to survive anything, but Nicole is right, I am changed inside, and I need to heal myself. But you have had a big change yourself, haven't you?"

"I did. Gérard showed himself to be who he really was. Fortunately he did it in time to stop me from making a big mistake." She shrugged, "An immature man. Our marriage would not have worked."

They went to get a glass of wine, then Josette looked at him with a puzzled look. "I'm curious. You said you have to heal yourself. What do you plan to do?"

"To be frank, I'm not sure. When I left Algeria, my captain told me I might have a problem re-adjusting to civilian life."

"Did he give you any idea on how to do it?"

"Not really. He told me to build on my strength, be proud of my service to my country, and keep my head high, regardless of what people might say about the war. He said that whatever I would do, I had to continue to lead and help people because it would make me focus on others instead of myself. He added that he knew that being in the mountains slowed my mind down between combat episodes, and said I should trust Mother Nature to help me with further healing."

Josette tilted her head. Her beautiful eyes grew even darker than usual and shot through Lucas' soul. The power of her gaze shook him up. "I'd love to help you, but this is not a plan," she said.

One never had to think twice about what Josette meant. She always spoke her mind, but it pleased him to hear that she would help him. She was right; Lucas did not even have an idea or a direction for a real healing plan. "That's true, Josette, I'm still confused. I will keep in touch and let you know how I'm doing. It's so nice to see you again. We have both grown up fast in different ways without really meaning to become who we are today. Actually we have both survived some form of trauma, and it warms my heart to see that you are doing well."

"It is nice to see you too. Give me a hug. I still think you're a great guy."

The hug went all the way to Lucas's heart. It gave him a jolt.

⁂

Over the next days, Lucas kept thinking about Josette and wondered whether it would be wise to call her. He did not remember her number, so he called Nicole to get it, thinking she could tell him if she thought it would be a good idea for him to call Josette.

Nicole was studying at home so she answered right away.

"I'm so glad you called," she said. "Josette is trying to get hold of you, and she does not have your number, and neither do I."

Lucas chuckled. "How strange, I wanted to call Josette, but I don't have her number, that's why I'm calling you."

Nicole laughed. "Okay, let's update our directories."

Lucas gave Nicole his number, and got Josette's.

"Do you know why Josette wants to talk to me?"

"No, I don't," Nicole said after a pause, "but she seemed quite anxious."

"I'll call her."

✒

Lucas was eager to talk to Josette. It had been a nice surprise to be with her this weekend.

"Hi, Josette, it's Lucas. Nicole told me you were trying to reach me."

"I'm so glad you called. After talking to you at Nicole's party, I realized that I'd like to know more about who you have become. I saw you're a lot stronger than before the war, and at the same time, I sensed you have been traumatized by your time in the infantry, and that in some way you are also a little fragile."

"You are very perceptive. These long months have been difficult, and I am struggling to regain my pre-war self."

"Would you like to talk more about it? I have a lecture I'm attending tonight, but I have all day free tomorrow."

"I'd love to, Josette. Let's have lunch and go to a park in the afternoon. I'll pick you up at your place at noon."

"That would be great. You remember where I live?"

"What do you think?" He chuckled. "55 Rue de Rennes, correct?"

"Of course. See you tomorrow."

✒

Josette greeted him at the door with a big warm hug. "How are you?" she asked. "I worry about you."

"I'm okay. I just need to put the last years behind me."

She looked at him, let her eyes smile, shook her head, and replied. "It's not as easy as you pretend to make it, and you know it. Let's go have lunch. There is that new place not far from here. It's nice and quiet, even at lunch time."

They were seated on the terrace, protected from the street by boxes of evergreen. It was peaceful and pleasant.

"Tell me about your life with and without Gérard," He said to her, "I'm curious, and concerned that you might be sad."

She shrugged. "No. I'm not any more. First, he made me mad as hell, and then it hit me that there would not be a Gérard in my life, and that made me sad. Now it's really behind me. He was the wrong guy for me. But other things happened that you need to know. You never met my parents because they lived in Germany at the time we were together, but my mom — you know she was British by birth — died in a car accident shortly after you left for Algeria. Although we were not really close, I missed her. I could no longer talk to her. My dad, who is now a full colonel, was very distraught, but he is okay now. Actually, he's now posted in Paris. We see each other more frequently now. He also has a new friend, Marlene, so he's not alone."

"What an awful three years. How are you doing now?"

"I'm fine. You know me; I am strong and I look at the bright side of life. I enjoy my residency, and I also got some extra training in other medical schools, some outside the country. I enjoyed that."

"What do you do when you're not at the hospital?" Lucas asked.

"I am also studying American literature. It is not very well understood in this part of the world, and I started writing a thesis about the nineteenth-century most influential writers in the United States. That keeps me busy. But enough about me."

She put her hand on his. "I worry about you, Luke. Is it okay if I call you Luke with the English pronunciation like I used to?"

Lucas smiled and reached out to put his other hand on hers. "Yes, I remember you did and I liked it. I still do."

"Okay, Luke. How are you, really?

"Confused might be an honest answer. For many months, I ran an infantry platoon of forty-five men. They were replaced at the end of their tour, but I also had many casualties, some killed, others wounded who were evacuated and I never saw again. I led them in battle and for some reason, I was never badly hurt. I felt guilty."

"Why guilty?" She interrupted Lucas. "You did nothing wrong."

"True, but I survived three years and during that time many of my men did not, or were wounded, some badly."

"I understand that to be some sort of trauma. Go ahead."

Lucas bent his head on the side. "I grew angrier at the rebels we fought, at the useless war, and at myself. Actually, I am still angry. I had a great captain whom I worked with daily all those months, and I had a close relationship with the colonel in charge of the regiment. Somehow I did good work in several operations and he and the captain trusted me. They assigned a lot of patrols and search-and-destroy missions to my platoon because they knew we would deliver. We ended up in many firefights, hence my casualties."

"What were the names of your captain and colonel? My dad might know them."

"Captain Dufour and Colonel de Castre. The colonel has been recently promoted to teach at Saint Cyr, the French military academy."

The waiter brought the dishes they had ordered and Lucas raised his glass of wine. "Bon appétit, Josette."

"Bon appétit and best of luck to you. I think you need some." She smiled.

After a while, Josette asked, "Do you have any idea what you want to do now that you're through with the military?"

"Only vaguely. I plan to meet with my alumni association of the engineering school and ask for openings in international companies. I might want to live overseas for a while. I'm still mad at the French leadership for having started, and then abandoned a war that killed so many. To me it's not just a number of victims; it's the long list of the soldiers I lost, the ones who were killed or injured in combat in this useless war. It's the same with the civilians, mainly the children who are now dead, or were maimed. These are memories I'm not sure I will be able to erase."

"I have spent time in foreign medical schools and enjoyed being abroad," Josette said, "So I understand your desire to go out of the country. But you are alone without a family to be with. Do you have any close friends?"

"I have Thierry and Nicole," he replied, then paused. "And I have you... don't I?" Lucas's heart stopped, waiting for her reply.

She did not hesitate. "Definitely."

His heart restarted at high speed.

Their eyes locked, an unblinking stare frozen for several long drawn-out seconds. Then she added, "And I will help you get back on your feet. It's a promise."

Lucas sensed a surge of blood go to his head and felt very warm all of a sudden.

After lunch, they went for a stroll in the Jardins du Luxembourg. In the quiet early afternoon, they stopped and sat by a playground where young kids who were not attending school yet went down slides, enjoyed rides on the free swings, and ran around playing tag.

"This is so peaceful. It's good for me to see beautiful trees, flashy flowers, and children at play and happy. Part of the nightmares I have…"

Josette cut in. "You have nightmares? Because of the war?"

"Oh yes. Different kinds of dreams: noise, explosions, screams, mayhem, or atrocities. Children are so often innocent victims of war. I have seen many children killed, some slaughtered, others shot, orphaned, terrified, or in utter despair. There were a few kids I protected whenever I could. It was so rewarding and yet so hard to see the trust they put in me. They are still in harm's way now."

"I see how much you need to heal. You can't berate yourself about the past. You have to look forward. Any child in particular on your mind?"

Lucas told Josette about Aisha. "I tried to stop by and see her whenever I drove or patrolled not far from the farm. My soldiers knew the routine and became quite friendly with her parents, Basira and Ahmed who worked the farm they owned. Aisha always ran to me shouting, 'Lieutenant Lucas!'"

"That's cute. Any other child you can remember?"

"Oh, yes. Let's not talk now about the many who did not survive, but there is Hana, my very special Hana."

He told Josette about her being orphaned and abandoned, and about the grenade incident. When he stopped, she frowned and asked him, "What did you do with Hana when you found out her parents were gone?"

He told her about Ahmed and Basira taking Hana in. Josette, her eyebrows raised, the hint of a smile on her face said, "So, what happened next?"

"After speaking with Mustapha, who he knew well, Ahmed decided that Hana could not be safe in the village, so he decided to keep her for good. Ahmed and Basira have been taking care of her ever since. I stopped as often as I could to see her. Francine, a friend of Ahmed, taught Hana and Aisha French. So we were able to talk."

Josette shook her head. "It's horrible what these kids have to go through."

They got up and started to walk down one of the shady footpaths.

Josette stopped and faced Lucas. "What you said earlier about children resonated with me. You knew I studied medicine to become a pediatrician. Well, I have evolved from that. For the past two years, I have been working on a special aspect of child care. I have opted to specialize in trauma in children: trauma from accidents, from disease, from mistreatment at home, and the most prevalent of all, trauma from war. That last one is what you have been talking about."

Surprised, he said, "That is a subject close to my heart. I see now why you called my guilt feelings trauma. What does specialize mean?"

"It means certification in treating children trauma cases. That is twofold: first the verification that there is a trauma and the diagnosis of what the trauma is and how it affects the child. It can be purely psychological, resulting from fears or environmental constraints, but also physical, causing flaws in the child's development, usually behavioral."

"I think I have seen that in some of the kids I saw hurt."

"Undoubtedly, but the certification goes further. The second part addresses how to treat the children and how to mitigate or suppress the harm they suffer, and potentially heal them, or at least minimize the long-term effect of the trauma. Science is in its first steps of this study area today. I'll be one of the first doctors to be certified in that new specialty."

They resumed their walk.

Intrigued, Lucas asked, "What made you leave pediatrics to immerse yourself in this new branch of medicine?"

Josette's face grew somber. "One day in the pediatrics emergency room, the orderlies brought in a young girl, maybe seven or eight. She had bruises on her face and on her body and also a broken arm. I worked on her right away and set her arm in a cast. She never said a word."

"Was she not in pain?" Lucas asked.

"No doubt, but not a peep out of her. Then I asked her how her injuries happened. She told me she fell."

"But she had bruises," Lucas said.

"She said she fell on a bush. I looked at her and asked her what her name was. She said Christine. So I said to her as gently as I could, 'Christine, tell me the truth.' In a way she did. She said, 'I can't. My father said he would kill me if I told anybody.' She looked absolutely terrified."

"Did you call the police?"

"No, the father was just outside of where we were. I was afraid of a confrontation. So I called one of the social workers. She talked to Christine and found out where she went to school. She talked to the head of the school and told them what happened. The school people knew she had been beaten before, so they decided that the next time Christine showed up in school hurt, they would call the police and have them and a social worker go to her home, arrest the father and whisk her away to a temporary safe place."

"What happened?"

"I don't know, Luke. I called the school and they would not tell me. I was not part of her family. But I felt bad. I could not think of anything that would help her and I kept thinking about the little girl and her daily traumatic life. Even if there was a way to get her in the hospital, there was no specialist trained to handle that type of psychological trauma."

"So that's why you changed your specialty?"

"Yes. And I also read some Ralph Waldo Emerson essays as part of my American literature study."

Lucas stopped and looked at her. "Who is he?"

"He is an American writer and philosopher of the nineteenth century. He wrote one sentence which changed the vision of life I had for myself. He said: *To know even one life has breathed easier because you have lived, this is to have succeeded.* I wanted to make Christine breathe easier, but I could not. I did not know how. There are children hurt by parents and by wars all over the world. I decided I would help them."

They went on with their walk. Josette's concern for and dedication to children moved Lucas. "That's wonderful. I like that saying from Emerson. I feel that I have done some of that too, although so much more should be done." He felt blood rush to his face. "I am touched by your compassion. What will you actually be doing?"

She continued. "I plan to formulate protocols and develop techniques to treat the different sort of traumas that have been identified, and find a way to treat the children who are affected." Josette looked at him tenderly."Maybe we can find out if Aisha and Hana need help."

"That would be special. I'd like to know more about your work."

She nodded vigorously. "Sure thing. This field of medicine is new. There are teams in various countries working on elaborate protocols to address the problem. I'm working with doctors and scientists in England and in the United States. There are others in Germany, even Russia and some of the Arab countries." And then she added, "You obviously have a tender spot for children. Do you think you would want a family, with kids of your own?"

"Absolutely. Three kids."

She laughed. "Not two or four?"

"No, three. So it's two against one when they fight, hopefully not always the same two. I'll teach them about Mother Nature, her mountains, her oceans, her deserts, trees, flowers, animals. I'll show them the night starry sky, the sunsets and the sunrises. I'll share with them the beauty of the wilderness, and tell them to look at rain as water from heaven; we will spend nights outside at peace with the world."

"Wow! That's sounds nice," Josette whispered. "When did you become so involved with nature?"

"The truth is that I spent many a day and many a night in the mountains and in the desert, chasing rebels, or hoping to find some. Thank God I did not have to fight every time, and often I ended up walking, inhaling the dry air, looking at the sun and observing the many changes of the gold, orange, and red colors of the desert, from sunrise to sunset, and staring at the moon and the stars, from sunset to sunrise. I observed the local fauna and the minimal flora."

"Fauna? What kind of animals?"

"I saw rabbits, hares, snakes, and scorpions come out in the cool of the night and go about their endless search for the food that would sustain them for another day."

"Snakes, scorpions? How awful!"

"Not really, they are part of nature; they let you be if you let them do their thing. Many a day and many a night I was part of that nature, I learned about it. You were with me when the only nature I knew could be found in the parks of the city of Paris; but there in Algeria, I discovered the Atlas Mountain Range, the Sahara Desert, and their sparse vegetation and few animals. Mother Nature helped me keep my sanity; I owe her, and I will respect her for the rest of my life."

"How beautiful! I think I want to be part of your nature too."

Her words gave Lucas a little bit of a shock. Did she really mean what she said? So he gently said to her, "I'll be honest with you. There is a side of me who thinks I want to start over with you, who wants to fall in love again, have three children."

Josette interrupted. "Three kids? You said that before; you mean it, don't you?"

"Yes, I do."

"Who would take care of the kids?" Josette asked and smiled.

"Both of us. But we'll be busy, we'll have someone help, and we'll chip in as much as we can. It'll be fun for all of us."

Josette got teary. "It sounds wonderful."

"And I'll take all of you to meet Mother Nature every day we can. We'll experience the smell of the forests, listen to the murmur of the streams, feast on the beautiful colors of the sunrise, the sunset, and any time during the day or the night, learn from the animals, taste the wild berries, and live a full life."

"That sounds nice, but what is the other side about?"

"I'm afraid of my memories, afraid of the anger that is hiding in me, of the guilt I can't seem to suppress, and I'm afraid of bringing gloom into the life of whoever shares hers with me."

"But you're so strong."

"I am, and I know how to fight; I can and will protect those I love from anybody and any threat, but the violent skills that I learned to use for months are buried deep in me; I hope I can and will control them, but I don't know if I will always be able to. The truth is I fear no one but myself. I need time to heal that part of me."

"My turn to be honest too. You have guessed that seeing you again brought back to me our happy time together. Listening to you today rekindled the deep love I had for you when we decided to go our separate ways because you were going to war in the infantry and thought you might not come back."

"I remember that time well." Lucas grew pensive and looked at the ground.

"Well now, you are back, in one piece and in a way I am, too," Josette said softly. "I don't know where we really stand and whether there are three kids in our future, but I know I am not ready to walk away from you."

"That's music to my ears, Josette."

"You take the time you need to heal and I will be with you all the way. I want to be part of your healing. Whatever you need me to do to help, I will."

"You touched my heart. I welcome your help, and I promise I won't walk away from you either. I guess we must let some time go by so I can slowly readjust to a normal life."

"We will. We have all the time in the world."

"I will curb my anger and eliminate my nightmares. I don't want to be depressed, I want to be normal — whatever that means."

Josette's eyes became misty. Lucas took her hands in his, and added, "And I will succeed."

The long kiss that followed brought back to him the memories of the soft skin of her cheeks, the sweet taste of her lips, and the warmth of her body, all of which he used to crave years ago. He hoped it was an omen of what lay in front of them.

When they both came back to their senses, she said, "I thought of a first step for my helping you. I would like you to meet my dad. He is a career officer, has been through many tours of duty, experienced all sorts of hardships, and faced all kinds of danger. He may have some ideas for you. Would you like to do that?"

"I'd be delighted to meet your dad, and if he can help, I'd be eternally grateful."

"Okay. Take me home; I'll talk to him, and I'll let you know what he says."

On the way to her apartment, she told him that Emerson believed in the divinity of Nature. "I think you do too. You call her Mother Nature like if she were a goddess."

"You're right. Actually I sensed she was a goddess because of the way she guided my mind back to sanity." They talked about other authors from American literature she had been reading. Lucas did not know any of them; he only read English novels when he spent his summers in England in the fifties.

Chapter 6

El Boussaid

March 15

Basira was ready for the short walk that would bring Aisha and Hana to Tom's ranch for their lesson with Francine, but Ahmed said to her, "Take the truck and drive them, it'd be safer."

Basira did not like to drive and replied, "Why? It's not far and it's a nice morning."

"I've seen men I don't know in the area lately. I'm not sure what it's all about. Algeria is not safe these days. Better watch out."

So, the three of them drove away.

A few minutes after they left, a group of armed men entered Ahmed's property. Two of them asked Ahmed to go into the house with them; the others took position outside.

Red in the face, his jaw clenched, Ahmed stared at the two intruders. "What is this all about?" He shouted at them.

"We're soldiers from the Front de Liberation National, the new regime in Algeria. We're here on government orders," the lead man responded.

"Do you have papers? Identification? Written orders?" Ahmed asked.

The man showed him a wrinkled card from the FLN with the stamp of the leadership of the rebellion against the French.

"What are you here for?"

The man said, "Your sons have been conscripted into the local FLN regiment."

Ahmed stood up as tall as he could make himself, his chin up and said, "There'll be no such thing. My sons are sixteen and fourteen. They can't be soldiers."

"It is not for you to say," the man warned him, "They have to be ready to come with us in an hour. We will wait by the gate so nobody tries to leave."

"I won't let them go," Ahmed shouted. "Get out of my house."

"Careful. Better think it over." He glared at Ahmed. "We can take you too," the lead man said; then he and his assistant rejoined the others outside. Ahmed went to get the two boys, who looked shaken. They had listened to the exchange between Ahmed and the FLN men.

"You heard what they said. I'm going to try to chase them, but in case they still take you away, obey their orders so they won't harm you."

"How long are we supposed to stay with them?" The older boy said.

"I have no idea, but if you can escape, or if you are released, go to Mustapha in the village, he will know where we are and if it's safe for you to go home."

Then Ahmed went to retrieve his rifle and walked outside. When he saw the group of men, he pointed the gun at them and shouted out, "Get out of here before I shoot you."

The head man moved toward Ahmed who fired a warning shot over his head. One of the other FLN soldiers fired back toward Ahmed and nipped him on the hip, drawing blood. Enraged, Ahmed fired back; two of the men fell. The riposte from the group hit Ahmed who collapsed on the ground, blood oozing from his chest.

The two boys ran out and held him. But the body had become limp and lifeless. Their father had been killed. They wept over him. Then they saw the men move toward them. They stood up. They were scared, but they could not run.

The head man who had not been hit said, "You are now soldiers of the FLN. Come with us."

The older boy shouted, "No. You're murderers. You killed my father."

"He attacked us," the headman said. "He fired first. Come. You would not want me to shoot you too. Would you?"

The younger boy told his brother, "Father told us to obey them.

I don't want to see you killed like him." So the older boy lowered his head.

One of the men who had been shot by Ahmed had been badly hurt, and the boys were ordered to carry him and put him on the first truck; the other wounded one limped back to join him. The boys were told to sit in the back of the second truck. They were about to leave when Basira came back. She had seen the boys get in the FLN vehicle, so she jumped out of her truck and waved. Before the yell could come out of her mouth, a shot rang, and she fell. The FLN party left in a cloud of dust with her two sons who were not aware she had been shot and was bleeding on the ground.

༝

Rafa, a neighbor, had heard the shots and came running with his farmhand. They found Basira in front of the gate, bleeding from her shoulder, not conscious. They also found Ahmed's body where he had fallen in the yard.

"We need to take care of her fast," Rafa told his helper. "She's bleeding. There's nothing we can do about Ahmed. Let's put her in her truck and drive her to Tom's ranch; he'll know what to do."

Supporting her left arm because of her smashed shoulder, they carried her gently on the back of Ahmed's truck. The helper sat next to her, holding her. Rafa drove slowly to Tom's place.

Tom saw Rafa coming.

"What's going on? I heard shots coming from the direction of Ahmed's farm."

"Ahmed has been shot dead, and Basira has been hurt in the shoulder. We thought you'd know what to do."

"Oh my God! I'll tell Francine; then we'll drive to the military hospital. Just follow me."

When they got to the hospital, a couple of nurses took Basira inside and were able to stop the bleeding. She had regained consciousness, but knew little of what happened. Tom and the nurse asked her who shot her. She replied, "I drove in, and I saw my boys get in the back of a truck. I got out of my pickup to ask what was going on and someone shot me. That's all I know."

The nurses told Tom, "We need to take care of her; you can check on her this afternoon. Are you her husband?"

"No. She's a neighbor. Her husband has been shot dead, but she does not know it. Take good care of her wounds. Her life is not in danger, is it?"

"No it's not. She'll be in pain though."

"For sure. Can you call me when I can see her, and tell me if I can bring her girls?"

"I will call you, but it'll be after lunch at the earliest."

"Thank you, ma'am," Tom told the nurse.

He then turned toward Rafa and said, "Thank you for helping. Can you drive the truck back to Ahmed's farm? I and the military will take care of the body and the farm. I have to talk to Captain Dufour. He needs to get involved."

"Thanks, Tom," Rafa replied, "I believe the boys have been taken away, but do you know where the girls are? I'm kind of worried."

"The poor things have no idea of what happened to their mother and father, but the girls are safe at my house with Francine."

"That's good to know. I'll drive the truck back. If you need any help, let me know." Rafa got back in the pick-up.

cᶊᴼ

Captain Dufour, to whom Lieutenant Lucas had reported before he went back to France, ran the infantry company that protected the area. Tom went to see the captain and told him what he knew. The captain told Tom that he knew the FLN had been forcing young teenage boys all over the area to become FLN soldiers.

"That's probably what happened at the farm. Ahmed tried to fight them and was killed. When his wife came back, she just saw the kids being taken away and tried to stop them."

The whole tragic event made sense to Tom now.

"What's next, Captain?"

"I'll take care of Ahmed's body and the farm. If there are animals, we'll bring them to another farm."

Tom interrupted him. "They do have goats. Have the neighbor Rafa take care of them."

"The nurses will take care of Basira. Not sure how much is wrong with her," the captain said, "Check with them; they'll know this afternoon. Go take care of the two little girls."

They shook hands, and Tom said to the captain, "I have a question."

"Sure. What's on your mind?"

"How much time do I have before I must get out of here?"

"Hard to say. But I'd bet that three months from today will be too late. Better make plans in a hurry, Tom."

"Thanks. Are you guys going to stick around for a while?"

"No order has come yet, but when the area is declared unsafe, civilians in the ranches and farms will be advised to leave or stay at their own risk. We will probably escort the ones who decide to go. But I don't know when that'll happen."

Tom left and drove slowly to the ranch wondering how to break the news to Aisha and to Hana.

❧

When he pulled in front of the house, Francine came out. "How's Basira?" were the first words out of her mouth.

"They're taking care of her at the military hospital. I'll go back there later; she's being operated on. Her shoulder was all bloody, but I don't think she's in any danger."

"What about Ahmed?" Francine asked.

"He's dead."

"Oh my God. How are we going to tell Aisha that her dad is gone? Even Hana, although he was not her dad, she's been with him for almost two years. Also, we don't know how Basira will be. She probably will not be able to run the farm by herself. "

"Let her get well first, and then we'll see. I believe the two of us should both tell Aisha and Hana about their parents," Tom said.

"Agreed."

❦

The two girls were finishing copying a fairy tale to practice writing in French. Francine sat next to Aisha and put her arm around her. Tom stood in back of Hana. When Aisha finished writing her sentence, Francine said, "Something happened to your mom, Aisha. Some bad men shot her in the shoulder and she is hurt."

Aisha froze and looked at Francine with a blank look, not reacting at all. Francine went on, "She's in the hospital being taken care off. She'll be all right, but it'll take a couple of days."

Tom had his hand on Hana's shoulder. He felt her shiver, but she also said nothing; she just shook her head from left to right, like saying no.

Francine added, "You will stay here until she is well."

Aisha frowned and ask, "Why can't we go home? Dad will take care of us."

Francine took a deep breath, had a little cough and said, "Well…"

Tom interrupted. "Aisha, your dad has been shot too, by the same bad men."

"He is in the hospital?" She asked

Tom shook his head. "No. They killed your father."

Again, Aisha said nothing, but Hana started to shake and mumbled, "I know these bad men. I hate them… I hate them… I hate them." And she turned to Tom, put her arms around his neck and started to cry on his shoulder.

Then Aisha raised her head. "Did the men kill my brothers also?"

"No, they did not," Tom replied, "They are now with the new Algerian troops."

"Are they gone forever?"

"No they're not, but we don't know when they'll be back."

Aisha nodded, and nodded, and nodded. Then she put her arms around Francine, and sobbed softly.

They stayed like that for a long time, and then all of a sudden, Aisha exclaimed, "Who'll take care of the goats?"

"Your neighbor Rafa will, don't worry." Francine smiled.

Hana did not want to let go of Tom, so he carried her around for a while until she got tired and went to sleep, or maybe she just closed her eyes. He gently put her in a bed, and tucked her in.

༄

The nurse called later and told Tom that he could come and see Basira for a short time, but not to bring her daughters.

"Basira has tubes and wires connected to her body monitoring her vital signs, and a huge bandage on her shoulder," the nurse told him. "It would frighten the girls."

So Tom went to the hospital by himself. When he went in, the army nurse told him, "The captain told Basira that her husband had been shot to death. She replied she suspected it, otherwise he would not have let them shoot her."

Tom went to the room where Basira lay, sedated but conscious.

"Thanks for bringing me here, Tom. Are you taking care of my girls?"

"Yes, we are. Don't worry about them. They have heard the bad news and are dealing with them now. They'll stay with us."

"Thank you," Basira replied, "One thing, Hana must have her old raggedy doll to go to sleep. She's dependent upon it. That has been true since she came to us."

Tom nodded. He remembered the doll from the day he first met her. "I'll make sure of that. Now rest. I'll be back tomorrow."

Basira's eyes were already closed.

Tom drove by Ahmed's farm and found two French soldiers guarding it. He told them the story of the doll, and the corporal accompanied him inside to retrieve Hana's precious friend. They found it and Tom went home and gave it to Hana who clutched it close to her chest.

They fed the kids, who were exhausted, and put them to sleep.

Tom and Francine sat in their living room.

"Now what?" Francine asked.

"Now, we have to plan our exit from Algeria. The captain told me that the area will probably be unsafe within a few months, if not a few weeks."

"It had to come to that. Luckily we have that new property in France," Francine said.

"True, but we have no plan for the passage yet. It will be difficult to get one, so many will be fleeing the area. But the main question is what about Basira and the girls."

"I thought about that. There are two answers," Francine said, "One, we bring them to Mustapha, the head of the village, and let him take care of them. It is where they're from. Or, two, we take the three of them with us to France. It would be complicated, but maybe Basira could work with us in the new property. The main thing is the girls would be safe. What do you think is best, Tom?"

Without any hesitation, Tom replied, "It is not for me or you to decide. We need to offer the two solutions to Basira, and to the girls, and let them decide. I know they'd be safe with us. God knows what would happen here."

Francine nodded. "You're right." Then she thought of something and said, "Tom?"

"What, Francine?"

"Do you know Hana's status with Basira? Could she legally take her out of Algeria? She is not her child."

"No idea. I'll try to find out." Tom replied.

ᑴᕐᕐᐤ

The next morning, at breakfast, Aisha said to Francine, "I want to stay in your farm forever, and I want Mom and Hana to stay here too."

Hana did not say anything but looked at Tom and at Francine, waiting for the answer.

Tom spoke up. "Girls, Francine and I are not staying here. We will be going to France to get away from the bad men."

Hana started to shake again. Tom saw that and quickly added, "I will ask your mom what she wants to do, come with us or go back to the village."

Aisha nodded, but Hana stared at her, and then shook her head. "Please, not to the village."

Tom added, "It's up to your mom to decide."

༄

Later in the morning, the captain showed up with Mustapha.

"Hi, Tom and Francine, I brought Mustapha," the captain said, "because he talked to Ahmed a couple of days ago about the situation. Go ahead, Mustapha. Tell Tom what's going on."

Mustapha said, "Ahmed knew about the potential conscription for his sons, at least for the older one. He told me he would fight any attempt to take his boys, but if it happened that they would be conscripted, he had told them to come see me if they escaped. I would know where the family is."

Tom said. "We are going to leave for France when we can book a passage. We have a place over there, and it is now time for us to go. Francine and I are going to meet with Basira as soon as she is well enough and offer her to go back to the village and work with you, Mustapha, to define a new future, or to come with us to France. The girls want to come with us, but it's up to Basira."

Mustapha agreed it was the right way to approach the future.

Then Tom asked Mustapha. "Remember little Hana? Do you know if she has any legal status with Basira?"

"Yes, I do. Ahmed came to get her birth certificate two years ago, and I wrote an addendum stating she had been adopted by Ahmed and Basira because her parents were both dead. I signed it and put a village seal on it. It is semi-official. At least it should be good enough to go to France. I did that for a rancher two months ago. It worked."

"Thanks, Mustapha. It's good to know." Tom felt relieved that Hana would have no trouble following Basira regardless of which way she went.

The captain turned to Tom. "I stopped by the hospital on my way to pick up Mustapha. Basira is wide awake. I believe you can talk to her today. The sooner the better. Time is running out; you have to make plans."

Mustapha said, "Basira might be reluctant to leave the boys, but you can tell her that I have connections and that if one or the two boys come to me, I know a safe way to ship them to France. That may help her make her decision. I personally think it'd be better for the girls to go."

❧

Late that morning, Tom and Francine went to visit Basira, who was up sitting in her bed.

"I'm glad to see you looking so much better," Tom said.

"The army doctors patched and immobilized my shoulder, I have little pain."

"That's good. Basira, we need to talk about the near future. Do you think you can do it now?"

"Yes, I do; and I think we must talk about where I am going from here."

"That's what we want to talk about," Francine told her.

Tom explained the possibilities for her to choose from and mentioned Mustapha's input.

Basira started to cry. "Are you in pain?" Tom asked.

"No. Not at all. I am touched. I want to go with you. My girls will be safe and have a life. Maybe my boys will come too." Tom went to hug her gently, staying away from the shoulder.

"Now I can tell you one more thing that will make you happy. The girls worried about where they were going to go and I explained to them what I just told you and told them you would decide. Both wanted to come with us to France. They'll be relieved."

When Tom and Francine got home, they told the girls the good news. Aisha smiled, but did not say anything.

Hana ran to Francine and hugged her. "Thank you," she said.

Tom was touched and said to Francine, "We have to make it work. We had better start planning our escape." And he added, "I need to write to Lucas. He would want to know what happened and I need to tell him what our plan is. We may need his help too."

"He'll be thrilled that Hana will be out of harm's way," Francine said.

Chapter 7

Paris

March 20

Thinking about the day with Josette, Lucas was torn between thinking of a happy life with her and his ability to erase the scars of the last three years so as to be able to live normally. Being alone with his memories in his small rented place proved to be hard for Lucas. He dreaded going to sleep every night.

A couple of days after their meeting in the park, he called Josette, hoping she would pick up the phone. She did and right away said, "I was just about to call you. What's up?"

"I just wanted to hear the sound of your voice."

After a long sigh, she was able to whisper, "Luke. Really?"

"Yes. But why were you calling me?"

"My dad would like to meet you. Can you have dinner with him tomorrow night?"

"Yes, I sure can."

"Okay. Come to my place at six. We'll talk and then go see him. Bye. You are a dear, but I have a class to go to. I got to run. See you tomorrow afternoon."

When he saw Josette the next day, she said, "We had better get going. I prefer not to be late when I go to see my dad."

"Okay. Let's go. I'm looking forward to meeting him."

On the way to her dad's place, about a twenty-minute walk, she said that her dad knew Lucas' colonel and that she thought he may have talked to him.

❧

A tall man with graying hair and a military haircut opened the door.

Lucas was relieved to see that the colonel wore casual civilian clothes. "My name is Peter," Josette's father said with a big smile. "It's nice to meet you, Lucas."

"Nice to meet you, sir."

"No 'sir' required. Relax. You can call me Peter. Come in." The colonel led the way to the living room.

They sat down in the spartan, geometrically spaced, identical, comfortable chairs.

"So you worked for Colonel de Castre?" The colonel said.

"Yes, he ran the regiment I served in. We had many discussions, debriefings, and operational planning sessions. He taught me a lot. He's a great guy. Do you know him?"

"He and I went to the War College at the Ecole Militaire in Paris together when we were majors; we studied there for three months. When we joined the ranks of superior officers, we went our separate ways, but I just talked to him today."

"You did? I trust he's doing well. I know he's now in Saint Cyr. He was promoted during my last weeks in Algeria. I thought he was in trouble when the brass called him to France because he had me run a mission which was borderline with the new rules of engagement."

Peter smiled and said, "I know. He told me about it. He said he did not get in trouble because you executed the mission perfectly. He had asked you for no casualties and you led a successful mission with none."

Lucas smiled and closed his eyes, reliving that day. "I remember it well. We almost had one casualty. A rebel shot at me with an AK 47, but it jammed. They usually don't, as you know."

"Sometimes, one is lucky. You think your colonel is a great guy? You should have heard him talk about YOU! He thinks you're the best infantry lieutenant who ever worked for him. He said he included some of the missions you ran in his teachings. That's quite a compliment. He asked me to shake your hand on his behalf."

Peter got up, walked to Lucas and extended his hand. "I'm so glad Josette knows you. You can ask me for her hand any time."

Josette jerked her head back and gasped. "What did you say, Dad?"

"You heard me. I just said I found out your friend is a great guy."

The next few seconds were awkward. In the heavy silence that followed Peter's statement, his significant other, Marlene, came in. A vivacious woman with long blond hair tucked in a bun, dark eyes, and a beautiful smile. She went toward Lucas, her hand extended out and a welcoming face. "You must be Lucas. I've heard a lot about you today."

"I'm almost getting embarrassed to be such a celebrity," Lucas chuckled.

After a brief exchange of banalities, they went to the dining room to have dinner. They chatted about Algeria, its beautiful mountains, the mesmerizing desert, and the beautiful Mediterranean coastline north of Oran and in Algiers. Peter had served in North Africa before the war, stationed in Setif on the eastern end of the country near the Mountains of Kabylie.

Toward the end of the meal, Peter turned to Lucas and said, "Josette told me you were having a difficult time readjusting to civilian life."

"Yes. I'm struggling trying to adjust back to a normal, non-combat life. In some way, it's hard." Lucas took a sip of wine to think of how to talk about his pain. "I spent my whole North Africa tour in combat. I lived with a rifle in my hand day and night. I lost soldiers, I saw civilians killed or maimed, so I have a lot of bad memories to get rid of."

Peter nodded. "Your colonel told me about the decorations you earned for your platoon. You are quite a guy. Bad memories are normal. I don't have a recipe to eliminate them but my advice to you is to immerse yourself in defining your new life: job, family, sports, arts, anything. Keep busy. Go to bed tired so you sleep without nightmares: He lifted his glass of wine and toasted Lucas. "You're strong; you'll do fine."

When it was time to leave, Peter said, "You know you have done well for your country, for your men, and for your superiors. But you must also believe that you have done well for yourself. Keep your head high regardless of what you hear people say about that war. Colonel de Castre showed me you served your country gallantly and led your platoon with total disregard to your own safety. He knows you are a great leader, and I'm sure your soldiers would say the same thing. You must believe them. Come back and see me any time. Now I want to shake your hand for myself, and say thank you for your service. I'm glad to have met you, Lieutenant Lucas."

Lucas choked up and stayed speechless for a few seconds, and then looked him in the eye.

"Thank you, sir. Your praise is that of a superior officer. It means a lot to me, and I'm proud to call myself your friend."

cro

Josette and Lucas left for their walk to her home.

After a few steps, Josette stopped, faced Lucas, took his two hands, and said, "I knew you were a great guy, but I had no idea you were a hero. I'm so proud of you. I thought I would cry when I heard what those high-ranking officers said about the way you conducted yourself."

"That may be, but I'm still your Luke, that is, if you'll have me."

She beamed. "Is that a proposal?"

"I don't know, Josette. I'm confused. All I know is that I think I never stopped loving you."

Tears cascaded from her beautiful eyes. They held each other and made a spectacle of themselves right there in the middle of the sidewalk. People had to walk around them. Some smiled, others shrugged. No one could ignore them.

"I believe I never stopped loving you either," she said, "And my guardian angel made sure I did not stray away from you with that Gérard guy."

They made it to her apartment and he did not walk any farther that evening.

cro

Josette and Lucas woke up the next morning, kissed tenderly and looked at each other.

"Here we are. What do we do now?" Josette asked.

"Good question. Let me ask you one thing before I try to answer you."

"Okay. Shoot."

"I think that last night I asked you to marry me, and I think you said yes. Am I right?"

Her eyes were riveted to his. "Yes you did, and yes you are. Do you want to change your mind?"

He pulled her close, brought his lips to her ear and whispered, "No Josette, I don't. I told you last night I thought I had never stopped loving you. This morning I am sure, and I trust you are too."

"Right again. But I'm a little bit scared. We have known each other for a long time. We were together for two years, we loved each other, and we obviously still do, but we were young and never talked about a life together. What will it be like?"

"I'm not really sure, but I think it should be an adventure: Say yes to life. Explore Mother Nature's domain; learn from people of different cultures and share ours with them; help children, have our own. Be part of the world and strive to make it a better place. 'Never say no to a child who needs help.'"

Josette sat up and clapped. "What a beautiful picture! Never say no to a child who needs help. I love that. Yes I do want to spend my life with you and I want to live those words with you."

"We will." And then he teased her, "That is, if your dad will let me have your hand?"

She burst out laughing. "He had better remember what he said last night, if he values his life."

⚬⊱⚬

She took his hand and led him to the kitchen, "Let's have breakfast, and talk about the start of our life. We need to make plans."

"Plans?' Lucas asked.

"Yes, plans!" She giggled. "Like whom do we tell? When do we have the wedding, and all those important questions."

"Now, who do you have to tell?" He asked Josette.

"My dad, and my sister, whom you have never met. Her name is Caroline; she's two years older than me. She lives in Geneva. She is a physicist and works at the European Research Center for Nuclear Physics."

"She is a nuclear physicist? That's impressive. You and your sister are powerful women. I look forward to meeting her."

"You will," she said, "and we must also tell Nicole and Thierry, and my friends and colleagues at the hospital. What about you?"

"Ms. Rooth, if you remember her. She's my surrogate mother; she lives near Torquay in Devonshire in the southwest of England. I spent all my summers there in the fifties. That's where I learned English. Unlike my mom, she truly loved me, and I loved her. She probably won't come to the wedding, but she needs to know. We might want to go to England at some point. Also, Madame de Sèvres, the Countess who was my uncle's friend. I have been close to her since he died. She gave me a lot of support when I fought in Algeria. I would like you to meet her."

"I do want to meet them too. Going to Torquay also sounds fun; I have never been to the southwestern part of England."

"You'll love it. It's beautiful. I guess I should let my mother know too, but she won't come. She is moving to Antibes. I have to think if there are other people I would like you to meet."

Josette seemed to hesitate, but asked, "Is there anybody from your Algeria years you would like to tell, if not invite?"

Lucas immediately thought of his friends, the ranchers, Tom and Francine. He told Josette the story of having saved their ranch and their lives.

"Tom owns a vineyard and large orchards of orange and fig trees a mile away from Ahmed's farm. One day Tom's ranch had been attacked by twenty well-armed Algerian rebels who were determined to kill everyone on the property and burn the buildings down, but because I had intelligence on their plan, my platoon was able to foil their murderous mission, and save everyone on the ranch and the property."

Josette opened her eyes wide. "Wow. That was some feat."

"That's not the end. Ahmed had heard the rifle shots and had come toward Tom's ranch to find out if he could help. I told him about the raid. Tom and Ahmed had been friends ever since."

"What happened to the rebels?"

"If I remember correctly, seven or eight were killed and about a dozen were taken prisoners."

"Have you kept in touch with Tom and Francine?"

"Yes, I have. Shortly after that episode my platoon went for some additional training in a camp near the port of Oran, and then the colonel sent my company near Aflou. It turned out to be a godforsaken place in the northern Sahara from where communications other than military were close to impossible. But when the platoon went back to Mascara, I could go to Tom's ranch and to Ahmed's farm mainly to see the girls."

"Did you save many people like these ranchers?"

"I could bore you to death with battle stories, but besides not being interesting, it would be hard for me to relive these times. I'd rather not."

"Of course. I want to help you heal yourself, not dwell on your painful memories."

Lucas was touched and realized that her medical research into trauma taught her much about how to deal with people like him who had been hurt as much as the children she worked with.

"What about these little girls you mentioned, Aisha and…?"

"Hana. Actually I believe they would be delighted for me. I'm almost certain they're unlikely to come to the wedding. Ahmed was on the side of the French and I'm afraid he might be now in some danger, but I'm not sure what his plans are. Tom will let me know if anything happened to them."

"Do you think Tom and Francine could come?"

"I know they were planning to leave Mascara and to move to a farm in France. They had found a property they liked. I don't know for sure, but I think they actually bought it. I gave Tom Nicole's address so he could let me know when his plans were firm."

"Do you think the little girls might be in danger?"

"Yes. I know they are."

"Can you get in touch with Tom or Ahmed?" Josette asked anxiously.

"I can write to Tom."

"What about Ahmed? I'd love to meet these little girls."

"I have really no idea how to contact them."

"But they'd like to know the good news about us."

"Tom will let them know; but I doubt Ahmed and the girls will find refuge in France."

Josette got up, stretched, sighed, and suggested, "All we have left to do is set a date."

"How about tomorrow?" He teased her.

"Why not, my calendar is open." And Josette came to take his hand and the two of them danced around the room.

Lucas felt no gloom, guilt, or anger this morning. He knew right then that Josette would heal him. The adventure had started.

೪ം

Finished with breakfast, Josette looked at the kitchen clock. "Never mind all that unscheduled excitement. I have to go to work. I am never late. What's your plan?"

"No plan. At what time will you be home, Josette?"

"About six. Do you want to meet me here? We have lots to talk about," she beamed at him.

"I'll be here. We should go tell your dad tonight. Okay?"

"Why not? I'll call my sister from the hospital. Enjoy your day."

Chapter 8

Paris

March 22

Just when Josette got home late afternoon, the phone rang. It was Nicole.

"Josette?"

"Hi. It's me. What's up?" "Josette said.

"I received a letter for Lucas from a Tom Somebody in Algeria. That's why I called."

"I know who that is," Josette replied. "Lucas will be anxious to get hold of it."

"The two of you come here tonight," Nicole replied. After a short pause Nicole asked, "Just curious. Anything going on between you and Lucas?"

Josette chuckled. "As a matter of fact there is quite a bit."

"Really? Tell me. Is it good?"

"Oh, my God. What shall I say? It's fantastic. Last night, I took him to meet my father. I promised Lucas I'd help him get over his war trauma and I thought my dad, with all his experience in the military could at least give him some advice on how to best deal with his dark memories. Well, I found out that Lucas is a real hero."

"What do you mean, a hero?"

"Lucas' colonel told my dad that Lucas was the best infantry leader he ever had under his command. Lucas earned all kinds of citations for leadership, bravery, name it. His soldiers would do anything he told them to do because they trusted him. He made his platoon into an efficient war machine. That's why his superiors respected him and had the utmost confidence in him. They all loved him from what I could gather. I was so proud of him."

Nicole exclaimed, "How great. And at the party he never let on."

Josette interrupted her. "No he did not. But that's not the whole story. The real answer to your question is that Lucas proposed to me on the way home last night, and we're going to get married."

"NOOO! How cool! I am so happy for you. What news! When's the wedding?"

"No idea of when, how, where we will live, where we will work. We just know we were made for each other. The rest will work itself out."

"Fantastic is the right word. We'll celebrate tonight when you come to get the letter."

"I'll confirm that when I see him. I'll call you."

✧

When Lucas got to Josette's place, she told him about Tom's letter.

"I hope it's not bad news," he exclaimed. "Let's go."

They hurried to Nicole's apartment. Lucas tore the envelope open. His hands shaking, he held the long letter from Tom and read the first paragraph.

"Oh my God. I can't believe it," he said.

"What? Is it bad?" Josette asked anxiously.

"I'm afraid so. Let me read it first." He raced through the neatly written lines. At first the words did not register in his mind. It was too painful to let them penetrate his brain. But the truth became clear; he sobbed.

"What is it, Luke? Tell me."

"Ahmed is dead. The insurgents killed him and hurt his wife. She's wounded."

"What about the children?" Josette asked.

"I don't know yet." His teary eyes did not make it easy to read on, but he had to. He wanted to know, but at the same time feared the worst. The next lines confirmed that the two sons had been taken away to be indoctrinated in the new Algerian military. He read on and then looked up at Josette whose eyes were begging for the answer.

"Aisha and Hana are alive, but the boys are missing."

Josette burst out crying, feeling the pain of the little girls she never met, but she knew were special to him. He finished reading the letter.

"When did that happen?" Josette asked him.

"A couple of days ago; I'm not sure exactly."

"What are they going to do?" Josette wanted to know.

"Tom said they don't want to get into a fight and end up like Ahmed, so they'll try to get out of there when they can get a passage to Marseille."

"Is that Tom and Francine, and the girls too?" Josette asked.

"Tom did not say anything about the girls. He said he'd write when his plans were firm."

Lucas asked Nicole to alert him the minute she got a letter from Tom if she did.

Josette put her arms around Lucas and, her eyes inches from his, smiled and said, "The girls will be all right, I am sure; and we'll get to hug them."

Then Nicole asked if Tom's letter explained who killed Ahmed and how.

"Tom only said that the rebels had gone to all the farms owned by Algerians they knew were supportive of the French and wrecked them, cutting trees, pulling up vineyards, burning buildings, and destroying everything in sight. Apparently Ahmed and his wife tried to defend their property with their weapons. A gun fight ensued and they were shot. A neighbor found her bleeding and took her to the military hospital. Tom did not say how the boys disappeared."

"That's awful," Josette said.

"And it makes me mad at the rebels I fought. I wish I had been there with my soldiers. I'd have saved them," Lucas said.

"This reminds me," he said out loud, "of the day I lost so many of my men, killed or wounded. That day changed me. I had had enough of the war, enough of the rebels, and enough of the carnage. I hated the enemy and I wanted to annihilate them. I had become a combat soldier, ready to kill, and I felt no guilt about doing it. I'm not proud of that, but the feeling was strong; it was real."

Remembering that day, his anger rose, and he clenched his teeth. After reading Tom's letter, he felt like he did after the battles in which he lost several soldiers.

"Don't torture yourself, Lucas, your war is over; you are no longer a soldier," Nicole said.

Nicole reacted to what she could see, but Lucas had to control his temper. Inside his mind, his war was far from over. He fought his anger. What could or should he do with regard to the rebels? Nothing! He had to focus on the children. He started sweating, his heart beat faster, and his mind started to drift back to Algeria.

Josette put her arms around him. "Try to distance yourself from the killing if you can. Think of Aisha and Hana."

"I'll try my best, Josette, but it's easier said than done," Lucas managed to mumble.

For the first time Josette saw the dark side of Lucas's soul. He had promised her he would curb his anger. He had to be able to do it. He sat down and held his face down, hidden in his hands, and stopped talking. Nicole and Josette were uneasy and remained silent, not sure what to do.

After a short time, he recovered control, and his mind went back to the sad news he had to accept, because it was real.

"I'm sorry," he said to the two women. "I'm all right now."

ఞ

Josette put on her medical researcher hat. "We'll have to help Tom and Francine with the two girls, and their mother, if they all come to France. The kids have been traumatized and will need special handling."

"Do you have any idea about what they should be doing?" Nicole asked.

"I'd need to talk to them. I'm sure Aisha's and Hana's traumas are different. Hana had to deal with the fright of being alone, abandoned

when her mother died, the memory of the loud explosion of the grenade in the village, and also the shock of being with a new mother. Both
girls have to deal with the mother's injuries, the loss of the father, and
the disappearance of the brothers. It's complicated."

"If I may add to that," Lucas interrupted Josette, "I'd think that the
children were already frightened by a war they did not comprehend at all."

"You are right. And the war also affects Tom and Francine, which
makes it more difficult for them to care for the girls."

Nicole asked Josette, "But what kind of protocol or treatment are
you talking about?"

"There are many possibilities, from playing or listening to music,
looking at or practicing visual arts, exposure to the calming effect of
nature, the companionship of a dog, and compassion from adults, psychological treatments, etc. It's not an exact science."

"So much for the celebration of your engagement," Nicole said.
"We'll try tomorrow or the next day."

"Right," Josette replied, and turned to Lucas. "And let's skip telling
my dad until tomorrow. Let's go home."

⁂

Lucas sent a reply to Tom's letter that night. He would mail it in the
morning, hoping it would be delivered the next day, but he had no idea
of the situation in the Mascara area these days. He could only hope the
letter would get there. He gave him his phone number and address so
that he could contact him directly and ask for any help he needed.

Chapter 9

Paris

March 23

The next day, on Friday morning, Josette and Lucas were having breakfast, and Josette suggested, "There's so much we need to decide as we begin our adventure. We need to make a list, don't you think?"

"Let's make the list, and then we'll prioritize," Lucas agreed and added, "Let's hear what's on your mind."

Josette chuckled and started to rattle her questions at high speed. "When is the wedding? Where will it be? Who do we invite? Where do we get married? Where do we live? Where do you work? Where do I work?" She stopped for an instant. "And there must be more when, where, who, how, and which questions that will come to our minds."

Lucas opened his mouth to venture a tentative answer, but before he got a chance to reply, she quickly continued without letting him say a word, "But before we talk about that, I have one question for you. Yesterday you almost lost it after reading the letter from Tom. Your mind went right to Tom's ranch. You were ready to go back there and fight, ready to pull the trigger."

Lucas sat up in his chair. "Well, that was not good news."

Josette shook her head. "Luke, you're just a few days back from the war and from traumatic experiences which lasted years. You need to recover from these difficult times. You have to erase the bad memories from your soul. You need to begin to reconstruct yourself to be ready for that world we will create, but which you are not quite ready for yet."

"What are you saying, Josette?"

She grabbed his hand and squeezed it hard. "I think you should take time off to begin with. Go some place by yourself, or better, with me. We need to reset your mind. We're going to spend our lives together. Let's start with a healing trip."

Lucas put his other hand on hers. "You really care about me, don't you?"

"Yes, I do. I want you to be well. But I'm not sure how to help."

"I love you for that. You're right. I need to slow down. I have some money; I don't have to rush into a career. I'm not ready to make decisions on anything."

చర్

His mind started racing, not sure of what he should do. Then he blurted out, "Could you take off for a few days now?"

"When? What do you have in mind?" Josette asked as they were clearing the breakfast dishes.

"I mean next week or the week after, really soon. You and I can go to some quiet place, and slow down our lives, look at trees, at lakes, at mountains, gaze at the sky, at the stars, immerse ourselves in Mother Nature's realm. We would forget the hustle, bustle, and the trappings of modern life for a short while. What do you say?"

"Actually, Easter break is starting the week after next," Josette replied. "I have no more classes and no hospital duty until the exam. I planned to use the time to study for my final, but I could take one week off. Where do you want to go?"

"Let me think about it. We'll discuss it tonight."

"Not tonight, Luke. Do you remember? I have to be at the hospital this weekend. It's part of the certification requirement. I have to spend forty-eight hours in the emergency room. Don't ask me why."

"I had forgotten. You'll need to sleep to recover from that on Sunday night. We'll discuss it on Monday."

"Let's do it," she said. She looked at the clock and got up. "I have to get going. We'll talk Monday. Come around lunch time."

చర్

Lucas thought about what Josette had said. He had to admit to himself she was right. After Nicole's obvious shock when she opened her door and saw him, his first morning back; after Thierry's face when he saw Lucas; and after Josette saying she wanted to help but did not know how. It was obvious that while searching for who he was, he seemed to give off distress signals.

Actually, deep inside, he felt lost. He had little enthusiasm for any of the jobs he could think might be available. His mind still focused on the ravages of the war, on savage scenes of combat. Worst, he was haunted by the images of the innocent victims of the conflict. His heart ached for Aisha and Hana for their loss, and he also feared that after losing her father, then her mother, this new blow of Ahmed's death might be too traumatic for Hana. She was so fragile. Both girls lived without any understanding of why terrible things were happening to them and to the world around them. They were not the only ones. He sadly realized that many other children suffered and that many did not make it, but these two were alive, at least physically, if not fully psychologically. He felt the urge to help them and others like them; but how? A big question he could not answer.

Josette had told him she did not know how to help. He started to think that if she started to work with him on answering that big question, it could be one of the ways she could help him. Treating traumatized kids had become her new vocation. She might be able to apply what she had learned to his condition. He decided to bare his soul to her. She would have ideas, if not the final answer.

At the same time, he did not feel strong enough to be by himself, so he thought it would be best to take Josette up on her offer of taking a week off and for the two of them to spend it together. He needed to make that one-week retreat happen, and he had to find the right place, but he only had a couple of days to discover the magical hidden refuge that would become the first step of their adventure, a step in which they would blend into one another with the single goal of slowing down, and enjoying nature.

The first place that came to his mind was la Chartre-sur-le-Loir, the village Lucas spent the summer of 1945 recovering from the deprivations of the war with his uncle. They were both in desperate need of rest and good nutrition. The sleepy little village in the Sarthre area happened to be the ideal place at that time, yet probably not what he had to have now. He needed peace, nature, and quiet, more than food.

The second idea was Benodet in the west end of Brittany. Swept by the Atlantic winds and waves, the Finistère area was a treasure of ocean vistas and salt air. He had been there and loved it, but again, it might not be the perfect place for their retreat.

Early that afternoon, he stopped by a travel agency and casually asked for a recommendation for a quiet place in the mountains, anywhere in France. Christiane, the clerk in the shop astounded him with the amount of information she gave him. She was originally from the back-country northeast of Nice.

"I know where you need to go," she said, "the Mercantour area. It is northeast of Nice, on the Italian border. It is a park with very few visitors, certainly now with the winter barely over. I would recommend staying in Sospel, which is the village I come from."

Christiane gave him a couple of brochures on the area. She mentioned a hotel, and a few hikes that they could do, for sure.

"If you're lucky, you'll meet all kinds of animals: Chamois, ibexes, marmots, foxes, wolves and many birds, including eagles."

She giggled. "I could talk to you about the park for hours."

He thanked her profusely, and went to one of the largest bookstores he knew and found a guidebook about the area. After reading it, he would be all set to talk to Josette. He had three options to offer her. All she would have to do on Monday is pick one.

Chapter 10

El Boussaid

March 23

The girls were excited. They were on their way to see Basira with Tom and Francine. So as not to frighten them, Tom spoke softly. "Now we have to be quiet, because in rooms next to your mom's, there are soldiers who have been hurt and are in great pain, so we can't make any noise."

The four of them entered Basira's room. She looked good, sitting in a chair next to the bed, her left arm secured to her chest so the shoulder could not move. She waved to the girls with her right hand and told them to come close to her. Aisha asked her if she was in pain, and beamed when her mom said she was not. Hana kissed her right hand, but was subdued, looking at her with a pained look like she was ready to cry. She did not say anything.

Francine saw that. She hugged the little Hana and said to her, "Basira is all right, she is coming home the day after tomorrow."

Hana started to panic. "The bad men are at the farm, waiting for her. I want her with me in your home," she said, almost sobbing. Francine caressed her cheeks, and said to her, "That's what I meant. She's coming to our home. We'll all drive here in two days and bring her to our house." Hana buried her face on Francine's chest and stayed quiet, breathing heavily.

They could not stay long. The military hospital was not meant to accommodate children, so they said good bye to Basira.

When they got home, the captain and one of his lieutenants were waiting in their jeep in front of the house.

"You know Lieutenant Marchand, don't you?" The captain asked Tom and Francine.

Lieutenant Marchand had replaced Lieutenant Lucas when he went back to France.

"Yes, of course. What's up?"

"First, can we have the girls not participate in this conversation? I know that, thanks to Francine, their French is pretty good. I don't want to frighten them."

Francine said, "I'll take them. Tom will fill me in on the plan."

Hana said to Francine, "Can I stay?"

"The captain prefers you do not. Tom will tell us what he said."

The captain unfolded a map of the regiment's assigned zone and looked at Tom.

"You asked me the other day how much time you had before you had to get out. Here's what's happening. A couple of farms have been ransacked east of here, not far from Tiaret." He pointed on the map at the locations of the buildings that had been attacked. "It's obvious that the future FLN government is not yet in control of the country. We are all potential targets for assaults from renegade rebels who are out for themselves and also possible intrusions from legitimate government troops. So the regiment's area has been declared unsafe and we need to plan to get out. I'm assuming you intend to go to France."

"Yes we do, Captain, and we have offered Basira to take her and the children with us when we leave, and we were thrilled when she accepted, not wanting to remain in the village. So Francine and I have precious cargo to bring to France. We have a destination because we have bought a property near Avignon. All we have to do is decide what to bring beside ourselves, if anything. The most difficult part for us is to find and book a passage to the European continent."

"Great," the captain said. "There's another difficult part for you and your family. That is to get to your port of embarkation in one piece. That's what I want to talk to you about. The regiment has put together a plan to evacuate all those who want to leave, starting with the most remote zones west of here. Those who don't leave will stay at their own risk. There are several steps to that plan. Step one has started for the Tiaret vicinity. We are next."

"What's step one?" Tom asked.

"We'll bring one container per family, in your case one for Basira and one for you, to pack personal items that can fit in it. No large piece of furniture. You can pack clothes, artifacts, family treasures, pots, dishes, etc. Once they're sealed, the containers will be picked up and shipped to a military base in southern France for you to pick up when you get there."

"That's terrific. We thought we would have to leave everything here."

"Step two, we need to discuss. My company cannot provide security to every farm and ranch in my assigned zone. So we have to consolidate the families who want to leave. The farmers and ranchers will have to live in fewer residences. Our assessment is that your ranch is one of the easiest to protect. Could you house three or four additional families for a few days?"

"Definitely. We can house three families in the quarters reserved for the staff which is no longer here, and squeeze another one with Basira and us in the main house."

"Excellent! Step three will be the transport of the families to Sidi Bel Abbès in an armed convoy. Once there, all the evacuated people will be housed in the Foreign Legion Headquarters in the officers' housing that have been vacated. Most families will go to France, some to Spain. All of them will leave Algeria from Oran or from Algiers. They'll communicate their plan to the Foreign Legion officer in charge and stay in the Legion buildings until the time of their departure from Algeria. That day, they'll be escorted to their port of embarkation."

"Sounds good to me," Tom said, "What time frame are we talking about?"

"Step one starts now and the containers will be picked up at the end of next week."

"Wow. That early?"

The captain went on. "The following week, the consolidation will take place. You will have to coexist with the other families for at most a couple of weeks. I can't tell you precisely how long. Plan to be in Sidi Bel Abbès in about three or four weeks. That should help you with booking your passage. End of April, early May should be your target,"

"A couple of last questions," Tom asked. "First, when and how do we get protected?"

"Troops will be stationed around your property buildings twenty-four hours a day starting the week after next. Then, you won't be able to leave your quarters unless escorted by soldiers. You will need to have a valid reason for your trip. A medical emergency for example."

"Thanks. Different subject. I have about ninety cases of wine that I could not sell. How about I give some to you, and some to the Legion?"

"We would gladly take some off your hands. I'm sure the legionnaires would be happy to help. I'll send a truck tomorrow to take forty cases. I'll make sure we load the remaining fifty when you all leave for Sidi Bel Abbès."

"Lastly. What about food?"

"I recommend you stock up on food for a month, and plan to share the meal preparation with the families housed with you."

"Thanks, Captain. No more questions. I'm all set."

"Better start sorting what you deem essential. When you take Basira to her farm to fill her container, let us know. We'll send an escort to protect her and the girls. Lieutenant Marchand is your contact point. Use your radio to communicate with him on your needs, or any unexpected incident. The entire regiment area is a powder keg. We hope there won't be problems, but be vigilant. Keep the little ones and Basira inside. You and Francine keep close to your weapons. There will be a squad on alert every minute of the day and night until troops move to protect your ranch. Help is about ten minutes from the time you radio us."

✍

Tom brought Francine up to date. She was pleased with the security the colonel in charge of the regiment had put in place. At the same time, she shared her anxiety with Tom. "The troops must anticipate incidents or an uprising of some kind; otherwise they would not have that elaborate a plan. I'm kind of scared."

"Their plan might be enough of a deterrent," Tom tried to reassure her.

"I hope so," she grumbled.

When Hana asked Francine what the captain said, all she told her was that the captain had a plan to help them escape from the bad men.

✢

The next day, soldiers brought one container to Tom's ranch, another one to Ahmed's farm, each measuring four by five feet around and three feet high.Tom shared the captain's plan with Basira at the hospital. She told him all she wanted to bring were clothes and a few utensils. "We'll go to the farm, get what I need and what the girls want, then we'll bring it to your ranch. There will be plenty of space left you can use."

The following morning, Tom, Francine, Hana, and Aisha got in the truck with joy. They were going to bring Basira home. Her doctors' instructions were for her to continue to rest, and keep her shoulder immobilized for another few days. For the last step, she had to go back to the hospital to remove the straps and the soft cast. Then it would be time to return home to begin a rehabilitation program. The doctor told her she should end up with no restriction of movement on her left side.

Tom called Lieutenant Marchand to get an escort to bring Basira to her farm. She and the girls went with Tom and selected what they would bring with them. Hana had a few clothes and all the books Francine had given her over the past two years. They left the rest and all the furniture for the next farmer. The soldiers would bring the container to Tom's ranch.

Basira had a heavy heart leaving the place where she and Ahmed had lived and toiled for almost twenty years. Hana, quiet as usual, kept looking at the gate obviously fearing that the bad men would come and harm them. When they left the farm for the last time, Basira said to Tom, "I don't know where my sons are. I hope they don't come back here. I'm never coming back to this farm."

Hana looked at her. Any time anyone mentioned the farm in front of her, Hana became sullen and looked at her feet. Having heard what Basira said about never coming back to the farm, she stared at her and gave a big, deep sigh. Her shoulders rose as if a burden had been lifted from her back. Through her usual sadness, her face showed a hint of a timid smile.

᪐

Tom went to visit the Picards, ranchers like themselves who had been close friends for several years. Tom suggested they be the ones joining them in the main house. They accepted happily. John Picard knew people in Oran who worked in the shipping industry. He told Tom, "I'll make some calls and see if I can get passages for the four of us." Tom told him about Basira and the two girls.

"That'll be more complicated, but I think my friends will be able to help." John said, "They had offered to take us across a few weeks ago, but we weren't ready then. I should be able to get passages for the seven of us."

"I'm not sure what you had in mind," Tom said, "but it should be easier to book cabins in first class. There should be less demand for expensive accommodations. So you need to know it would be okay for us."

"Great. That's what I wanted to ask you. I think it can help a great deal."

᪐

Tom wrote his second letter to Lucas to apprise him of the new developments.

Chapter 11

Paris

March 26

Lucas got to Josette's place at lunch time on Monday, and before he could utter a word, she announced, "I talked to one of my professors this weekend. He has started a study on combat trauma, focusing on soldiers who were hurt in Algeria in fights like the ones you were in with rifles, machine guns and grenades. He told me that he concluded that for the most part, soldiers recovered well from the physical injuries and trauma they endured. That is because medical science had made great progress in surgery to repair organs and lacerations, bone splinting, limb replacements, and more, and even rehabilitation programs were effective. But it is not quite so for the psychological wounds."

"Did he mean like what I have?" Lucas asked.

"Exactly. He called the menu of treatments for those wounds limited, and stated that a full recovery was problematic. He asserted that choosing the correct protocol for a specific trauma is a difficult problem because the effectiveness of the healing depends much on the psychological state of the soldier's mind and his emotional needs. Most treatments are essentially designed to slow down their brain, but there are few approaches to doing it. In some cases lowering the brain activity is not sufficient, the memories have to be obliterated, or at least dulled so they are no longer painful. This is a science which medicine is just starting to study."

"You're a pioneer, my love."

"Yes, I am. And the professor told me that my work was key to solving the problem."

"So your work is leading-edge."

"You're right. When I get my certification, I will know all that the world has learned about trauma, and that's not much."

"Question? What does he mean by slow down the brain? Is it sleep?" Lucas asked her.

Josette smiled. "Let's sit down."

She took Lucas' hand. "The answer to your question is no. It has to do with the immediate environment the patient lives in at the moment of the treatment. For example, suppose you're on a boat on a peaceful lake in a remote mountainous area. If your boat is a small sailboat, a canoe, or a kayak, the impetus on your brain is mild. On the other hand, on a motorboat, there's the noise of the engine, the fumes of the exhaust that makes it difficult to breathe, the speed of the boat which demands concentration not to hit any obstacle. All these stimuli make your brain work fast."

"Well I can assure you that in combat the stimuli, as you call them, are legions."

"That's what he said. In a battle, your brain has to deal with multiple threats at the same time, as well as deafening noises, and blinding colors from explosions, all of which trigger reactions in the soldier's brain."

"Not to mention trying to figure out where everyone is: your buddies and the bad guys trying to kill you and shooting at your troops," Lucas added.

Josette continued, "Although not as threatening as combat, the motor boat demands instant responses to different stimuli while the canoe demands few instant reactions. It lets you act leisurely. It lets your brain slow down."

"Ah. Okay, I get it."

Lucas got up. "By the way, I stopped by my place and there was a letter from Tom."

"What did he say? I hope not more bad news."

"Why don't I let you read it?"

He gave her Tom's note.

Josette became excited as she read. "The girls are coming to France. They'll be safe if they can make it to the ship."

"Lieutenant Marchand is my replacement. He's a good guy. He and the captain will make sure they get all the protection they need. I'm confident they'll sail."

"I'm so relieved," Josette said, "Are we going to go down to meet them at their new place?"

"Tom did not have a date for his trip to Marseille, so we don't know when they'll be in the new home. We'll see when it makes sense to go see them, but I do want you to meet them, and I'm dying to hug Hana; she's so precious. Now let's talk about our retreat. I have three potential destinations I came up with."

Josette leaned forward on her chair. "I'm dying to know what they are."

The first choice of la Chartre-sur-le-Loir did not impress Josette. "We don't need special food; and it seems pretty boring: no lake, no mountains, no park, little wild life," she commented. "What's the second choice?"

The setting of Bénodet, its huge bay, the wild rocky shore and crashing waves, the roar of the surf, the sting of the wind and the salty air did not trigger an enthusiastic response either.

"It's nature and it's wild. It sounds beautiful but will it slow down your brain, with the noise, the active waves, and the strong wind?" she asked.

Lucas had to smile. Josette did not shy away from sharing her opinions. "I have a soft spot for these two places because of the past memories I have from there," Lucas replied, "but I think you're right, they're not what we want. The third choice I have is the Mercantour Park north of Nice."

"What's there?"

"I have never been to that park, but it's in the Alps and it's remote. There are mountains, lakes, and many trails. That would be a first for me. The woman who told me about it was born near there and swore it would suit our need for peace, quiet, and raw nature."

"That sounds more like what we're looking for. Any idea of where to stay, how to get there, etc?"

"Yes. She recommended the village of Sospel which is close to the park and is itself a little sleepy town of less than two thousand people. We can take the overnight train to Nice and rent a car there, or drive all the way from Paris."

Josette clapped. "I love trains. Now, can we be gone? What if Tom needs help?" Josette asked.

"I thought about that," Lucas replied, "From reading his letter, I figured there's no way he can get to France at least for another four weeks. Francine's brother Robert will pick them up when they get off the boat. I'm not sure they'll need help but if they do, it won't be for a while, so I say let's plan the trip and book it. Okay?"

Josette jumped up. "Let's do it."

Then she gave Lucas her most mischievous smile. "One more thing, Luke. I have no doubt we're going to get married, no matter what. I know I said we should wait for you to heal from your war memories. Forget that. We're ready. I know I am. We should get married as soon as we can."

Lucas embraced Josette tenderly. "I agree wholeheartedly." And he kissed her.

"When do you think we can do it?" He asked her.

"We need to get a civil marriage license from the city and book a date. It only takes a couple of days to get it scheduled. Also, I know you're not religious, neither am I, but it seems that, although it has no legal or official standing, everybody gets married in the church as well, so why not comply with the norm? If we do, it takes a couple of weeks to schedule a religious wedding. What do you think?"

"If you want to do the church ceremony, I'm all for it."

"Good. My father would like that, and although I have never met Madame de Sèvres, I bet she would approve too."

"For sure, she is a traditional French aristocrat."

"What we should do," Josette suggested, "is go to the church now, tell them about us so they do whatever they have to while we are gone. When they are done, we'll be free to pick a date that works for us without having to wait."

"Great idea," Lucas replied. "Let's do that before we go."

⁂

The following day they went to Eglise St. Augustin, the church near the Cercle Militaire, a club for military officers, where Josette was certain the colonel would book the celebration luncheon. The church was also close to Lucas's rental apartment, therefore within the church territorial jurisdiction. They talked to a priest and filled out forms. The church would research baptism certificates, and make their marriage request public to give time to anybody who might want to object to it.

Lucas also wrote to Ms. Rooth to tell her about Josette.

They booked themselves for the next Friday on the train bleu, the overnight sleeper train from Paris to Nice. Lucas booked a room at the hotel that Christiane recommended in Sospel, and found a topographic map of the park which showed all the trails and elevations of the area. Josette got herself good hiking boots — Lucas had his treasured army boots that served him so well for months. As it was early April, they made sure they had enough warm clothes. They were all set.

A new dawn was about to arise for Josette and Lucas.

Chapter 12

Paris

March 26

Colonel Dubois had not heard from his daughter since last Wednesday when she introduced Lucas to him and he wondered if anything was happening between her and her infantry lieutenant friend. He had been impressed with the young man. The colonel sensed Josette had been deeply hurt by that Gérard doctor two years ago. He admired her dedication to the medical profession and her trauma project. He applauded her focus on helping children, but he wanted her to be happy and live a full life.

He asked his companion, Marlene, who sat across the living room from him, reading today's newspaper, "What did you think of this guy Lucas?"

"He looks to me to be a perfect mate for your daughter. She needs to have a life. Medicine is great but… you know." She opened the newspaper to another page.

"That's exactly what my thoughts are," he replied, "Do you think we should try to find out if they're up to something?"

"Like what?" she asked, still reading.

"I don't know. Find a pretext to invite them over?"

"Any idea?" She put her paper down. "We don't want to be too obvious, but I'm kind of curious too."

"How about, we're celebrating my new job?"

"You have a new job? That's news."

"It happened today. It's a temporary assignment. I'll report to the general overlooking all non-active soldiers, meaning the ones who are recovering from injuries and the ones who have been discharged and have been put in active reserves. With all the guys coming back from Algeria, it's a mess that needs to be cleaned up."

"Well it sounds wonderful. Congratulations, dear, but is it cause for celebration?"

"Not really, but it keeps me in Paris for a while. "

"I see." Marlene paused for a brief moment then asked, "Why not just tell her we're having a drink because of your new job and suggest they drop by?"

The colonel thought for a minute. "It looks a bit obvious, but let me call her."

He did and surprisingly, she answered the phone.

"I'm glad to find you at home," he said to her.

"I'm cramming. My final exam is getting close. What's up?"

The colonel suggested they drop by for a drink.

"Lucas is coming in a few minutes. We were thinking of coming to see you. He has news from Algeria. We thought you might want to know what's going on there."

"I sure do. Come on over."

On the way to her dad, Josette suggested, "We can tell him about the wedding. Okay?"

"Great idea. That'll be more of a surprise than if we had suggested coming to see them."

❧

As soon as they were seated in her father's living room, Peter asked Lucas, "What news from Algeria do you have? I'm curious."

Lucas said. "Before I share what I heard, I could use a little bit of help from you."

"Sure thing. What can I do for you?"

Lucas stood up. "It's not because of the suggestion you made when I met you last week," Lucas said with a broad smile, "but I would like to ask you for your daughter's hand."

The colonel jumped up from his chair grinning and said, "You know the answer to that." They shook hands. Marlene hugged Josette and came to hug Lucas.

The colonel said, "We have a confession to make. Marlene and I were curious about you two and we tried to find an excuse to invite you over to find out if anything serious was going on. Now we have the answer. Congratulations to both of you." He turned to Lucas. "And to you, I say, welcome to the Dubois family."

"Do you have a date in mind?" Marlene asked.

Josette answered right away. "We don't have a date, but the sooner the better. We want an intimate wedding. There will be few people to invite."

"Then, we can have the reception at the Cercle Militaire," the colonel suggested. "They cater to officers, and they do a good job for that sort of thing."

Josette winked at Lucas. "That's a good idea, Dad. We need to work on a date which works with everyone's schedule," Josette said, "and think of who you might want to invite. We want to keep it small and simple."

"Fine. Let me know, so I can book a private room. Now Lucas, what about the news from Algeria?"

Lucas told him what he learned from Tom. The colonel shook his head, "What a rout. Damn. That war was a big mistake."

The evening went on with more talk about North Africa. Then Josette shared with them the Sospel plan.

"When are you leaving?" The colonel asked.

"We get on the train Friday night and come back a week later," Josette replied.

⁂

The next day, Lucas called Josette who was working on her preparation for the final exam.

"We have told your dad about the wedding, so I need to go tell the countess, and then I'll introduce you to her. Okay?"

"Yes. Actually, I'm anxious to meet her. She has been important to you."

"She has. I know that she'll be happy for us. Work hard. I'll see you at dinner time."

The Countess was home.

"What a nice surprise to see you, Lucas. Come in and have a seat."

"I'm going to spend time in the wilderness. It's a step to help me recover from that war. Wilderness is restful and healing. I'm going next week with my friend Josette. We will go to the Mercantour area in the Southern Alps. The reason I came today is to tell you about her."

"Oh," the countess's face lit up. "Am I to expect some kind of announcement?"

"Yes, you do. Josette and I are going to be married, and I would like to introduce her to you whenever it is convenient."

"Congratulations! I'm so happy for you. How long have you known Josette?"

"Actually, Josette and I were in love when I was in the engineering school." Lucas told her about the separation and the reunion when he came back from Algeria, and then he added, "She'll get her trauma medical certification in a couple of weeks."

"So she's a doctor?"

"She is, and she is finalizing a specialization in psychological trauma treatment focused on children, mainly those hurt by wars."

"Intriguing," the countess said, then she asked, "How old is she?"

"She's a year older than me."

The countess paused for an instant, then continued. "That's perfect, I already like her. Wars do so much damage to soldiers, and to children."

"When would it be convenient to bring Josette?"

The countess replied, "I have quite a few meetings scheduled. I'd rather have my assistant call you. If I pick a time, it will be the wrong one. When is the wedding?"

"Not sure. Soon, but we don't have a date yet."

"Let me know as soon as you know."

Chapter 13

Sospel, French Southern Alps

March 31

Midmorning on Saturday, Josette and Lucas got off the train in Nice, rented a car, and drove up toward the Mercantour area. Hairpin turn after hairpin turn, uphill after downhill, the road to Sospel made them dizzy but lifted their spirits with its splendid panoramas. They reached their modest but quaint hotel before lunch. They could finally breathe the clean air of the mountains. The lushness of the landscape surprised Lucas. This did not resemble the arid, rocky, and sandy slopes of the Atlas Mountains.

They had a leisurely lunch at the hotel, enjoying the crisp mountain weather and the welcoming sun.

"Where do we start?" Josette asked. "It's your show; we're here to help you slow down."

"You are the trauma expert. What do you suggest?"

She laughed. "I only know about children. You're beyond that age."

"Seriously," he said, "Let's use the afternoon to explore the village, and maybe meet some folks who can recommend hikes. You see, I need to sleep better, get rid of nightmares if I can. Your dad said it's more likely to happen if I'm tired physically. A day's walk in the mountains is not only enthralling, it is also demanding, so it'll be helpful."

"That makes sense. But you're in great shape, and I'm not. I'm not sure I can do too much of that."

"Get out of here. You'll do well. You're strong. We'll do it gradually."

"Tell me, Luke. Do you still get nightmares?"

"Not too many anymore. I don't think I'll keep you up during the night."

The two of them set out strolling in the narrow streets of Sospel.

The village used to be a gate into Northern Italy during the Middle Ages. As early as the thirteenth century, a toll bridge collected a fee from travelers going from what was then the County of Nice to Turin.

Walking slowly through the old twisting lanes of the little town, they were awed by the yellow, pink, and green pastel colors of the houses. They looked at the balconies, some of which held the morning laundry drying on the railings. Their eyes were attracted to the flowers gracing windows framed by faded greenish shutters. Peaceful and cheerful as it was, the medieval village brought smiles to their faces. Lucas saw a little café tucked in the corner of a plaza close to the old toll bridge.

"Let's sit and have a beer," he suggested.

"Good idea. Let's," she agreed.

A young woman came to take their order. "Welcome to Sospel. My name is Beatrice. What can I bring you?"

They both ordered a cold one.

"Your first time in Sospel, is it? "The waitress asked.

"Yes, it is," Josette replied. "What a beautiful village!"

"It is, and the Mercantour, our Alpine park next door, is spectacular. Have you been there yet?"

Lucas replied, "No, we just got in, and we're here for a week. We plan to do some hikes. That's why we came here. Any recommendations?"

"Let me ask my dad to come talk to you. He's the expert on the park."

A strong-looking man in his forties came, held his hand out, and gave Josette and Lucas a firm handshake.

"Name's Bernard, welcome to Sospel. Where are you two from?" He looked at Lucas and added, "You look nice and tan."

"My name is Lucas and this is Josette. I just got back from Algeria. I spent almost three years there. They get some sun in that country."

Bernard laughed heartily. "I bet they do. Thanks for your service. I heard it did not turn out to be a piece of cake for some. What branch of the military were you in?"

"Infantry. Did a lot of patrolling."

"Must have been hot," Bernard nodded. "What are you in Sospel for? Hiking?"

"Yes. We want to go up in the mountains, but we have to do it gradually. We have a week."

"What I can do, is drive you around the perimeter of the park, show you the accesses to the trailheads, and explain where they go, how difficult the hike is and how long to plan for. This way, you can pick what you want to do and not waste time trying to figure out where to go and what's there to do and see. How does that sound?"

"That'd be terrific." Lucas turned to Josette inquiringly. She nodded back. "We'll take you up on that. It's very generous of you. Thank you," Lucas replied.

"You gave three years of your life on our behalf, that's my way to thank you. I'll pick you up at nine tomorrow morning. I guess you're staying at Le Chalet. There are not too many other options."

"Yes, we are."

Bernard got up. "I'll see you in the morning."

That evening, inhaling the cool pine-scented light breeze, the couple cuddled up on their balcony, looking at the rugged mountain slopes outlined by a dark sky dimly lit by a half-moon.

"Do you want to share what's on your mind?" Josette asked Lucas.

"I'm just enjoying the mountain air and the crisp evening. I love the silence. It makes me feel safe and content."

"Was it like that in Algeria?"

"In some ways, but there always had to be a part of me which had to be on alert. So the silence, although welcome and comforting couldn't make me feel safe. This is good for me."

As the sky darkened, the stars appeared. Their twinkling and familiar pattern was exactly that which he saw much farther south in the Northern Sahara. The familiar sight warmed Lucas's heart.

"Is not Mother Nature's night display beautiful?" he asked Josette.

She put her head on his shoulder. "It is magnificent. I've never been this close to the stars."

"They are part of the wonders of nature. But you can only see the stars when you're away from city lights. The modern world generates much light pollution as well as other disrespects of Mother Nature, such as noise, air, and crowd pollution. When we hike in the wilderness, you'll breathe and drink the real, unspoiled nature's menu. You'll love it."

 would

The next morning, Bernard drove to several high, picturesque villages from which narrow roads led to trailheads: Saorge, Coaraze, Entreveaux, etc. Lucas had his topographic map and marked the spots. Josette noted on a pad the distance, elevation, time estimates, and destinations of the different hikes. Bernard explained the highlights of the trails, and the many lakes like Lake Allos, the largest in the Alps, and Lake De Fenestre, and high passes: Col de Fenêtre, 2,200 feet, col de Verns, 3,400 feet. Summits: Mt. Pelat, 10,000 feet, and summit des Garrets, 6,000 feet. All these tantalizing hikes would take anywhere from four to ten hours. He recommended the Valley of Marvels with its prehistoric markings on several rocks, a five-hour roundtrip from the trailhead.

They had lunch with Bernard at his café. He wished them luck with the hikes.

"Take water and warm clothes. It's still the end of March and there's plenty of snow up there. You'll enjoy it. You won't see any tourists. The mountains will be yours."

That afternoon Lucas and Josette stocked up on bottled water and food to be carried in Lucas's daypack.

The next day, to get acclimated, they set out to go to Lake Allos, only a four-hour easy hike with limited elevation gain at low altitude. They were awed by the beauty of the blue lake with its background of snow-capped summits. They sat on a cold rock admiring the scenery. They saw Mt. Pelat which happened to be on the list for a later hike, at the end of the week. Birds flew over their heads, eagles and other large birds Lucas could not identify. They didn't talk for a while. Then Josette asked Lucas, "What are you thinking about?"

"This is so beautiful and so different from the Atlas Mountains. There are no lakes there, and no snow. Yet, I feel at home."

"That's wonderful. It must be calming for you."

"Yes it is. That's what I need. I want to remember the good images of the past months. But I can't help but think of my girls. I hope they're safe. Tom and his friends will take good care of them, and my soldiers are there too. I know they loved Hana and Aisha."

"What do you plan to do with them when they come to France?" Josette asked.

"Nothing much. They will be safe. I just want to welcome and hug them. I also would like you to meet the two girls and look at them with your professional eye. You may recommend that they do certain things that will ease their settling into their new life."

Josette nodded. "I'm curious to meet them, because of you, of course, but also because of the trauma that they both endured. Aisha who dealt with the fear of the war and lost her dad, but more so Hana who, in addition to being rejected by the people in her village, lost both her parents and then her new father." She looked at him tenderly and asked. "You said you have fewer nightmares. Are you getting better?"

"It depends. I am handling the combat memories pretty well, but it's the images of the atrocities against innocents that still bother me. I have been asking myself a question for some time. Do you think that combat veterans could have a trauma similar to that of these two little girls? And do you think that the treatments or mitigation you would suggest for them could apply to me?"

"To be honest, since I have been looking at your struggle in re-entering civilian life, I have wondered about that very question. I don't know of any study addressing this. I wonder if I should investigate similar protocols to the ones I have for kids."

"That could be an important study. I know my soldiers were affected by the war as much as I was. It is probably true of all combat troops.

Sometimes, I wonder if I should not dedicate myself and my career on helping veterans returning from war."

"You'll know as you get more settled." Josette shivered. "Let's go back to Sospel. I'm getting cold; I need to walk."

On the way down, they stopped at the Refuge d'Allos, a wooden structure where one could stop and shelter overnight. They talked to the couple running the place. They told Lucas and Josette, "You can spend the night here anytime if you wanted to venture a bit farther into the mountains and shorten what could be a long day."

"We'll keep that in mind," Josette replied.

ও৲৹

They hiked every day, taking longer hikes each time and enjoying every single one of them. On the next to the last day, they decided to hike to one of the passes beyond Lake Allos and spend the night in the lake refuge on the way back, so as not to make the day inordinately long and exhausting. After trekking close to Mt. Pelat, they stopped to enjoy the marvelous views. Sitting, drinking some water and having a nice lunch, they heard the sharp piercing sound of marmots. Then not far in front of them, three yellowish brown rodents emerged from their holes. They were the ones they had heard. They saw Josette and Lucas, but did not seem to feel threatened. They did not acknowledge their presence and proceeded to look for food. They must have come out of hibernation recently, because there was still much snow on the ground, not far above where Josette and Lucas sat. Squealing and gathering pine cones from the ground, the little rodents went about their chores, ignoring their audience.

Josette and Lucas relaxed, enjoying the entertaining spectacle when all of a sudden, running and jumping from rock to rock a small herd of ibexes came toward where the couple sat. The goats saw them and stopped. Surprised at being so close to the beautiful animals, Josette and Lucas kept quiet and grinned from ear to ear. The males flaunted their long curved horns and stared at Josette and Lucas as if wondering what they were doing there. They all had their dark brown winter coat, but they were hungry and were coming to the area where snow had melted and blades of grass started to show up. Lucas and Josette did not move, neither did the marmots bother with the goats, so the ibexes went farther down and started grazing.

But when the time came to go down, Josette and Lucas had to startle the wildlife. As soon as they stood up, the ibexes jumped back up the slope and the marmots scattered and disappeared into their holes.

"Wow! What a treat," Josette said. "The animals did not mind us."

"It's early in the season. They have not seen tourists yet, and they're hungry, so we shared that moment with them. Mother Nature shares her treasures with those who respect her, her animals, and her flora."

They stayed at the refuge as planned, so that evening they gazed at the starry sky. They looked at the reflection of the moon on the almost black lake. Warmly bundled up, they were at peace with the world. The rhythm of life had slowed down for Lucas, and Josette thanked Mother Nature for that.

"Would it not be nice to live not far from here and have the park in our backyard?" Josette said.

"I had the same thought, but the only city where we could work would be Nice. The town is beautiful, but it has limited opportunities in medical research, or corporate businesses. It will depend on what we end up doing."

⁂

On the train back, it became clear that the week had been good for both Lucas, who had slowed down and for several days did not revisit the nasty memories of the past years, and for Josette, who rested, away from her upcoming final exam. But at the same time they had not made much progress toward deciding the direction their lives were to take.

When Josette and Lucas got back to Paris, a letter from Ms. Rooth congratulating him and Josette awaited them. Not surprisingly she said that she would not come to the wedding. "I think I remember you talking about Josette the last summer you were here. I can't come to congratulate you on the big day, but I'd love you to come and spend a few days with me. I'm dying to meet her. Let me know when you can find the time to do that."

Lucas told Josette, "I'd really like to go see her."

"Let's plan on it."

Chapter 14

El Boussaid, Tom's Ranch

April 6

Aisha and Hana had withdrawn into themselves after the shooting that killed Ahmed and wounded Basira. Hana was sad to have lost the man who had given her a refuge away from the bad men of the village and had protected her from them, but Aisha had become even more subdued. She missed her father, the farm where she was born and raised, and the only way of life she knew. She stayed close to her mother after Basira came out of the hospital.

At the farm, for the past two years, Hana had mostly kept to herself, tending to the goats who seemed to enjoy her companionship. If she was not with the animals, at first she read the book that Francine used for her teaching. Later Francine gave her other books. Hana only came alive when she was with Francine, studying French and learning how to read and write. Since she had moved to the ranch, she tended to speak more with both Francine and Tom than to Basira. She almost exclusively used the French language. She was curious and eager to learn. Hana wondered where France was. So Francine had showed her an atlas. Hana studied and asked questions about the maps. After a short time, she started to grasp the concept of the world atlas. She asked questions about the countries she discovered going through the big book. Aisha was less interested in learning and had started to distance herself from Hana.

Hana had never seen the ocean or the Mediterranean Sea but she dreamed of sailing to Marseille. She could not visualize what being at sea would be like, but she would be gone from her current life, far away from the bad men. Although she was now two years past her last days in the village, she was still traumatized by that time. She tended to cling to Tom or to Francine whenever she saw strangers nearby and heard harsh Arab voices or unexpected loud noises. Whenever Ahmed and Basira had taken Aisha to the village, they had dropped Hana at Tom's and Francine's place.

Hana did not know the captain's plan, but she quietly observed the many changes around her, and she had become more alert. She followed the happenings with keen interest, hoping they would bring her to safety.

There was much to be done on the ranch and much going on. First, the container delivered by the soldiers had to be filled with the possessions that could fit. Tom and Francine sorted through their belongings and selected what would go to France and what would stay. The containers were picked up at the end of the month of March.

ఌ

As planned, the neighbors who were scheduled to occupy the staff quarters moved into the ranch property, and the Picard family settled in the main house with Basira, the girls, and Tom and Francine.

There was a sense of excitement combined with an underlying feeling of angst in the now full house. John Picard, with a permanent smile sculpted on his face, and his wife, Anne-Marie, a happy person too, joined Tom and Francine in the main house. Both were armed, he with a submachine gun, a French Mat 49, and she with a rifle. Like Francine and Tom, they were both good shots. The families who had moved into the staff's quarters a few feet away from the main house also had weapons. The newcomers established a schedule whereby two of the new residents, men or women, would act as sentries, one by the front gate, and one in the rear of the main house until the soldiers assigned to the protection of Tom's ranch came. They were due in two days.

Although the occupants of the ranch knew they were in danger, they felt they were as safe as they could manage to be. In spite of the fact that they were all abandoning their properties and their way of life, their mood was good. At least, the decision to leave Algeria had been made and they had a detailed schedule for their escape. They had done their best to be as secure as possible, and safety was in sight.

❧

Hana watched the comings and goings in what had become crowded surroundings. Francine had noticed the change in Hana's behavior. She mentioned it to Tom who was also aware that Hana showed less fear, and looked happier.

"I can't be sure," he said, "but I have a feeling Hana has started to believe that she's about to leave the place where she endured so much trauma and constant fear. We have no idea of what happened to the little girl before her mother died, and we may never know how many days she struggled between her mother's death and when Lieutenant Lucas rescued her. All we know is that Mustapha told us that the villagers ignored her. But I suspect there must have been nastiness aimed at her and possibly threat of violence or worse. That would explain her visceral fear of the villagers. I saw her when Basira said good-bye to her farm; Hana had a little smile when she knew she could forget the farm because she would never go back there."

Francine replied, "It's hard to believe that she's almost eight but knows war. She does not understand why there is a war, but she knows it kills. She has been traumatized by her losses, and she knows that death takes people away forever. She was scared from morning till night, but she kept it to herself and dealt with it, probably secretly dreaming of a life without fear, not quite knowing what that meant or whether it was possible or not."

"She seems more affected by the happenings around her than Aisha is," Tom said.

Francine nodded. "Definitely, Hana is very smart. I saw that the first days she came with Aisha for the French lessons two years ago. Not quite six at the time, she was curious, and it became obvious to me she wanted to learn, and also wanted to know how to read. Basira said she was glad that I would teach the girls how to read and write, but she added she could not pay me for doing it. I thought it was cute of her to say that."

Tom asked, "I should know, but I don't. How did they both do?"

"Hana learned fast. She made quick progress; she could read quite a bit after a few months and her comprehension is outstanding today; even her writing is good. Her French is flawless. Her mind can process solutions to problems. She managed her fear, and trained her brain to analyze what was happening around her. She changed her behavior accordingly, to make herself as safe as she knew how. Aisha was a lot slower in learning French, and she's way behind Hana in reading and writing although she's about the same age. They're both dear, but Hana is as smart as a whip."

❧

John Picard used Tom's phone, which worked today by some kind of miracle, to check on the passages he was trying to secure for the five adults and two kids. He hung up the receiver, shaking his head, and turned to Tom.

"Tom, I can get tickets to sail from Oran to Marseille on April 29th, a Sunday. The best I could get is one suite-cabin made to sleep four and one double cabin which accommodates two, all in first class. Is that okay with you?"

"It's perfect. We can take the suite with Basira and the two girls. Thank you so much."

"Okay. I'll book it," John said.

Hana had listened to the conversation, and looked intrigued.

"What's a passage?" she asked Tom.

"It's a trip in a ship over the sea to go to France."

Her smile let Tom know she liked the answer.

"And what's a suite?" she added.

"On the ship we will have a big double room. That's called a suite with enough space for the five of us to sleep in, because the trip will be overnight."

She looked at Tom. Her eyes were smiling as much as her lips.

"Does that mean we are going on the ship? We're really leaving?"

"Yes, little one. We are going to France. We'll first drive to Sidi Bel Abbès, in a couple of weeks, and by the end of the month, we will be on the ship."

"When do we leave on the ship?" Hana was eager to know.

"It'll be on the 29th of April."

She ran to his arms and said, "Thank you." She rested on Tom's shoulder and sobbed softly.

"Why the tears, Hana? Are you sad?" he asked.

"She raised her head, tears rolling down on her cheeks, but her face radiating joy, "No. I am happy." She looked at him with her bright blue eyes, and with a shy little smile, she whispered to him, "I'm going to live."

Tom was so touched, his eyes watered.

"Yes, you will, Hana. You deserve it."

Tom told Francine about his conversation with Hana. "A bit less than a month, and we'll all be safe. That sounds good to me too."

Francine smiled at him. "Amen." Then she said, "It amazes me to see how mature she is for an eight-year-old, yet she is almost as vulnerable as she was the first days we met her; but to her credit, she manages her fear and does what she thinks will keep her safe. Maybe one day we'll know what happened in her last days in the village, but I'll never ask her."

ༀ

The next day, Mustapha came to the gate of the property. Whoever stood guard by the gate knew him. All the soldiers did.

"I need to speak with Tom," he said to the sentry.

The sentry went into the main house to get Tom, who greeted Mustapha.

"What brings you here, Mustapha?"

"I want to talk to you about the properties. I think it would be better to have someone live in Ahmed's farm."

"Who do you have in mind?"

"Rafa wants to move into the farm. It's better than his. He's willing to give Basira thirty thousand francs to move in now. Rafa's farm hand will pay him twelve thousand francs for his."

"Why?" Tom asked, "You can do that for free when we are gone."

"Not that easy," Mustapha replied. "Many others are eyeing French farms. But if I can vouch for the new ownership, there will be no fight. They won't be available for anyone to just take them over, or wreck them."

"I see," Tom said. "Let me get Basira."

"You don't have to. I have the money with me. I can give it to you now."

Tom remembered that Mustapha, like all the elders, was not comfortable talking with women. "I know Basira does not care what happens to the farm. We're going to be gone," Tom told Mustapha. "So I'll give the money to Basira, if that's what you want to do."

Mustapha said, "I like Basira. She's a nice woman. She can use the money. I'll sign some papers to make it official. In case the soldiers try to stop Rafa, I'd tell them to talk to you."

"That's fine." Tom said.

"Also," Mustapha added, "I thought that when you leave, I might move into your ranch."

Tom laughed. "I don't mind, but you know we grew grapes and made wine. Are you going to do that?"

Mustapha shook his head. "No, but I like your house. I have fifty thousand francs for you. That will give me title to the property."

"Okay by me. Thanks. Enjoy the place."

"I have four wives," Mustapha said. "There'll be room here for all of them."

Tom had a good laugh. Then he became serious. After money changed hands, Tom asked, "Have you heard from Basira's sons? Do you know where they are?"

"They are in a training camp near Saida, south of here. I visited the facility a month ago after the French troops had left it. It's quite nice. I'm sure the boys will be okay. Give me an address where I could send a message to you if there is news from them."

Tom gave him the address of the property he and Francine had bought in southern France, and then went back into the house. He told Basira what Mustapha had done and gave her the thirty thousand francs.

Basira exulted. "I never expected this. How honest Rafa is. I'd like to thank him, but I won't have a chance. If you can find a way to convey my thanks to him, please do."

Tom told Francine about Basira's money and theirs.

"I'm so glad for Basira. She has not lost everything. Our fifty thousand are totally unexpected. That's a surprise. Why do you think Mustapha did that? Being fair?"

Tom shook his head. "That would be a first. I think he and Rafa are going to go into Ahmed's farm and be stopped by the soldiers. Mustapha will tell them to talk to me. I'll tell them about the transactions."

"So what?"

"So, Mustapha is going to tell them how fair he was and ask them to protect the properties until the troops leave. Then the FLN troops will be the ones to protect them. Clever?"

"You're probably right. He is shrewd."

Chapter 15

El Boussaid, Tom's Ranch

April 7

The next day, the troops came and established defensive positions around Tom's ranch.

At first apprehensive when the troops come, Hana relaxed when she saw Lieutenant Marchand. She had been devastated when Lieutenant Lucas had come to say good-bye when he left for France, but he had convinced her that she'd be safe with his replacement, Lieutenant Marchand. Hana was getting excited and confused. All the people moving around in the ranch and the boisterous meals with so many people made her dizzy. Used to being by herself a lot, she needed to be calm for a while. She asked Francine if she could borrow one of her beautiful books.

Francine asked her, "Would you like me to teach you some French spelling, help you read, or read to you? Or do you prefer to go hide in my bedroom and be quiet?"

"Your bedroom would be good."

Francine gave her Le Petit Prince. Hana had already started to read it and was enjoying it.

"Thank you," Hana said, and she went to sit by herself.

Reading and trying to imagine what life in France would be, she wondered if Lieutenant Lucas would live near her. Her heart secretly hoped she would see him again.

Aisha was shying away from the strangers who now lived with her, and kept close to her mother. Francine wondered why both Aisha's and Hana's behavior had changed so much in opposite directions. She mentioned it to Tom, who thought for a moment.

"Aisha has spent her whole young life in the same farm, with the same mother and father," he said. "She has had a nice simple life in spite of a couple of scares, but her dad died, and now she faces a new life in an unknown place. She is apprehensive."

"I agree with you, but what about Hana? She is facing the same unknown."

"But she has a different background. She lost her dad when she was too young to remember him. We might not know how her mother died or how Hana spent her days and nights until Lieutenant Lucas picked her up, but Hana does, and she survived that terrible time. Then, she only spent two years at the farm, mostly with the goats and her books. She lived scared of the bad men all the time, so she does not have a happy past. She looks at her future in an unknown destination as a different, more secure, and hopefully much happier way of life. In other words, a hope for a change away from her bad memories sounds good to her."

"You're probably right," Francine nodded. "What a nightmare for these poor kids."

⁖

The days went by. Everyone was on alert, but there was no attack. The families on the ranch became more and more confident they were going to make it.

A couple of weeks following the crowding of Tom's place, the captain came and gathered everyone. Aisha and Hana, the only children of the group, were there too. Aisha was nearly shaking from fear, but Hana had her eyes wide open, eager to hear the news which she figured would be about leaving the ranch.

The captain said, "It's now time to go to the next step, which is the transfer to Sidi Bel Abbès. We have moved a few families who lived closer to Tiaret, west of us. It did not go smoothly. Two groups of men, one from the FLN, and one from a local village were waiting for the convoy to depart to occupy the properties. But one group jumped the guns, a fire fight between the two factions ensued, and a couple of civilians and one of my soldiers were hurt. We don't want that to happen here."

Tom said, "Captain, you should know that Mustapha came here and talked about his plans for who gets to live where."

"I know," the captain said, "I talked to Mustapha, and we are now protecting the properties he and his friends have just acquired." Tom winked at Francine who smiled back. "My troops have helped make the move secure," the captain continued, "Mustapha has also conscripted a few men from the village to help guard them." He looked at everybody in the room, and announced, "You will be leaving this place for Sidi Bel Abbès in two days."

Hana wiggled and squirmed in her seat. Francine held her hand and whispered, "Shush. I'm excited too, but we need to listen to the captain."

The captain went on, "We'll be here at seven in the morning. We'll back up two trucks into the property and load the three families from the staff buildings with their luggage. The cover will be on the trucks so no one will be able to know what and who we are transporting. The third truck will be for Tom and the occupants of the main house, same scenario. One more thing, you will have to bring your weapons and ammo and leave them in the trucks for your escort to collect. You will have no need for them anymore, certainly not in the Foreign Legion compound, and you would not be allowed to bring weapons of any kind on the ship. I doubt you would have any use for them where you're going."

"How about on the way to Sidi Bel Abbès? Don't we need them for the trip?" John Picard asked the captain.

"You will have an armed escort all the way to the Foreign Legion buildings."

"Why don't we just leave the weapons in the house?" Tom asked.

"Absolutely not," the captain replied. "Bring them in the trucks. We will take care of them. We don't want to leave them to the locals. Okay, guys, good luck. Start packing. See you in two days." The captain saluted and left.

~

The families who had moved into Tom's ranch were already packed for the next leg of their trip, but Francine, Tom, Basira, and the girls had to select what they would bring. Everyone could only take bags they could carry, with a little help from soldiers and porters to get on and off the ship. Francine gave Hana and Aisha each a small back pack and asked Basira to help Aisha set aside what she wanted to bring. Hana selected her precious raggedy doll first, and also the books Francine had given her, her new shoes and two cute dresses that made her look like a quite sophisticated young girl. Francine looked at Hana's pile.

"That's a nice dress," Francine said pointing at the light blue one with a white border.

"Do you want me to wear it for you?" Hana asked her.

Francine knew right away that the correct answer had to be yes. So Hana put it on. Tom walked into the room and stopped. "You look wonderful, Hana. You look very European."

Her face brightened instantly. "I do?"

"For sure. With your blue eyes and a beautiful dress, you look like a Parisian." Hana blushed and beamed with pleasure. She wanted to shed any remnant of memory attached to where she had spent the first eight years of her life.

On that last morning on the ranch, everyone was up, dressed, packed, and ready early. When the first truck backed up, the first two families who had stayed in the staff quarters climbed in the back of it with their luggage. The driver brought the canvas down, and the vehicle moved out and parked behind the two lead jeeps, already waiting on the road. The third family of four and their luggage went into the second truck which moved out. A larger truck backed up. Tom helped Basira, not yet one-hundred percent healed, climb into the back. Aisha went up and sat next to her. The Picard family went in, and Francine sat with Hana. Tom loaded the luggage and turned around, looking at the ranch for the last time. He and Francine had heavy hearts. They knew it had to be done; they had to restart their lives, and they were lucky to be able to do it. Many, like George and his family, had been slaughtered; Ahmed had been shot as had scores of others. Yet this was where Tom and Francine had started their life together.

"Time to go, sir," the sergeant who would be in the last armed jeep said to Tom, the last one to board the truck. He shook hands with the captain who stayed to oversee the departure.

"Thanks for everything, Captain. Stay safe and come home soon."

✢

The convoy, which included a small truck loaded with Tom's wine destined to the Legion, followed the twisty road west to Sidi Bel Abbès where they arrived late morning. They all got off, and thanked Lieutenant Marchand and his soldiers for all they had done to ensure their safety in the past few months. Then legionnaires led each family to comfortable quarters in the officers' buildings. Later, they all gathered downstairs to meet Captain Goddard, the Foreign Legion officer in charge of the evacuation.

He greeted the families warmly. "Welcome to Sidi Bel Abbès. You will find the city to be reasonably safe. You can walk around, and stroll through the parks if you feel like a little exercise. I would avoid markets and restaurants because that's where there is potential trouble. The food in the officers' mess in the compound is quite good. When you go out of the compound, get a pass; the sentry will request it when you come back in, so we know you belong here. Senior Sergeant Schmidt will take you outside to show you the legionnaires' areas which are off-limits to you. Lastly, if you know your departure date and specifics, stop in my office in the command post and give me the information so that we can schedule transportation. Also, thanks for the wine. It won't be wasted. Relax. You're safe here."

Aisha and Hana were overwhelmed by the three-story buildings and the severe geometric layout of the complex. Hana stayed close to Francine, and Aisha to her mother.

Tom and John Picard went to meet with Captain Goddard.

"There are seven of us, five adults and two children," Tom said. "We are scheduled to leave a week from tomorrow on the ship Provence leaving the port of Oran on Sunday the twenty-ninth, early afternoon."

"The departure areas tend to be crowded and a bit unsettling. What class are your passages in?" The captain asked.

"We're booked in first class."

"That's great. The process will be a lot more orderly for you. Yet I'd like to bring you to the check-in area late morning. I would not want your little girls – they're very cute by the way – to be flustered. I am sure this evacuation is difficult for them."

"I appreciate that, sir. At what time shall we leave here?"

"We'll have a small bus that will fit all of you ready at nine. Your escort will be ready too. You're all set. Stop here if you need anything. Try to enjoy your week here as much as possible. These are hard times for everyone."

After thanking the captain, the two men rejoined the rest of the group and they all went to the officers' mess for lunch.

They were delighted with the quality of the food. After the meal they retired in their respective rooms to rest. It had been a long and stressful morning.

⋞⋟

John Picard had arranged with his friends to have the ship passage certificates delivered to a common friend in Sidi Bel Abbès, so he went to retrieve the tickets. When he met his friend, he found out the documents were not there. He panicked for a moment.

"I hope our trip is still booked. Damn! What do I do now?"

His friend said, "Let's call Oran."

They finally located the man who was in charge of the tickets who said, "I'm sorry, I have them here, but I have not sent them yet."

John said, "Can you drive them here, and bring them to the Foreign Legion headquarters? Ask for me, I'll tell the guards to expect you."

"I can do that. I'll be there tomorrow morning."

"Thanks. I'll meet you at the entrance guard post."

John told Tom about it. They spent an anxious night. The guy in charge of the tickets did not seem to be too reliable. Yet the next morning he showed up at the Legion compound, and gave John the tickets which were as promised. "Sorry about the mix-up," he apologized.

With a sigh of relief, John thanked the man for making the trip.

The escape was still on. "Thank God," Tom said.

Chapter 16

Paris

April 8

The two days for Josette's certification exam were Thursday and Friday, May third and fourth, less than a month away.

"I better buckle down and get ready because I don't have many days left before the exam. I'm not really worried, but I want to shine for my professors and for my mentors," Josette told Lucas when they woke up the morning after their return.

"Anything I can do to help, just ask. Otherwise I'll stay out of your way," Lucas said.

"Don't worry. I will ask you if I need anything. But before I get into it, how about Saturday May twenty-sixth for the wedding if it works with everybody?"

"I'll check and we'll talk about it tonight. I'll also look for a larger apartment. If I find something I think you might like, I'll show it to you and you'll decide."

"Thanks, Luke."

True to his word, he went to his studio to give Josette the space she needed.

First, Lucas wrote to Ms. Rooth to inform her of the date of the wedding, and to tell her more about Josette. Then Madame de Sèvres' assistant called and proposed this Thursday at six for him to introduce Josette, and asked that Lucas stop in before that for a short visit.

Later in the morning he called Josette.

"I'm sorry," Lucas said, "I hate to disturb you, but I want to verify that you are okay to meet the countess on Thursday at six."

"Don't worry. Of course, Thursday is fine."

"Good. Go back to work."

"I will. I love you, Luke."

"Love you too."

༄

Lucas went to call on the countess. She welcomed him warmly, and asked him if there was a date for the wedding yet.

"The tentative date is the twenty-sixth of next month. We are checking with everybody."

The countess buzzed her assistant and asked him if the date was open, mentioning the potential wedding. His answer was positive.

"I wanted to share with you a project I started last year. It would interest you because it affects veterans, and because of Josette's working on trauma."

She proceeded to tell him about the Maligny family property, and how it had been transformed into a rehabilitation center for wounded warriors.

"The treatments the army provides in the facility are for physical traumas, broken bones, missing limbs, internal injuries and so on, nothing related to psychological trauma, but it does help soldiers to get back on their feet, some literally."

"That is great news, I wonder if any of my soldiers are or went there."

"We could find out."

"I'll think about it. I'm curious to know how you managed to find your way through the military bureaucracy."

She smiled and said, "I'm not sure you know, but my former husband, who died over ten years ago, was a major in the colonial infantry during the Indochina conflict. That's where he was hit, and he never recovered. One of his lieutenants, a nice man, now a colonel, kept in touch with me over the years, and I thought he might know some retired military heavyweight who could navigate the bureaucracy for me. I called him, and he put me in touch with retired General de Vangarde who has connections and got it done."

"That was a coup," Lucas said. "This colonel knew the right guy."

"I had known Colonel Dubois since he served as a lieutenant with my late husband."

Lucas could not believe it, and looked at her, his mouth opened. He shook his head, "It can't be."

"What can't be?" She asked.

"Josette's last name is Dubois, and her father is a colonel. I just met him for the first time a couple of weeks ago because he got back to Paris from Germany recently. That has to be the same man. Dubois is very common name, but a Colonel Dubois is not."

"This is a marvelous coincidence and a fabulous omen for your wedding. We have to get together. Have him and his wife come with you when you introduce Josette to me. Now I can't wait to meet her. Come give me a hug."

She gave him a real hug, full of warmth and affection.

"I have things I need to attend to. I'll see you, Josette and her parents on Thursday."

⁓

Lucas went to the church to find out the status of their application, and to inquire if they could schedule the wedding for the last Saturday of the month. The priest looked at the agenda book and said it was possible.

"We are not quite done yet, but I could put you down to reserve the spot. Would you like me to do that?"

"Please, do."

"You and your bride will have to come in a few days to fill out the final paperwork, but you are all set."

Then Lucas went to the *mairie*, the 7th Arrondissement city hall, and got the form they had to fill out to get the license. The clerk said there would be no problem in scheduling the signing for May twenty-fifth, one day before the church wedding. Lucas did not find a suitable apartment, but there was time for that.

Lucas was still incredulous about Colonel Dubois when he saw Josette.

"You'll never believe what happened when I saw the countess."

"Try me. I'm very gullible."

They both laughed.

"Madame de Sèvres has donated her Maligny property to the Veterans' Administration to create a rehabilitation center for wounded warriors. The center is now fully operational."

"I believe that," Josette said, teasing Lucas. He ignored her.

"When I asked her how she managed to negotiate that with the government, she told me that a certain General de Vangarde made it happen. The incredible thing is that the person who hooked her up with the general is a colonel who knew her late husband."

"So?" Josette interrupted.

"So, the name of that colonel is Colonel Dubois, your dad."

"NOOO! That I can't believe. Really?"

"She has invited him and Marlene to join us when I introduce you to her on Thursday. She also said it was a good omen for us."

"It is. And you know what, Luke?"

"No. What?"

"I love her already. A person of her rank, caring for wounded warriors. That's grand. I also have some news, although not nearly as dramatic. My sister Caroline called me back. She just got back from a business trip to America. She is excited about our wedding and dying to meet you. She said in jest, I hope, 'I'll be honest, after the Gérard adventure, you're not the easiest person to get along with, so if he agreed to marry you, he's got to be a great guy.' So I told her a bit about you and how much you impressed our dad."

"Will she come to the wedding?"

"She said she wouldn't miss it for the world."

Chapter 17

Paris

April 12

On Thursday shortly before six, Josette and Lucas met the colonel, dressed in his crisp uniform, and Marlene on boulevard Malesherbes in front of Madame de Sèvres' residence. They proceeded through the inner courtyard and walked up the steps to ring the bell. The butler smiled at Josette. "My congratulations, Ms. Josette. You picked a good man. We have great admiration for him in this house."

She smiled and thanked him. He turned to Lucas and nodded. "Very pretty lady, Mr. Lucas. Congratulations to you too."

He turned to the colonel, bowed his head and said, "Please follow me, sir. Madame la Comtesse expects you."

They all went up the elegant spiral staircase into the countess's parlor, Lucas' favorite room.

The countess walked in to greet the colonel. "What a surprise I had the other day when Lucas and I realized that his beautiful bride-to-be is your daughter."

She then looked at Marlene. "And you must be Marlene. Please sit down. I'll have some refreshment served to celebrate this great occasion."

She turned toward Josette and said, "Please come and give me a hug. I love your husband to be, and I love you already. I must say you have chosen a good man."

"Indeed, Madame, Lucas is a great man," the colonel said. "Also you might not know he's a hero who distinguished himself leading his platoon in successful military operations."

The countess nodded, "Undoubtedly." Then she turned toward Josette. "And I understand you are dedicating your life to treat trauma in children. I respect your compassion, and if I can do anything to facilitate your quest to help the little patients, do not hesitate to tell me. I suppose most traumas you see result from wars?"

"Yes, Madame." Josette responded. "To witness kids who are innocent victims of conflicts they have nothing to do with is heartbreaking. There are also some unfortunate children who are abused by their families. But I understand you are yourself compassionate about soldiers who were wounded in battles."

"Indeed, your father knows my despair in seeing so many local conflicts which kill and maim people, and accomplish absolutely nothing."

The colonel nodded. "This Algerian war is a sad and vivid example of that."

A waiter in a white coat came into the parlor and poured Veuve Cliquot into five champagne coupes. Everyone stood up. The countess proposed a toast.

"To Josette and Lucas. Many years of happiness, and thank you to Lucas for your service to our country, and to Josette for your help to the young victims of man-made cataclysms."

They all lifted their champagne. Then they chatted about the Maligny facility. The colonel had checked on it and reported that it was doing a great deal of good in helping soldiers literally walk back into civilian life with few restrictions.

"I thank you much, Madame, for this important contribution," the colonel said.

"We'll look at the potential need for more facilities, and," she turned to Josette, "maybe adding treatments of soldiers' trauma. They might need it as much as the children."

"You are right, Madame. Science is just beginning to look at that aspect of trauma. Medical scientists have started to look into what generals call battle fatigue, which I am convinced has little to do with fatigue, but a lot with stress. Lucas here can vouch for that,"

"I'm sure you and I will talk more about this. Maybe you can help me and I can help you."

The countess turned to the colonel.

"Colonel Dubois, what is the plan for the twenty-sixth?"

"After the ceremony, we will gather and have lunch at the Cercle Militaire, Place Saint Augustin."

"I approve. It is a grand place for celebrations."

With that, she rose from her chair signaling it was time to leave.

"Josette, my dear, I am so glad you and Lucas found each other."

⁂

On the way home, Josette asked Lucas, "Who do we have to tell now that we have settled on a date for the wedding?"

"Your sister, Thierry and Nicole, your doctor-friends, and Ms. Rooth, if she writes that she'll be coming after all. Your parents and Madame de Sèvres already know. I think that's it."

Early the next day, Josette said to Lucas, "I know I must buckle down and study, but I have to have something to wear for the wedding. I'm going this morning with Marlene to get a dress. What are your plans?"

"I guess I better get a nice suit. I need to have something to wear too."

"That would be nice." Josette smiled and said, "When we're both back we'll go over who's coming and make sure they all know when and where to go. Once that's done, I will study."

"Deal." Lucas agreed.

When they were back, they went down the list.

"When is Caroline coming?" Lucas asked.

"She'll come early in the week of the ceremony. She'll be staying at our dad's place. Hopefully, we'll spend time with her before the wedding. And you have not heard from Tom, have you?"

"No. He must not have a date for the trip yet. It must be hard to get. Okay, Josette. Get to your books, I'll leave you alone."

Chapter 18

Sidi Bel Abbès, Algeria

April 29

The morning of the twenty-ninth, Hana and Aisha were awakened earlier than usual. Once they were fully conscious, they both remembered that today was the day. Aisha was anxious. With her blue dress on, Hana was ready and excited.

The seven of them piled into the little army bus. A jeep with a machine gun led the convoy, the bus followed next, a truck with a squad of legionnaires behind it, and a jeep ran as the last vehicle. They drove all the way to the dock where the Provence had moored. A checkpoint manned by armed French troops stopped them and verified the passages of everyone on the bus. The police checked each adult's identity, but did not ask for any document for the two children. Tom let out a sigh of relief. They drove to the first-class gangway with no delay. Stewards were there to help the passengers with their luggage, and led them to their cabins.

They went out on the deck to look at the port of Oran. They were on the ship, almost out of Algeria. They had done it. The adults, of course, had some regrets leaving the place where they lived mostly happily for many years. Aisha clung to her mother, not knowing what the future would bring her, but Hana became ebullient, her face displaying utter joy.

A steward walked around with a tray of sandwiches, and in the middle of the afternoon the ship left port. All the passengers watched the coast disappear, most with mixed emotions. Basira had left her sons in Algeria. Aisha felt rudderless unless she held Basira's hand. The Europeans had left their life of many years. They remembered their recent past with some regrets, but they looked with some anticipation at a new experience. On cloud nine, Hana held Francine's hand.

The weather was a bit rough with strong winds and high waves so the ship rolled and pitched a bit. Basira, Aisha, and John Picard elected to stay in their cabin and to skip dinner.

Hana went to the dining room with Tom, Francine, and Anne Marie Picard. Hana was in a great mood.

Francine remarked on that and said, "Hana, you are happy tonight. I've never seen you so talkative."

Hana grinned. "That's because the bad men can't reach me anymore."

"Who are these bad men?" Anne Marie asked gently.

Hana looked at Tom, then at Francine, and down at her plate. She almost whispered, "Men from the village."

"Anything bad happened there?"

Hana wiggled on her chair and looked down again. "Shortly after they killed my father — I don't remember when it happened — these men moved in with my mother. They were always trying to touch me, but my mom pushed them away. When my mother died, the men tried to take me to their house saying they had food for me. But I didn't want to go. They sat me on a chair, took my shoes off and started to pull my clothes off. I screamed." Hana looked at Tom, "Their hands were in bad places, so I jumped from the chair, grabbed my doll, and ran outside. I went around the back of the house and ran to a shed a few houses away and I hid behind the tools and stuff."

"You were safe there?" Anne Marie asked.

"I thought I was, but an older girl I knew, had seen me enter the place and came after me. She asked me what I was hiding from. I told her I ran away from those men. 'I know them, they're bad', she told me. 'But you have to go in the barn where the goats are.'"

"Why did she say that?"

"She said 'Men don't go into that barn. It's for the women to take care of the animals. You'll be safer there. I'll bring you food.'"

"So, how long did you live with the goats?"

"I don't know. I hid in the straw when the women came to look after the goats. I slept in the barn with the goats. They kept me warm. But one day, the girl came and told me there were soldiers with a jeep parked in the plaza. An officer was talking with Mustapha. She told me to run where they were. 'Mustapha will tell them you're an orphan and maybe the soldiers will help you,' she said. So I went and stood by the jeep. The officer was Lieutenant Lucas." Then Hana looked down at her plate again.

Francine and Tom recognized the distress in her eyes. They had seen it before. Francine took her hand in hers. "I knew something had happened in the village, you were so afraid of going there, but I did not know it was that bad. I am sorry, little one. You are right. It's over. The bad men can't get you."

Hana gave her a timid little smile, and tears rolled down on her cheeks.

Francine gently wiped the tears and said, "It's over. Let me cheer you up. Let me tell you about the place we are going to, would you like me to?"

"The farm? Yes, please."

"The farm is not really a farm. It is a winery, and there are also orchards on the property. It has a beautiful main house where you'll live, and two guest cottages. Because it is a winery, there's a large building with a wine-tasting room, and caves dug into a hill where the wine is made and stored. There are barns for gardening tools and equipment, a chicken coop and housing for the staff. I'm not sure if there are goats."

"Is there a village?" Hana asked.

"Yes, a nice little village with lots of great people. The village has a good elementary school where you will be able to go and learn like all the other kids. You'll love it, so when we get there, we will go see the teachers and figure out the grade that suits you. How is that?"

Hana's face gave her the answer. She got off her chair and went to put her arms around Francine's neck. She whispered, "Thank you." Then she did the same for Tom.

The next morning, the passengers disembarked and, after a cursory documents check, were admitted into France. The luggage was unloaded onto the quay, and Francine's brother, Robert, arrived to pick them up with the winery truck. The Picards said good-bye, and left in a cab to catch a train to Bordeaux where they had family.

Tom, Francine, Basira, and the two girls piled in the truck, and Robert drove toward the new property. It would take about two hours.

Chapter 19

Beaumes de Venise, South of France

April 30

When the car pulled up to the gate of the new property, Francine and Tom had tears in their eyes. They had made it. Aisha's mother, still hurting from her shoulder and from the loss of her husband, turned to Francine and thanked her for having brought her and the girls to safety. "I can't ever thank you enough for having saved our lives. It is now time to look at a new future."

Robert opened the gate and proceeded on the long driveway to the main building. The drive to the beautiful house was lined by a grove of several-deep olive trees on the left. The smell of the orange blossoms from the orchard of orange trees on the right welcomed them to their new home. Hana jumped out first when the car stopped in front of the two-story residence. A man greeted the new owners.

Tom told Hana, "This is Armand. He runs the winery."

She smiled at him.

"I'm Hana."

"Welcome, Hana," he said.

Hana looked around her, and sighed.

"Do you like it?" Francine asked her.

Her face radiant with joy, Hana surveyed the hills covered with vineyards, the great big house with an ivy-covered wall, and looked up at Francine.

"Yes. It's beautiful."

Then she saw a big, beautiful German shepherd at the end of the courtyard who, his head held high, looked at the little girl. The two of them stared at each other for a while; Hana seemed fascinated by the animal, and showed no fear at all. The dog started to walk toward her, so she walked toward him. When he sniffed her legs, she bent over and took the dog's neck in her arms. The dog let her do it. Both did not move for a long time. She kissed him, and put her cheek on the fur of his neck. He stayed by her side. Armand said to Hana, "This dog showed up last week. He has no collar, no name. He was hungry and thirsty. I gave him food and water, so he stayed. He is a chien-loup, in English a wolf-dog so I called him Wolf. You can keep him and give him another name if you want. He can be your friend." Hana looked at Wolf and at Armand, and with a big smile looked at Basira who did not say anything, so she turned to Francine, who smiled back and said, "You can have him. Wolf is yours, little girl. He will be your friend and your protector."

She ran to hug her and say thank you; the dog came to Francine too.

"Can you think of another name for him, Hana?"

Hana whispered, "I like the sound of Wolf. He is beautiful."

Tom said, "He is a big proud dog. Wolf is a good name for him."

Hana sat down on the step leading to the front door, and Wolf went to sit next to her. Two lost souls had found each other. This augured well for the young girl's rebirth in a new country. Both Francine and Tom looked at Hana; they felt even more affection for her, now that they understood the ordeal she had been forced to go through.

૪ఌ

Tom said to everyone, "Let's go in the house. There are plenty of rooms. You can select which one you would prefer."

Robert said to the new arrivals, "Let me show you inside."

They all went into the two-floor building. They walked into the comfortable and welcoming living room. "Oh! My piano is here. I'm so glad," Francine exclaimed.

"It came in last week. It took a long time to get here, but it did," her brother said.

Robert showed them the second floor, where the master and three other bedrooms were. Tom suggested Aisha and Hana share the one with twin beds, and Basira take one of the two with a double bed. Robert said, "The third one can be a guest room. I'm staying in the guest cottage for now until I leave."

Aisha said, "I want to stay with my mother."

Basira said, "If Aisha prefers to share the bedroom with me, we could take the one with twin beds, and Hana can have one with a double bed." She looked at Tom and Francine, "If it's all right with you."

Tom nodded. "That's fine. You okay with that, Hana?"

Hana nodded and asked, "Can I have the room with the bed and the desk too?"

Francine agreed. "Of course, Hana, and we'll put a pad on the floor for Wolf to keep you company."

Hana's face radiated joy. "Oh. Thank you, thank you."

Tom then said, "Let's get our luggage in and have lunch. Julie, Armand's wife who worked in the kitchen, had prepared a meal for all to have after their long journey. After lunch, Tom said to Francine with a broad smile, "I think you should try a few notes on the piano to see if you remember how to play."

Francine had played a few times in Algeria, but not frequently. Hana and Aisha had never heard her. Francine bowed, adjusted the height of the piano bench and sat on it. She looked up at the ceiling, and said, "Any special requests?"

When no one proposed anything, she started to play the Ode to Joy from Beethoven's ninth symphony.

The uplifting piece of music filled the whole house. All loved it, including Wolf, who listened to the music, his chin resting on Hana's lap.

Everyone clapped, and Francine said, "Time to unpack and get settled."

എ

When Francine and Tom got into their room, Francine asked Tom, "Do you think there's anything wrong with Aisha? She seems overly quiet."

"She's lost without her familiar environment of the farm she grew up in," Tom replied, "She does not have any idea of what's ahead for her."

Francine agreed. "Undoubtedly, but Basira is not that cheerful either. I'm not sure how this is going to work out."

Tom added, "She probably misses Ahmed too. But I also believe that the winery is much more upscale than what she's used to. She is not relaxed. They're both intimidated by this place. On top of this, France is a foreign country for them, and they dread the future."

Francine added, "At least we made Hana happy, the poor thing."

"Yes, and actually, she's no longer a poor thing as I see her perky, curious, and full of energy. I feel good about that," Tom replied.

ఛ

Francine sat on one of the easy chairs in their bedroom and said, "I'm looking forward to a less threatening and more relaxing life here. Aren't you?"

"It'll be a nice change not to have weapons within reach all the time."

Francine and Tom had married near Avignon in their early twenties. Tom's parents had died shortly after from tuberculosis, a rampant disease after World War II, and Tom had inherited his parents' money. Young and eager to lead an exciting life, Francine quit her school teaching job, and, looking for an adventure, they purchased a vineyard near Mascara in Western Algeria in 1950. When they found out they were not able to have children, they decided it would not be wise to look to adopt little ones because of the outlook for the political instability of the French territory. They were successful in growing their wine business, selling cases of the strong Mascara red wine in Algeria, but also in France. They also had fun growing oranges and figs for the Algerian market. After tumultuous and difficult years, ready to settle in France, they had purchased the property they just moved to today.

Although they were called ranchers, they had been more owners and managers of the Algerian property than actual hands-on farmers. The same would be true of the Beaumes de Venise fully-operating winery.

"Our new business will demand hard work, but it will be fun," Tom said. "I also believe we'll enjoy having Hana around, but I wonder how Basira will feel in an environment entirely different from her earlier life."

"I'm afraid it'll be difficult if not impossible for her to adapt to her new life. She has the money Rafa gave her, but it's not a lot. She has no education, and although she's not a stereotypical Algerian woman in her dress and religious habits, she is Arab, and unfortunately will have to face prejudice. I am afraid it might not work."

"Agreed," Tom said, "And the same goes for Aisha. She looks North African, her French is far from perfect and, if she goes to school, which she should, the local kids might not accept her as one of their own. Her birth mark will not help either. Hana is different."

Francine added. "That's so true. I remember that when you saw her before we packed for our trip here, you told her she looked Parisian."

"She did. And she is smart."

"That, she is," Francine asserted. "I plan to take the two girls to meet the head of the local school to discuss how they could best fit in, because they have had no formal education so far."

Then she added, "Hana looks French, doesn't she?"

Tom looked serious and turned to Francine. "Do you think we should adopt her?"

Francine smiled. "I'm not sure how to do it. Basira's adoption is probably not a legal adoption, but I don't want to hurt her."

Tom said, "Neither do I, but it might come as a relief to her. Let's wait and see."

Francine went to see her brother to thank him for keeping an eye on the property.

❦

Armand, who had taken a liking to Hana, asked her if she liked animals.

Her face brightened up right away. "Yes, I do. What kind?"

Armand said, "We have a bunch of chickens and some ducks. You can go with my wife when she goes to collect the eggs. She does it every morning."

"I'd like to. Do you have any other animals?"

"We also have a small paddock and a barn where we keep goats because my wife makes goat cheese. Do you like cheese?"

"I do. I like goats too. I used to take care of them. Can we go see them?"

"Sure." They went up a hill, behind a small orchard of lemon trees. There were a half-dozen goats. When she entered their paddock, Hana spoke to them in Arabic. The goats looked at her, as if they understood what she said and came close to her. She kept talking to them and caressed them. Armand was amazed. "You're a magician, Hana. Usually the goats ignore everybody who comes into their compound."

"They're smart. They know I like them, so they like me."

"Do you know gardening?" Armand asked.

"No, can you teach me?"

"I'll prepare a little plot for you, so you can grow flowers. I'll show you how to do it."

In these first hours, a strong bond had been established between Hana and Armand. Hana went back to her room happy. She had befriended Armand, Wolf, and a bunch of goats.

Chapter 20

Paris

May 3

The exam was to take place in Necker Hospital, where Josette worked. The first morning of the certification exam consisted of a series of written tests that Josette had no trouble with whatsoever. In the afternoon, she met one-on-one with six professors, four of whom she knew and who admired her. The two new ones had heard of Josette and were quite intrigued by what they had learned about her. One did trauma research in an Aix-en-Provence hospital. The other man ran the psychology department of the University of Lyon. They had maneuvered to be able to administer the oral exam because they were eager to meet her. Every single interview went well. Josette had great command of the subject and impressed the medical brain trust which had been selected to assess her knowledge.

The second day was a public session where Josette had to give an exposé of the findings she had made during her current internship. She had chosen to report on her methods for detecting the traumatic events and diagnosing their physical and psychological effects on the children she followed for months. The second part of her talk addressed the effectiveness of the treatments she had prescribed for the patients. She planned to add recommendations for further studies.

All examining doctors had some knowledge of trauma, including Doctor Stanislas, the head of Necker Hospital. As it was open to spectators, Lucas, Madame De Sèvres, and Josette's father and Marlene were in the audience, as well as several of Josette's doctors and student-doctor friends. Dressed in her white lab coat, Josette looked professional, her posture projecting confidence and command of her subject matter.

Josette started with the story of two young girls, one five-year-old and her ten-year-old sister, who had been hurt by the explosion of a bomb hidden in one of the many trash baskets placed on every street corner of a busy Paris boulevard. In addition to the multiple physical injuries they received from flying shrapnel, they suffered multiple behavioral and psychological impacts from the explosion. Josette explained how, although painful, the wounds they suffered healed fast and did not cause lasting damage. The psychological effects of the blast did not go away fast.

She discussed in detail how the light, the noise, and the force of the detonation resulted in various manifestations of trauma, the one most significant of which came from the memory of the noise of the explosion. The most lasting effect of the blast turned out to be fear; the fear that resulted from the realization that the bomb had not been visible until it exploded, and that such devices could be hidden any place. That visceral fear proved to be the most challenging to treat in the young girls. Josette used many complicated, unpronounceable words, opaque to the neophytes in the audience, but triggered much nodding from the panel.

She continued by describing how the counseling by trained specialists helped mitigate most of the trauma within six to eight weeks, but she explained that although lessened over time, the older girl's reactions, such as fast heartbeats and the urge to run away when she heard any loud noise, did not change much while the younger one lost her phobia of loud sound almost completely.

"And I plan to study the reason for that," Josette said, then added, "After nine months, the fear of walking in the street never abated for either girl."

Her second report discussed a nine-year-old boy who, held with a knife at his throat in a farm in western Algeria, was rescued by French soldiers and freed. His trauma was only psychological, and an easy diagnostic. At the conclusion of her presentation, the audience, including the judges' panel, burst into applause.

When the audience quieted down, Josette said, "There is one more statement I would like to make. Trauma-generated fear in children depends much on the age of the child, but seems to be the long-lasting effect in most cases, while reactions to sensorial events are second. Although I have not studied the effect of trauma on adults, I have observed the impact of combat for soldiers back from North Africa."

She turned and pointed at Lucas. "My fiancé Lucas has recently come back from leading an infantry platoon in the mountains of Algeria. I have observed his struggle with his memories of that time. Fear does not seem to be part of what troubles him, reactions to sensory events are some of what he is trying to control, but it seems to me — and again, it is just a casual observation with no scientific foundation — that dealing with anger and hatred of those who perpetrated atrocities against innocent people, mainly children, is the most difficult inner battle he is fighting within himself."

Josette paused for a moment. "What to do about that? You might ask. Studying the difference in dealing with similar trauma to adults and to children might give us answers to how to deal with both the older and younger people. There are many soldiers returning from combat with physical wounds. They benefit not only from expert military surgeons, doctors, and nurses, but also from the rehab center where they relearn how to walk, to tie their shoes, how to live. I submit that the many who suffer from psychological trauma — and it is NOT battle fatigue, or cowardice — would be able to adapt faster to civilian life if they had a psychological rehabilitation program tailored to their needs."

She looked at the panel of examiners. "So I propose to request a grant to define this program and develop appropriate treatments for these soldiers. Thank you."

She gave the panel a thick file. "This is the detailed plan for my proposed research."

❧

Everyone in the audience cheered. Lucas had tears in his eyes. The countess put her hands on his shoulders, "You picked a gem, Lucas." She then turned to the colonel, "Your daughter makes you proud."

The panel would reconvene after lunch to share its assessment of Josette's readiness to be certified in this important new branch of medical science.

ℭ⁊⸍

At two o'clock promptly, the panel came in. Everyone in the audience had already gotten into their seats, and waited with anticipation for the conclusion of the last two days.

The head of Necker Hospital, Doctor Stanislas, who was also the chair of the panel, stood up. He addressed Josette.

"None of us was surprised by your superb command of this new specialty in the science of medicine, but none of the members of the panel expected such a formidable exposé of your understanding of the trauma affecting children. So the panel awards you your certification with the highest possible rating."

People started to applaud. He raised his hand. "That is not all. The panel has decided to start a search to fund a two-year-grant for your proposed study and for the development of a rehabilitation facility for traumatized soldiers. Thank you and congratulations to you, Josette."

The applause would not stop for a long time.

Doctor Stanislas came down and shook Josette's hand, He then turned to Lucas. "She'll have you fixed up in no time. Thank you for your service and for your sacrifice."

Josette went to meet the doctor from Aix-en-Provence. "It's nice to meet you, sir. I did not know you were interested in trauma in your city hospital."

"It's mainly me. The hospital is private, so I'm not constrained by the Ministry of Health. We're getting quite a few people and children coming from Algeria. Trauma is rampant among them."

"If I need a place to expand my research and my treatments, I might give you a call."

"By all means. I'd welcome it."

Chapter 21

Beaumes de Venise

May 7

Tom and Francine busied themselves setting up their belongings in the new house. They went to the military camp near Marseille to retrieve Basira's and their containers, unpacked them and returned them to the depot where they had gotten them. They bought another car, so both Francine and Tom could go about their chores. Hana was particularly happy to get her books back. Armand installed a bookshelf in her room so she had easy access to them.

On the Monday of the second week in the new house, Francine went to meet the head of the local elementary school to talk about the girls. In the remote villages of Algeria, boys received minimal formal education, if any, but girls were not entitled to any schooling. Aisha and Hana learned reading and writing as well as French from Francine, but although about the same age, they had reached different levels of fluency.

Francine explained the girls' backgrounds to Madame Leroi, the woman in charge of the primary education in the small village of Beaumes de Venise.

"Are you a trained teacher?" she asked Francine.

"Yes. I used to teach in a primary school before we left for Africa."

"How far did the girls get with your teaching?" Madame Leroi asked.

"In French, one of the girls, Hana, who just turned eight, is fluent. She has an extensive vocabulary and speaks with no accent. Not so for Aisha, who is a few months older. She has a pronounced accent and a limited vocabulary."

"What about reading and writing?"

"Same. Hana is very curious. She is an avid reader and reads well. Her writing is flawless. Again, Aisha is far behind her."

Madame Leroi, in her late fifties with graying hair, was a kind person. She smiled at Francine. "You believe that Hana is very smart while Aisha is limited, right?"

"I do. But Aisha might make progress in an environment with more traditional teaching and a school setting. I hope so anyway."

"What I think we should do is for me to give the girls a quick evaluation, so that I know in what grade to place them. Can you bring them tomorrow afternoon after class?"

"I will. Is three a good time?"

"It is. See you then. I admire you for your efforts to save these girls, both physically from a threatening environment, and intellectually from discrimination against women."

Francine smiled. "You'll see how lovable they are."

On the way out, Francine saw a few of the school kids and noted that their clothes were simple, and all about the same, also different from what Aisha and Hana were wearing. She decided to buy them new outfits so that the other children would not make fun of them.

That afternoon, Francine, Basira and the girls went to a local store and got simple dresses, cardigans and light sweaters which had seemed to be the uniform all children had on that morning.

ন্ত

The next afternoon, Madame Leroi met Hana and Aisha. She gave them a cursory and non-threatening test. She spoke to the two girls, testing their fluency in French. She verified that it was excellent for Hana, and passable for Aisha. Then she had each of them read a couple of pages from a second grade text book, and asked them to write a short paragraph that she dictated to them.

Hana passed these tests with flying colors, but Aisha struggled. Francine told Madame Leroi she had not taught them any math. Then the head of the school asked Francine to come inside her office. The girls were left by themselves.

"Here are my thoughts," Madame Leroi said. "Hana is ready for third grade, the normal one for her age with regard to reading and writing, but she needs to catch up with math. I can arrange for one of the teachers to tutor her during the summer, and she will be ready when school starts in September. You are right, Hana is very bright, and will be a pleasure to teach."

"That's great," Francine said, "But what about Aisha?"

"I'm afraid Aisha has to be held back. Her vocabulary seems to be limited. I'm not sure she can make the second grade, even with tutoring during the summer. She might have to go to the first grade. There are two problems with that. First, she'll be with kids much younger than she is. She'll feel out of place in school and may be teased. Second, at home she will be visibly way behind her sister, and may resent that."

Francine thought for a minute and said, "You know they are not sisters, and I think they're drifting apart from one another."

"I'm not surprised. Hana is much more alert and active than Aisha."

Francine nodded. "I don't know who her parents were, but Hana has incredible resilience. She managed on her own to survive a terrible environment and escape threats and dangers, some I know but do not fully understand. She is strong and at the same time vulnerable when she thinks of the bad times she went through. Hopefully, that will pass. I fell in love with this little girl over the past two years. I want the best for her, and I will help the tutor you recommend so I complement her teaching."

"The best will be for you and me to meet with the tutor and devise a plan. But what do you want to do about Aisha?"

"Aisha is a different case," Francine replied. "Her mother Basira came with us to escape the village where the rebels killed her husband. She is a very kind woman who welcomed Hana and took her into her family when everyone else in her village rejected the little girl with blue eyes; but Basira is not educated, and frankly, I'm not sure she will be able to fit here. Although she speaks reasonably good French, she is visibly Algerian. She and Aisha will encounter prejudice. So let's give Aisha tutoring throughout the summer if possible, and at the end determine if the best is for her to enter second or first grade. If her mother decides to go back to Algeria once the country is stabilized, there will be no issue."

Madame Leroi nodded. "I will talk with my teachers and see which one is interested in tutoring Hana. I know who is best suited for Aisha. Can you bring the girls again tomorrow after school? I'll have the tutors meet the girls. Then we will all meet and discuss schedule and details. Now, I will have to charge you a fee. School is free, but this tutoring is outside the teachers' duties. It won't be much."

"That's fine. I'll take care of it."

✤

The next day, Francine was back with the two girls. Madame Leroi greeted Aisha and pointed to one of three teachers who were in her office, a young brunette with a delightful smile.

"Aisha, this is Mademoiselle Dumas. She is going to talk to you about what she can help you with this summer. When she is finished, we will decide what we want to do. Don't be shy, and ask her as many questions as you want."

Aisha took the teacher's hand and smiled at her. The two of them left the room.

Madame Leroi told Hana, "You know that you need to catch up on your knowledge of math, so we have to schedule a program to do that. But I would like to know if you would also like to improve on reading, writing, or anything else."

Hana beamed. "I'd like to read more books, I'd like to learn the countries in the atlas, and I'd like to learn more about animals."

"What do you want to know about animals, Hana?" One of the teachers asked her.

"I don't know many. I have a new friend, a dog. His name is Wolf, and I used to tend to goats. I have seen camels and read about wild beasts. I want to know about all animals, where they live, what they eat, what they look like, everything."

"That's interesting, isn't it," the teacher said. "By the way, my name is Mademoiselle Roger."

The other teacher said to Hana, "I'm Madame Laurent. What do you want to know about the countries you saw in the atlas?"

Hana squirmed self-consciously. "I don't know. I guess, where they are, who lives there, do they have a desert or mountains. Everything."

Madame Leroi said to Hana, "Why don't you continue to talk with Madame Laurent, and Mademoiselle Roger in the next room? I need to speak with Francine."

The three of them left the room, and Madame Leroi went to sit next to Francine.

"Before we discuss the summer plan, let me ask you a question. Hana is an Arabic first name, but she has no real Arabic feature. There's quite a lot of resentment here against Algerians as a result of the war. Prejudice is not nice, but it exists, and children are not immune to it."

Francine replied, "It goes both ways where we come from, so I agree."

"I think Hana should change her first name from Hana to Anna. The French pronunciation would be the same, but the stigma of an Arabic name would disappear. She would not suffer discrimination which would be better for developing her social skills, one of the main ingredients of attending primary school."

"I guess I'd be okay with that. I would clear it with Basira. Then I'll try to figure out how to make it official, if it's necessary, or if it would be helpful to her."

"Why don't you. I will talk to the teachers, and we can meet tomorrow again and agree on a plan for this summer."

On the way back to the house both girls said they liked the teachers they talked to. When she got home, Francine looked for Tom and found him in the cellars of the winery discussing the 1962 plan with Armand.

"Honey, when you're through, I need to talk to you."

Tom followed her to their bedroom.

"How did it go at the school?" he asked.

"That's what we need to talk about."

Francine related the conversation about Hana's name alteration.

"What do you think we should do, Francine?"

"I have an idea. I believe that Basira is not going to stay here, and that she will go back to Algeria."

"That's possible, so what then?"

"I also believe that Aisha will want to go with her, and also that Hana will refuse to return to the village. Basira has no legal right over Hana. Mustapha's scribbling on a birth certificate is not a legal document."

"I think I know where you're going with this, but go ahead."

"If we were to get Hana an identification card, we could add Anna as a given name."

Tom grinned and finished the sentence, "And if we were to adopt her, we'll change her last name too. Am I correct?"

"Yes, you are." She went to give him a hug. "And I would very much like to see it happen. I love this little girl, and she does not deserve to go back to that village."

"Let me suggest that we would need the consent of both Hana and Basira, and I would also tell Lieutenant Lucas. If all three agree, let's do it. I love the little girl too."

"All right then. The first one to talk to is Basira. The question is do we ask her about the name change or the adoption?"

"Just the name change. I think it would be wise to consult a family attorney about the adoption first. I'm not sure what it entails and whether it would be almost automatic or if it would be a legal challenge."

"Okay. I'll tell Basira we'll change Hana's name for the school. But she'll ask about Aisha."

"Tell her that Anna is the French spelling of the same name, and that the pronunciation is the same. In French, the H is silent."

Francine saw Basira in the living room. "Did Aisha tell you about the teacher she talked to?"

"Yes, she did and she liked her very much."

"Good. I will see the headmistress tomorrow and see what she proposes. Also, so it does not come as a surprise, the school will use the French spelling for Hana, it will be Anna, which is pronounced the same way in French and they have one other Anna in the school."

Basira started to shrug, but winced when her left shoulder moved up. "I have no problem with that."

༕

The next day Francine confirmed that Anna would be the new name for Hana. "That'll make life easier for Hana and for everyone in the school," Madame Leroi asserted. "But there's no French equivalent of the name Aisha, and the little girl does look Algerian, so there would be no name change for her."

Francine nodded.

"I understand."

Madame Leroi continued. "Now, here is what I'd recommend for her summer tutoring: Mademoiselle Roger will see Anna a couple of times a week to teach her basics of zoology. It will satisfy her thirst for knowledge and develop her vocabulary. There are tons of good books about animals, so it will develop her reading skill further. She's already pretty advanced. Madame Laurent will see her once a week and teach her geography. She'll use good books as well. Mademoiselle Roger will also teach Anna the math she needs to know."

"I am in total agreement with your program. Can I tell Hana?"

"I'd prefer you bring her tomorrow and have her teachers tell her. Also, there's another gifted girl named Brigitte. She could benefit from Mademoiselle Roger's teaching on animals. She is also good in math and could help Anna with this subject. I would like her to go through the same program as Anna. It would be good for her to have a friend when she goes to the school for the first time. It'd make it easier for Anna to blend in."

"That's a terrific idea."

"I'll have Brigitte and her mom come tomorrow; bring Anna. Brigitte's mom's name is Juliette. You'll enjoy them. They are nice people. And by the way, that will cut the fee down for you."

"Fine. What about Aisha?"

"What I recommend for her is Mademoiselle Dumas five days a week for a couple of hours. It might be a good idea to have some of the sessions in the school. Mademoiselle Dumas is teaching second grade remedial reading to a couple of kids about to enter second grade three days a week. It would be good to put Aisha with them, and have her socialize a bit. I believe Mademoiselle Dumas could pick up Aisha at your house. It's only a fifteen-minute drive."

"Shall I bring Aisha tomorrow too?"

"I don't think it is necessary."

Francine and Madame Leroi agreed on a fee.

✃

The next afternoon, Madame Leroi had Mademoiselle Roger, Madame Laurent, Anna, Brigitte, Francine and Juliette sit in her office and explained to them the tutorial plan and schedule she had in mind.

"Brigitte and Anna are gifted children. Anna needs to catch up with her peers in math, and she's eager to read more and learn more. I thought that Brigitte would enjoy the same program and at the same time get Anna accustomed to the ways of the kids of Beaumes de Venise."

Francine offered to have the sessions at her home, and Mademoiselle Roger proposed to drive Brigitte to the winery to make it easier for her mother. All agreed to the plan, and the teachers and students went to another room to get acquainted and to discuss the objectives of the summer program.

Francine and Juliette stayed in Madame Leroi's office. Brigitte's mother was a visual artist who, at times, taught art seminars and workshops on drawing and painting.

"I am having what I call an art afternoon for kids once a month during the summer. It is designed for children of Brigitte's age. They learn the basics of drawing and the fundamentals of colors. At the same time I introduce them to a bit of art history. I love doing it because I can see the enormous differences in creativity and in hand control between the kids." She looked at Francine. "Do you think Anna would like to attend some of those?"

"I will ask her. I would think so. Her life so far has been a story of terror. She's much more relaxed and positive since she left Algeria, but I believe art would help her mind settle into a more rewarding exposure to a life she missed so far."

"Poor thing. War is such a horror," Juliette said.

Madame Leroi added, "I agree with Francine that art would be good for Anna. She had a difficult struggle growing up, but she dealt with it. She developed her mind to find solutions to overcome the adversity that pursued her. I think that, however dismal her life had been, her mind sharpened in order to survive."

Francine added, "Learning how to read at a young age allowed her a healthy retreat into a world she could enjoy. That's what made her curious. She also drew the pictures she saw in the books she read. I'm sure she'd want to participate in the art afternoon."

Francine thought about telling the two women that she played the piano. But she let it go for the moment.

Madame Leroi said. "With my years of experience in the education profession, I see these two young girls as the most promising students I have ever taught or met. I have great expectations for them."

Francine said, "Amen. I hope you're right."

The girls and teachers came out of their caucus, all with smiles on their face. They had a summer plan which would start in mid-June.

Chapter 22

Avignon, South of France

May 14

Francine and Tom had found a family lawyer in nearby Avignon. Her name was Madame Tabris. On their way to meet the woman, Tom said, "What we want to understand from her is what is possible and not. I don't think we can start any work on this until we have cleared it with everyone involved."

"I agree," Francine replied, "I'd also like to understand how long the adoption process will take, if we want to go ahead with it."

Madame Tabris, a fairly young woman, dressed in a conservative grey suit, greeted them warmly.

"I'm glad to meet you. I understand this is about an adoption."

"It is," Francine said. "Let me tell you the background for our inquiry."

Francine and Tom explained Hana's background, the two years with Ahmed and Basira, Ahmed's killing, and the escape from Algeria. Francine also mentioned the distancing happening between Hana and Aisha. They also told Madame Tabris about Mustapha's inscription on Hana's birth certificate.

"I am a family lawyer, and I have been involved with several cases of immigration, or shall I call them transfer, from Algeria to France. So I understand your dilemma. First, let me state that Mustapha's scribbling on the birth certificate does not make an adoption by Ahmed and Basira legal. The only thing that I can use is his statement that both her parents are dead." Tom asked the lawyer, "Have you seen many similar cases of adoption?

"Unfortunately, this is far from being unique, and the courts are keen on helping orphans settle in a new family. I can definitely bring an adoption request to court. Would you want Hana to have your last name?"

"Sure. We want to change her first name from Hana to Anna, and she would be a Segal like Tom and me. Actually, we don't know what her last name is. It may be on her birth certificate. We have not seen it. I'm not sure Hana knows it. "

"The next question is to have the authorities grant her French nationality," Madame Tabris asserted. "That is a bit tricky. She was born in Algeria, I assume from Algerian parents. Now, you're probably aware that native Algerians had many of the benefits awarded to the French people, but they never had all the rights of French citizens. Now that Algeria has been given its independence, the rules are not clear yet for Algerians moving to France. Some judges do not see it as an obstacle, while others are more hesitant in granting citizenship."

"It would make her life easier if Hana were to be a French citizen. Her features are not that of an Arab girl."

"I'll have to work on that. Maybe I can pick the right judge, but otherwise, it seems to me the case is straightforward. I can put together the request. Hana would have to meet with the judge. The process would take about a month once you sign the petition. Social services would have to visit your home."

Tom said, "Thank you so much, we'll talk to Barisa and to Hana, then we'll decide if we want to proceed. We will be in touch."

ॐ

On the way back from the lawyer's office, Francine bared her soul to Tom. "I could not bear seeing Hana go back to Mascara. It would destroy her. I'm also convinced that Basira will not stay here and that Aisha will be happy to return to Algeria with her mother. So I think I'd like to talk to Basira about making Hana, Anna Segal."

"I'm getting all mellow thinking that, although you and I could not have a child, we can make this precious Hana, our Anna. Like you, I love her. Let's talk to Basira," Tom said, and he embraced Francine tenderly.

ॐ

After supper, when the girls were in bed, Tom said to Basira, "There is something Francine and I would like to talk to you about. Is now a good time?"

"Yes. What is it?"

Tom took a deep breath. "It's about Hana."

"You want to adopt her? Is that it?" Basira asked.

Startled, both Francine and Tom rose in their chairs, opened their eyes wide. Francine had her mouth open, and Tom managed to say, "What made you say that?"

"I have seen Hana get closer to you in the past weeks. She has blossomed while Aisha has not. I also think Hana is more comfortable with you than with me. You're educated, I'm not, and she is smart. She wants to learn. I think that it would be the best thing that can happen to Hana. I think she is a dear, I am fond of her, but I can't give her what she needs."

Tom smiled at her. "Do you remember the day Ahmed and Lieutenant Lucas brought Hana to the farm in his jeep? You took her in your family with no hesitation. I saw that and that day I said to you and to Ahmed that you were special." He broke into a big grin. "I want to say it again today, Basira. You are really special."

"I want what is best for Hana. Let me give you the papers Mustapha gave us, the birth certificate and some other stuff."

Basira came back and gave Tom Hana's birth certificate, and an envelope marked with Hana's name on it. The certificate listed Hana's birth date as April 29, 1954. The father's name was listed as Maurice Martin. The mother's name was Farrah with no last name.

"Martin looks like a French name. What's in the envelope?"

Basira answered she did not know. "I'm not too good at reading official papers, so I never opened it."

Francine looked at Tom. He opened the envelope. In it Tom found a marriage certificate between Farrah and Maurice dated 1952 which listed Maurice Martin, nineteen years old, born in Montelimar, France in 1934, and Farrah Rahim, seventeen, born in Mascara.

Another yellowing paper recorded the sale of a house in Tiaret in 1938 to a Frederic Martin from France.

Tom and Francine hugged Basira and told her they would talk to Hana, and to a lawyer. They promised to tell her when they reached a decision.

&

In their bedroom, Francine said, "I'm no legal expert, but I think that if her father is French, born in France, Hana has the same nationality. I'll call Madame Tabris tomorrow and find out. That might make the whole process simpler."

Tom agreed, and then he said, "When you said you thought Barisa might not want to remain in France and might want to go back to Algeria, you did not know she was illiterate, or at least limited in her reading ability. But that is a serious handicap if she were to live in this country. It's more acceptable in El Boussaid."

"That's for sure," Francine said, "Now we want to talk to Hana and to Lieutenant Lucas. If we all agree, we'll start the process. We'll let Basira tell Aisha, unless she wants us there."

Madame Tabris welcomed back Tom and Francine. "I understand you have more information that can help us. Correct?"

Tom gave her Hana's birth certificate with the mention of the death of the parents, and the record of the marriage of her parents, "We think that her father being born in France should make Hana French."

She looked carefully at the documents and said, "If I can prove that the father was indeed born in France, the child is definitely of French nationality. I will request a copy of the birth certificate of Maurice Martin. Montelimar is only a few miles north of here. That should be easy."

"What else do you need before we can proceed?" Francine asked.

"I think, Aisha's mother could be considered by a judge as a temporary guardian of the child, and her approval would be required. Would that be a problem?"

Tom smiled. "Not at all. We talked to her and she said she thought that would be the best for the child."

"Good. Although she's far from her majority, the judge may ask Anna if she wants to be adopted, or if she feels she is coerced into it."

"We have not yet talked to her, because we don't want to give her false hopes, but we're convinced she'll say that she wants to be adopted by us," Francine said.

"One last question. Do you have anyone who could be a witness and support the adoption?"

Tom thought of Lieutenant Lucas. He reminded the lawyer of the lieutenant who got Hana out of the village, and said, "We were going to try to talk to him and ask if he had any thought of adopting her himself."

"It would be good if he could come to the hearing, or send an affidavit stating he supports your adoption of the little girl."

Madame Tabris sat up in her chair and said, "I think we have a clear road. I will request Maurice Martin's birth certificate, and you talk to the lieutenant and to Hana. What joy for the little one. Also, next time you come, bring Basira and Hana. I will ask them if they support the adoption. That'll be a semi-rehearsal for the judge asking the same question because they won't know me and might be intimidated."

∽

Madame Tabris was curious about that Maurice Martin from Montelimar. The town was not a long drive from Avignon, so she decided to go there and talk to the civil records people to find out what they knew if anything. She pulled up in the parking lot of the little town city hall and found the office of records. A man of about fifty greeted her.

"Good morning Madame. I'm Pierre Bellot, how can I help you?"

"I would like a copy of the birth certificate of a Maurice Martin, born in 1934."

"Martin? It sounds familiar. Give me a couple of minutes."

He came back after a short time. "I have a Maurice Martin, born

September 18, 1934, son of Frederic Martin. Is this the person you're looking for?"

"I think so."

"May I ask the reason for this request? Are you a relative?"

"No. I'm not." Madame Tabris proceeded to explain to Pierre about the adoption request for this man's daughter.

"I see. I happen to remember Frederic Martin. He lived close to where I did, and we went to school together. I remember that he got married when he was twenty to this gorgeous woman, a blue-eyed striking brunette. Unfortunately, she died when she gave birth to their son. That must have been Maurice. Frederic went back to live with his parents and his mom took care of the baby. But Frederic was devastated by his loss, and when the rumors of a coming war with the Germans became credible, he took his son, probably an eighteen-month-old baby at the time, to Algeria to get away from a France at war and from bad memories. That was the last I heard from him."

"I guess we will never know what happened to him and how the baby became integrated in the Algerian culture and ended up in a remote village in the Atlas Mountains."

"Let me make a copy of the birth certificate. It'll take me only a minute."

When he came back with the official piece of paper, Madame Tabris asked him, "Would you be willing to come to the adoption hearing and tell the story you shared with me? It would make Hana's request more credible, and would help me secure her French citizenship."

"I would be delighted to do it. This little girl's odyssey is touching."

"One last question, if I may," the lawyer asked. "Are there members of the family left in Montelimar? Anyone who could have a blood relationship with Hana?"

"No. I'm afraid not. The father died in the Ardennes at the beginning of World War Two, and the mother passed away shortly after. I don't know of any other relative."

Madame Tabris drove back to her office and called Tom and told him what she had found out. "We're good to go. I'll draft the application and when you're ready, I'll file it."

Francine reacted to the story by saying, "It's possible that her dad spoke some French to her when she was little. That would explain her facility with the language and her desire to learn it."

Tom nodded. "And we now know her blue eyes come from her grandmother, and why she looks so French. I wish I knew what happened after her grandfather Frederic came to Tiaret to buy that property in 1938. I guess we'll never know."

Francine frowned, trying to determine whether to share that story with Hana or not.

"We should ask her if she wants to know more about her father," Tom suggested. "My guess is that she would. But I think that when we talk to her about becoming Anna Segal, a French girl, we'll have to at least tell her that her dad was born in France."

Francine said, "Let's talk to her about the adoption today. I think we're ready to start the process. Don't you?"

"Yes. I do."

⁕

Francine and Tom went to Hana's room. They found her reading at her desk, Wolf lying next to her. "Hana," Francine said, "can we talk to you about something important?" Hana shivered and her eyes swelled with tears. "Is it bad?" she asked.

"Not at all, my sweet," Tom said with the kindest smile.

"I'm happy here, but I worry all the time something might happen and I would have to go back to Algeria."

"That's not going to happen." Tom said, "On the contrary, we want to ask you if you would like to become our daughter."

Hana burst into tears. She ran to Tom and jumped into his arms. She wept for a long time. Then she stopped and with a little voice asked," You mean you will be my father and Francine will be my mother forever?"

"Yes. And we'll love you forever," Francine told her.

She started to cry again. Wolf got up and went to Francine, wondering if Hana needed help. Francine petted him. "She's all right, Wolf," she told him and he sat.

"Am I going to be French like you?"

"Your name will be Anna Segal, a French citizen. And your first name pronounced without the h sound in French will change to Anna, A.N.N.A."

Hana took time to comprehend the words, and asked, "What about Basira?"

"Basira also wants this to happen to you."

"Why is that?" Anna asked.

Francine said, "It is because Tom and I love you that we want to be your mother and father. And it is also because Basira loves you too, and thinks we are better suited to guide you because you want to learn and we are more educated."

"How do I become your daughter?" she asked with a timid smile.

Tom answered. "We have to go in front of a judge who will make it legal. He will ask you if you want to be adopted. When you say yes, it will be official. Now I have to ask you the same question. Do you want us to become you parents?"

"Yes. Yes. Yes," she said loudly.

She hugged Tom, who put her down and she ran to Francine and said, "Thank you, Thank you. I love you."

Wolf wanted to be hugged too, so he went to Hana and put his nose up and got his hug also.

When all the tears were wiped away, the three of them went to see Basira who hugged the little girl. "I'm so happy for you," she whispered in Hana's ear.

Hana went to sit in the living room with Francine, "Does that mean I can call you Mom?" she asked Francine who smiled and tearfully replied, "Yes, my sweetheart. I'd love it if you do."

Hana smiled to herself and very softly said, "Mom, would you play the piano for me, please?" Choking and unable to talk, Francine went to sit at the piano and let her fingers say I love you to her new child.

ﾟ℀ﾟ

Meanwhile, Tom went to the phone and called the number Lucas had given him. The phone did not ring twice and Lucas' voice said, "Hello. This is Lucas."

"Lieutenant Lucas, this is Tom."

"Tom? You can drop the lieutenant bit. So you made it to France?"

"Yes, Francine, Basira, Hana, and Aisha are here with me in our new place in Beaumes de Venise."

"I'm so relieved. Welcome home."

"Lucas, a lot has happened in the past weeks, but the most important news I want to share with you is that Francine and I want to adopt Hana. We were not sure if you had any thought of doing that yourself."

"That's fantastic. No, I had no intention of doing that. What about Basira?"

"She is very happy for her. Now we need to make it legal, and I would like you to come for the hearing where the judge will make it official. I think Hana would love to have you there."

"I certainly will. When is it?"

"It's not scheduled yet. It may take a month or so. By the way, we discovered that Hana's father was French, and therefore she is too. Her name will become Anna. She'll be looking forward to a hug from you for sure."

"Tom, please tell her that I will be there to witness her happy day. I have news too. Just let me know the date and I'll be there with my new wife Josette."

"Fantastic! Congratulations to you too. When did that happen?"

"It didn't yet, it's scheduled for May 26." Lucas paused for an instant and asked, "Could you make it to our wedding?"

"There's much going on here." Then Tom thought about it, and said, "Let me talk to Francine. Anna would love that. We could come for the day."

"That would be fantastic."

"I'll call you in a few minutes."

"Good. You can stay in our place Friday night."

Tom went to talk to Francine, who replied, "I'd love it and Hana would too. Let's do it."

Tom called Lucas. "The three of us are coming."

"What about Aisha and Basira?"

"They're not coming. The two of them have trouble adjusting to being out of Algeria. They might go back there."

"That's too bad. I'm so happy to have you celebrate with us on our happy day. Call me with your train arrival time. We'll pick you up." After that phone call, Tom called Madame Tabris, and said, "We're all set here. Hana is in high heaven, and we spoke to Lieutenant Lucas; he will come to the adoption hearing and show his support. Can you start the process?"

"Yes I can. As a matter of fact I spoke to the court. They promised to expedite the case. I know Judge Moran, who will chair the hearing. He is a friend of mine and when I told him Hana's story, he was pleased and said, 'At least one outcome of that bloody war is positive. I'll be honored to welcome Hana, I mean Anna with no H to her new family.'"

"Great. Any idea when we can anticipate the hearing will take place? Lieutenant Lucas promised he would come."

"I think two to three weeks."

Chapter 23

Beaumes de Venise

May 19

Toward the end of the week following the meeting with Madame Tabris, Tom, Francine, Basira, and Hana went to Avignon for the adoption rehearsal with the lawyer. Madame Tabris greeted Hana. "You are the Anna-Segal-to-be. Aren't you pretty?" Hana beamed at her. Then the lawyer focused on Basira. She smiled at her. "And you are the kind soul who took care of this precious young girl for two years."

Madame Tabris continued, "I have to tell you that I am honored to meet the two of you, a gritty young girl, and a compassionate woman with a big heart. I admire both of you for your courage. You have both suffered, but showed tenacity and you both survived."

Then she shifted her gaze to Tom and Francine. "I must add that I'm also touched by you two for bringing them to safety."

Her voice had quivered at the end of her last sentence, so Madame Tabris shuffled some papers on her desk, regained her composure, and became her lawyer-self again. She looked at Hana, and smiled.

"Now I need to tell about the day of the hearing for the adoption. We will all go into a courtroom. It might be intimidating for you. It's a big room with lots of seats, an elevated desk behind which the judge will sit, and a few other tables with clerks. The judge will be dressed in a black robe, and will ask you and Basira a simple question. I'm going to ask you the same question so you'll know what to say." She looked at Basira.

"Basira Habib, you and your husband were Hana's guardians for the best part of the last two years. Do you support the adoption of Hana by Tom and Francine Segal?"

Basira replied, "Yes. I do with all my heart."

"Very good. The only thing you have to change in your response is to start by saying Yes, Your Honor."

Basira nodded. Madame Tabris turned to Hana. "Hana Martin, do you want to be adopted by Tom and Francine Segal?"

Hana's smile gave away the answer. "Yes, Your Honor. Yes, yes, yes."

"Perfect," the lawyer said.

"Does anybody have any questions?"

Hana raised her hand.

"Yes, dear."

"You called me Hana Martin. Is it going to be my new name?"

"No, it won't. Hana Martin is the name on your birth certificate. Once the adoption is completed by the judge, your name will become Anna Segal –that's A.N.N.A., daughter of Tom and Francine Segal."

Hana clapped her hands. "Thank you."

"Do you have any other questions?"

"Am I going to be alone with the judge when he talks to me?"

"Good question. The answer is no. On your right will be Francine and Tom, your parents to be, and on your left the two witnesses who will sign the adoption papers."

"Thank you. I did not want to be alone with the judge."

"Not to worry. He's a very kind man who is delighted to make you happy. And that brings me to the question of the witnesses."

She looked at Tom and Francine. "I will need to have two adults who have known Hana for some time and can affirm that they support the adoption. They will enter their name and enter their current address on the official Adoption Record, then sign it."

"One for sure is Lieutenant Lucas, who rescued her from her village," Tom said. Madame Tabris nodded and asked Basira. "Would you like to be the other witness?"

Basira got red in the face, and almost whispered. "I can't write."

Embarrassed by the answer, the lawyer looked at her. "I'm sorry. I did not mean to upset you."

"I know, but I can sign my name."

The lawyer thought for a minute and then said, "I'll inform the judge of the situation. He will appoint a clerk to record the names and addresses on the document. When that is done, you and Lucas can sign your name on the official document."

Basira nodded and smiled. "Thank you."

"Thank you so much. This is very thoughtful," Francine told the lawyer.

"The adoption will be a happy occasion. We must all feel good that day," Madame Tabris replied.

She smiled at everyone, and told Hana. "You are going to be a happy Anna Segal, young lady. I'm so glad to have met you."

She looked over her audience. "Thank you, all. The date for the adoption has been set by the court. It'll be on June 11, at ten in the morning. I'll see you then at the courthouse."

Later that day, Hana was reading a new book at her desk in her room when Aisha came in. She spoke in Arabic to Hana. "My mom tells me you're going to be adopted by Francine."

Hana smiled. "Yes, that's true. Isn't that great?"

"What's great about that? You were adopted by my mother and father. Aren't they good enough for you?"

"Francine said your mother didn't really adopt me, and it's better to have parents in French schools. It's not my fault. It's adult talk."

"You think you're French and therefore better than me?"

"Aisha. There's no reason to be mad at me. My father was French, but you and I will go to the same school. You'll learn and have fun."

"The teachers are putting me down already because my French is not as good as yours."

"I can't help it," Hana replied, "but you'll catch up. Don't worry."

Aisha stuck her tongue out at Hana and left the room. Hana caressed Wolf and said to him, "She's mad at me because I speak better French than she does. I don't get it." Wolf wagged his tail in total agreement. Hana decided to go talk to Francine. She found her in the winery reception room which was not yet open to the public.

She smiled when she saw the young girl. "Hi, Sweetie. How do you like your new book?"

"I like it a lot, but there are new words I don't know. You'll have to help me with them."

"I will when I'm done with my work here."

Hana looked at Francine and said, "Aisha knows about the adoption and she's mad at me because her mother adopted me before and she said I think she's not good enough for me. I don't know what to do."

Francine put her hand on Hana's shoulder. "I'll ask Basira to talk to Aisha. You have heard Basira at the lawyer's office. She is delighted for you, and she supports the adoption."

Hana did not say anything, then smiled and asked Francine, "Is it true that Lieutenant Lucas will be with us when we go to the courthouse?"

"Yes he is, and he'll bring his new wife. He said he'll be thrilled to be with you for the adoption. He had a lot to do with it."

Hana's face showed her happiness. "Yes he did. I'll never forget it. That day, he saved my life and made it possible for Ahmed, Basira, Tom and you to help me."

"Also," Francine added, "You, Tom and I will go to Paris for Lucas's wedding."

Hana did a little dance. "Yeah!"

On the way back to her room, she ran into Armand and told him about the adoption.

He lifted her and said, "That is perfect. They are great people and you belong with them." He smiled and said, "Do you think we should go tell the goats?"

She laughed. "Yes, they have to know. Armand and Hana ran to the paddock and Hana told them in Arabic she was being adopted. With a cute little grin, she told Armand. "I have to speak to them in Arabic. They don't understand French."

Chapter 24

Paris

May 11

While Josette was preparing for her certification, Lucas had found a nice apartment on Rue Guynemer. It had three bedrooms on the third floor. The quiet street bordered the Luxembourg Gardens. The certification exam behind her, Josette happily went to look at Lucas' find. The third bedroom would make a good office for her while she decided how her career would proceed. She loved the quiet street, the balcony, and the floor-to-ceiling windows overlooking the Gardens.

They signed the lease, then purchased additional chairs, couches, and beds to complement Josette's minimal furniture. They scheduled to move in the following week, a few days before the wedding. Lucas terminated his lease for his furnished studio, forwarded his mail, and packed his things so he would be ready to move into the new place.

༄

One morning, Josette told Lucas she hoped to get some money for the grant she had requested when she spoke to the doctors of the certification panel.

"If I get it," she told Lucas, "I'll have to stay in Paris for the next year of my career, maybe more. Is that going to work for you, Luke?"

"Sure thing. I'm going to get a job in Paris too. Hopefully I can find a career starter, which will give me a solid background with potential avenues for growth. I plan to go talk to the dean of the engineering school I graduated from. Mr. Boucheron helped me at the time of my uncle's death. He always gave me good advice, and I have much respect for him."

"I remember the name. Good idea." Josette agreed.

❧

A couple of days later Lucas went to meet with the dean. In his familiar grey austere office, dressed in his usual black jacket and black-striped grey pants, Mr. Boucheron greeted him warmly.

"Back from Algeria? I remember you chose to serve in the infantry to honor your uncle who had been decorated during World War Two. You're the only one from your graduating class who volunteered for that branch of the service and served in combat assignments. I'm happy to see you back, looking strong and healthy."

"You have a good memory. I'll never forget how much you helped me at the time I struggled with accepting my uncle's death. Indeed, I did join the infantry, and my platoon became so efficient that it received Special Forces training. Believe it or not, I became an elite infantry lieutenant, but I had no idea it would be a life-changing experience."

Lucas told him about combat, casualties, and dark memories. He added that he had spent over two years living in the open air in the Atlas Range and in the northern Sahara, and that he wondered if it would affect his ability to live in a civilized world. Then he shared with the dean his feelings of having been betrayed after having lost some of his men in a conflict that no one in France seemed to care about any more. Mr. Boucheron advised him to stay out of politics and suggested to Lucas that he might want to look for an international company and let them guide him toward the best opportunities for his future. Then he looked him in the eye.

"Now, Lucas, I'll be frank with you. I see from the way you talk about your war that you have paid a heavy price for having volunteered to serve your country like you did. I sense a deep trauma in your soul and you need to heal yourself. I don't have a recipe for that; you'll need professional help. You were a leader in school and you must continue to guide other people and help them be successful. It will make you stronger."

"I know that, and I'm not sure what I want to do with my life. I have ideas, but I have no plan and no burning desire to do anything in particular."

"Don't be in a hurry," the dean said, "You have to let time tell you who you are going to be. You can't launch yourself into a career in your state of mind. Lastly, I believe it would be a great help if you were to meet a woman with whom you could build a future, a family. You need to settle down." He chuckled. "But I can't help with that either."

"I'm ahead of you on that count," Lucas smiled broadly, and added, "I am going to get married to my fiancée Josette on the twenty-sixth of May. She's a doctor who just earned her pediatric trauma care certification."

"Congratulations. Maybe she is the best positioned to advise you in your re-entry into the business world. You want your first job to be in Paris. Most international companies have their French headquarters in Paris. I would look at the data processing industry. Computers are new, and they're the key to the future."

Comforted by those wise words, Lucas thanked him for his kindness and thoughtful advice.

"You are right; I may have escaped physical wounds, but I suffered psychological damage that I need to repair. Josette has committed to help me."

Lucas walked away from the meeting full of energy and ready to face life.

That evening, Josette asked Lucas how the meeting with Mr. Boucheron went.

Lucas replied enthusiastically, "Very well. He gave me good advice. He suggested I try to get into the computer industry, asserting it was the future. He also recommended international companies, saying that I could get an understanding of the future opportunities in the world market for me."

Relieved to see some kind of fire in Lucas' attitude toward his future, Josette said, "That's great. You should start interviewing after our wedding. I might know by then the status of my grant."

❦

They had barely moved into their new place when Caroline showed up at the door.

"Caroline!" She gave her sister a big hug. "How nice to see you," Josette exclaimed. "You look fantastic."

"Thank you. You look radiant too. Where's your sweetheart?"

"He's out running an errand. He should be back in a few minutes."

"Dad told me over the phone that you aced your certification. That's great. Congratulations," Caroline said.

Lucas came in and saw Caroline. "You must be Caroline," he said. "You look like your sister."

They chatted briefly, but Caroline said, "I left my luggage at Dad's, and I only saw Marlene. I need to go back there and see Dad. Can we have lunch tomorrow? My treat."

"It works for me," Josette said.

"I'm not employed, my schedule is wide open." Lucas chuckled.

⁂

At lunch the next day, Caroline talked about her life in Geneva, working in the exciting new European venture doing research for harnessing nuclear power for peaceful purposes.

Josette asked her what she did for fun. "Do you work all the time? Do you play? Do you have a boyfriend?"

"My work schedule is pretty full and I have to travel abroad quite a bit. I go to the U.S. mainly, also England and Germany. Work is what I do. I have had a couple of semi-romantic involvements which went nowhere."

Josette put her hand on Caroline's wrist. "So you don't have a man-friend?"

Caroline chuckled. "Now I do have some sort of a boyfriend. His name is Helmut. If you remember Sophia, Dad's half-sister who lives in Geneva, Helmut is her daughter's brother-in-law. He's from the German part of Switzerland. He's a ski instructor in the winter and a mountain guide in the summer. We don't see each other often in the heights of either season."

Incredulous, Lucas stared at Caroline, "You mean you don't ski with him and he does not take you hiking in the summer?"

Caroline blushed. "I'm not a skier. In the ski areas, there are crowds, T-bars, lifts, and gondolas; that's not for me. In the summer, mountains give me peace, beauty, and intimacy with nature. They also offer grand vistas, immense skies, wild flowers and animals. I go for hikes, but Helmut climbs mountains. That's not for me either."

Then she asked Josette, "Do you two ski?"

Lucas shook his head and laughed. "Aside from the Mercantour area where Josette and I just spent a week, the only mountains I know are the Atlas Mountains of the Northern Sahara. There is very little snow there."

"I can imagine."

The waiter brought their food, and Lucas poured some wine into their three glasses.

Josette looked at Lucas. "We should plan an outing with Caroline one of these days. This is the kind of trip which is beneficial to you, Luke."

"I'd love that," Caroline said. "I like to carry a tent and enjoy remote areas, but most trails in the Alps are well used. I tend to go to the Jura or the Vosges. These may not be spectacular mountains, but very few people go there, and one can have a communion with nature. It is good for one's soul."

Lucas looked up to the ceiling and agreed. "Sleeping under the stars makes one feel at peace with oneself."

"Is it in your trauma response kit?" Caroline asked Josette, who laughed. "It may very well be part of my tool kit. I'm still working on what works."

Changing the subject, Lucas looked at Caroline. "How do you like living in Geneva?"

"I love the job. I don't love the climate, but I spend most of my time at work. It's all right, I guess. What about you, Lucas? You said you were not employed."

"I'm taking my time to get over the months I spent in North Africa."

"Yes. My dad told me about your war. Sounds scary."

"Some of the time. But also boring when nothing happened."

"But I can't comprehend how did you get used to being shot at?" Caroline asked. "Dad said you were in many fights."

With a knowing grin, Lucas made eye contact with Caroline. "You really never get used to it. You learn the tricks of the trade from your troops and sergeants. You try to understand how the people you fight operate, and the most important thing is that you have to be lucky."

"But is it not hard to fire at people?"

Lucas looked down at the table. "At first it's difficult, almost impossible, barbaric, and it feels wrong." He hesitated. "But you see terrible things like soldiers who are killed or maimed; you witness innocent people who have been attacked. Then you get mad, and you want to eliminate those who do these things. The worst of it is that, if you survive, you get used to it. Once you get home, you have to fix your mind. That's not easy."

Caroline shivered. "Let's talk about something fun. Who's coming to the wedding?"

"We'll be a small number, mainly friends. You may remember Eric Tallec who you met when I graduated from medical school?"

"Yes, I do. A nice guy. Who else?"

"Friends of mine, Tom and Francine I helped in Algeria," Lucas said. "They'll bring a little girl named Hana. She's an orphan they plan to adopt in few weeks. They brought her to France, nobody in her village wanted her because she was a girl. You'll love her. She's very bright."

✧

The Thursday before the wedding, while at work, Doctor Stanislas, the head of the hospital where she worked and studied, summoned Josette. Anticipating there might be an answer to her plea for a grant, she got a bit flustered. With a pounding heart, she ran to his office. His secretary, said, "He's anxious to see you. You may go in." Josette knocked and opened the door. Three of the judges who were members of the panel the day of her certification were waiting for her with Doctor Stanislas. She did not expect that, and her face got flushed.

"You asked for me," she said awkwardly.

Doctor Stanislas said, "We know the wedding has not happened yet."

Josette shook her head. "No sir, it's this Saturday."

"We have a wedding present for you. Your proposed research study has been approved, and a grant has been awarded to you."

Josette started to say something.

The doctor raised his hand. "Let me explain some of the details. It is a little complicated. There are three components to the grant. The first one concerns the soldiers affected by combat trauma. This grant is offered at the Val de Grace military hospital, Rue Saint Jacques in Paris. The second component is earmarked for further research in trauma treatment for children, staff, and office space at Necker Hospital, where you work. The last one is for the rehabilitation center in Maligny."

"The three grants are concurrent?" Josette asked.

"Yes. They are because the need for diagnostics and treatment is pressing. Each of these three grants contains funding for research staff, office and patients' facilities, and also support personnel. All three components have a provision for further money upon substantiated request. You will be awarded a generous salary for the next two years, and a monthly stipend for travel to consult with other trauma information centers around the world. Your research will be published in the Journal of Medicine so that other scientists can easily follow your work and communicate with you. The last item is that we will advertise your research in the hospitals and ask for volunteers, so you can select the doctors and the students who are qualified and eager to participate in the study and possibly get certified like you were."

Josette was stunned. Usually not at a loss for words, she finally said, "I don't know that saying thank you conveys my gratitude for this stupendous grant. Who do I need to thank for this and for the confidence placed in me?"

Doctor Stanislas nodded to acknowledge her gratitude. "This is a substantial grant that has been funded by several donors: first, the French military. That has been spurred by retired General de Vangarde, and several officials of the Veterans' Affairs, second by the French Ministry of Health. The third is someone familiar to you, Madame la Comtesse de Sèvres. Other additional anonymous donors contributed various amounts of money."

One of the judges who worked at Necker Hospital, Doctor Joly, said, "My congratulations to you, Ms. Dubois. Obviously, the panel and the relevant authorities acknowledged the importance and the urgency of your research. Your spectacular presentation the day of your certification gave us the material to persuade the donors of the merit of the work you outlined."

Josette thanked him, and he added, "We're working on allocating and outfitting space at the hospital for you. We expect it to be ready in early July."

Doctor Stanislas added, "The Val de Grace people are working on their end. I believe they'll be ready with facilities and potential staff for you by the end of that month."

"That's fabulous," Josette said.

"One more thing," the doctor added. "Madame la Comtesse de Sèvres would like to congratulate you."

The countess entered the room and went to hug Josette. "It is my pleasure to be able to contribute to your research. It will add another dimension to the work that has been accomplished in the Maligny facility on behalf of those who gave so much to our country. Congratulations, Josette. I'm looking forward to be working with you."

"How can I thank you, Madame?" Josette asked.

"Let the three studies you will run save lives, and develop the science that can help victims of war around the world. That's the thanks I want."

Doctor Stanislas got up. "This concludes the meeting."

He came to shake Josette's hand. "This is a terrific research project. I am glad you'll be leading it. Your father has invited me to your marriage ceremony. I'll see you then. We are all proud of you."

❦

Too shaken by the news to continue any useful work, Josette decided to go home. When she unlocked the door, she shouted, "LUKE. You'll never guess what happened."

He went to greet her. She put her arms around him. "I got the grant. It is ten times bigger than anything I expected." She proceeded to describe all the facets of her new project.

"This is so exciting, Josette." Lucas said. "Congratulations. So the countess funded you to develop her facility?"

"She did. What a Grande Dame. And I think my dad did some work with the military also. He's involved with the veterans."

"So we'll be staying in Paris for the foreseeable future," Lucas said.

"Yes we are. On top of everything, this apartment is perfectly located for me. The military hospital is a ten-minute walk from here, and Necker, where I go every day, is at most twenty."

That evening, Josette shared the news with her sister. Her dad knew about the grant because he had worked with the grant team to help define it.

Chapter 25

Paris

May 24

The colonel and Marlene invited Josette and Lucas to have dinner with them two days before the ceremony to go over the final plans for the wedding. Caroline attended as well.

"I have invited a couple of new people to your celebration," the colonel said. "I want to make sure it's okay with you. First Madame la Comtesse would like to invite Retired General de Vangarde, because they both got involved with and participated in the funding of the grants. He would also be her escort. The second surprise is due to my interference. I reached out to Captain Dufour who is now back in France. He would like to celebrate his favorite lieutenant's happy day. Do you have any objection to these additions?"

Lucas and Josette looked at each other. Lucas shook his head. Josette told her dad. "No, they would be great guests."

"I would add that when I left Algeria," Lucas said, "Captain Dufour and I did not say much to each other. Instead of saying good-bye, we choked. We could not talk. So many months on the front line forge strong relationships, respect, and trust. I would love to see the old man again."

"Now. A bit more controversial," the colonel continued. "Captain Dufour would like to invite Private Vidal, who got a bullet through his neck, was air-lifted to a field hospital and then to France. He had sent word to the captain that he had survived and been discharged. The captain has kept in touch with him. The private had praised Lucas for the way he had him swiftly evacuated from the battlefield and expressed the desire to thank him personally. He could be helpful to Josette in her research on soldiers' trauma. What do you think?"

Without hesitation, Josette asserted, "I would want to meet him, but it does not have to be at the wedding. Would that be okay with you to have him at the celebration? You're a colonel and he's a private."

"I have no issue with that," the colonel replied. "He's a courageous soldier who served his country well. What do you think, Lucas?"

"I'd love to have him come. But I'd also like to add three people, if that is possible. Tom, Francine, and Hana, the little girl I rescued from her village. They made it to France, and Tom and Francine will adopt Hana in a few weeks."

"That is fantastic." The colonel said, "You told me about her and I want to meet this young girl. A gutsy kid."

"That she is, and also the sweetest child. This is not a formal wedding. There'll be just family, a few close friends, and a supporting theme of trauma recovery. I kind of like that."

"Okay. It is settled," Josette asserted. "The civil signing is on Friday at three and the church service at ten Saturday morning at the Eglise Saint Augustin. Lunch at the Cercle Militaire right after."

⚜

On Friday night, after the civil marriage at the *mairie*, Josette and Lucas went to the train station to pick up Hana and her parents to-be. Hana was thrilled to see Lucas, and jumped into his arms almost like she did over two years before in El Boussaid. "You have changed so much in the last three months, Hana. You look very French."

Hana beamed and whispered in his ear, "Thank you."

"Hana. I want you to meet my future wife Josette. She has heard all about you and she loves you already."

Josette put her arm around both the young girl and Lucas. "You're so precious. I'm looking forward to knowing you, Hana. And congratulations on your new mother and father."

The adults greeted each other with much joy. They had a delightful evening, catching up on Mascara and the odyssey that brought the trio to France, and getting acquainted.

Josette fell in love with Hana when she saw how excited the girl was to be with Lucas again. She asked Hana what she liked best about her trip from Algeria to France.

"Everything," was Hana's answer.

"Do you like Paris also?"

"Yes. I do. It's like nothing I have seen before, so many people, so many cars, so many buses, so many... everything."

༄

The day of the wedding was a bright sunny Saturday. The wedding party walked leisurely from the church to the lunch venue.

It touched Lucas that Captain Dufour made a special trip to be there. The captain met Josette, and saw Tom, Francine, and Hana. He hugged Hana. "I'm so glad to see you here, little one. You look great."

"Also," Lucas added, "You'll be happy to know that Hana is going to be adopted by Tom and Francine in a few days. She will be called Anna Segal. I have been asked to come to the adoption hearing as a witness. I'm so happy for her."

Captain Dufour shook Francine's and Tom's hands. "Congratulations and welcome back to France. I'm glad you made it."

Private Vidal came to shake hands with his former leader. He said, "Lieutenant, I'll be forever grateful to you for the speed with which you got me airlifted from that ridge. That's what saved me." He showed them a pretty ugly scar on the side of his neck. "See. I'm all fixed up. My arteries work, and I can turn my head, and breathe."

Lucas introduced Josette. The private shook her hand. "So happy to meet you."

"Same here. I'm a doctor and I study the effect of trauma on children, but I will soon start a research project on soldiers' trauma." She tilted her head toward the private. "May I ask you a personal question?"

"Sure thing."

"You said you are all fixed up. But..." She stopped and said, "This is the wrong setting for such a conversation, I apologize."

Private Vidal smiled. "Not a problem at all, ma'am. Go ahead, ask me."
Josette went on, "I was just going to ask. Is your head all fixed up too?"
The private had a good laugh. "The answer is I'm doing okay...
most of the time."

"I'd like to talk to you and maybe help you. Do you live in Paris?"
Josette asked him.

"I do, and I'd like to benefit from your knowledge. The war memories still bother me."

"I'll get in touch with you when I am better organized to treat combat veterans."

⁕

Madame de Sèvres introduced Josette and Lucas to General de Vangarde, who congratulated the new couple but was especially happy to meet Josette.

"I did want so much to meet you. I admire you, a young woman, a talented doctor who is focusing on soldiers who served their country with valor and on innocent children. All of them have suffered traumas through no fault of their own. As you know, I have helped Madame de Sèvres set up the Maligny center where you have been awarded one of your grants. If you need any help, do not hesitate, call me. I'd be glad to do whatever I can. Your work is so important."

Madame de Sèvres met Tom, Francine, and Hana.

The countess bent down to talk to Hana. "I heard about you, little one. I am pleased to meet you. Do I look like I could be your grandmother?"

Hana smiled. "I never had a grandmother, Madame," she replied. "I didn't even have a mother."

"I heard. But I've been told your guardian angel will bring you a mother and a father soon."

"What's a guardian angel?"

The countess smiled and sighed. "It's someone who loves you, and makes sure good things happen to you, but you can't ever see him."

"Do I have one?"

"Everybody does. But you have to let him do his thing when he's ready."

"I didn't know that. Tom and Francine will adopt me soon. Then I'll have a mother and a father."

"You deserve it. I hope to see you again, Hana."

✧

Doctor Stanislas came to congratulate the bride and groom and said to Lucas, "I have talked with your captain. I learned a lot about your military record. It is impressive, and I suspect you might be the most evaluated, diagnosed, and treated traumatized soldier on earth," he said jokingly. "Really, hearing about what you and these young men accomplished during that war illustrates the definition of the word valor."

Caroline was fascinated with all the military and the medical guests. She spent some time talking with Doctor Tallec. They both met Hana and were fascinated by her energy, her openness, and her happiness at being there.

✧

At the end of the luncheon, the colonel asked if anyone would want to say a few words.

Nicole stood up. "I'd like to congratulate Josette and Lucas. These two human beings were in love but parted when he went to war. Unsurprisingly it didn't take more than three weeks upon his return to France for the old flame to re-ignite. Best of luck and happiness to both."

Doctor Tallec, the handsome young colleague of Josette who helped her in the trauma research, got up next and praised Josette's dedication to helping traumatized children. "She's pioneering a new branch of medical science; and watch out, she'll make a splash. Lucas, you aren't a child, but she'll find a way to fix your mind after your difficult war. We all want to work for her."

Doctor Stanislas got up next. "All I want to add to what Doctor

Tallec said, is that, as everyone in this room knows, Josette is about to undertake significant research on trauma. The benefits of her work will reach soldiers and children victims of severe trauma, in France and in all countries of the world. All of us will follow her lead and become better people for sharing her dedication to mankind."

Private Vidal got up next. "I had the privilege to serve in Lieutenant Lucas' platoon. I drove the jeep which brought him to take command of the second platoon on his first day in North Africa. The minute he got there, his senior sergeant got the platoon together, and the lieutenant told us, 'I'll never ask you to do anything I'm not willing to do myself.' He lived true to his word. At the end of his first week, our platoon had to check an abandoned farm. Lieutenant Lucas, brand new to the business of war, decided to go into the structure himself in spite of his sergeants urging him to let one of them do it. There were rebels hiding in a pit inside. Lieutenant Lucas entered first and almost lost his life. A corporal took care of the threat with a grenade. When that corporal told the lieutenant he had guts, his response was, 'I have to learn the job before I get soldiers killed.' And that he did."

Captain Dufour told Private Vidal, "Tell everyone why you're here."

"A year-and-a-half later, we got entangled with a bunch of rebels. I got hit by a bullet in the throat and lost consciousness. The lieutenant radioed for emergency air evacuation. Nurses took me away. One of them, I'm told, pinched my carotid artery with her fingers so I would not bleed to death. They got me to a hospital where they stopped my bleeding and from there they transported me back to France where they fixed me up." His voice faltered, but he continued. "All the doctors and nurses I thanked for helping me told me that the quick reaction of my lieutenant was what saved my life." His eyes locked onto Lucas. "Thank you, sir."

Private Vidal said, "There's one more thing you need to know about Lieutenant Lucas. He was a courageous and gifted platoon commander. Everyone respected him, but we also looked at him with affection, yes, affection because of the way he reacted to the children hurt by the war: we saw his steely warrior eyes tear up when he told us he and the first squad had killed the murderers of little Michael and his brother René. We saw his smile when he told us he had rescued that little girl Hana." He pointed at her and clapped his hands. Everyone else did too. She again blushed and beamed, obviously thrilled by the attention. "Welcome to France, Hana."

He turned to Lucas. "We all loved you with all your kids."

General de Vangarde got up. "It is my privilege to be here and meet young people who performed their duty with courage and honor. Doctor Stanislas must be proud, too, to train and guide doctors, therapists, and nurses who dedicate their lives to helping children recover from traumatic events. I admire and pay my respects to all of you, with a special mention to Captain Dufour, Lieutenant Lucas, and Private Vidal for their service to their country. But what strikes me is that that around this table, we have a wave of young people who are determined to make the world a better place. Today is a special day for Josette and Lucas, but also for all the people old and young who have encountered, or will face, the terrible hardship and pain of trauma."

Everyone applauded the speakers, and then the countess and the colonel got up.

Madame de Sèvres said, "I, as Lucas' surrogate mother," and Colonel Dubois added, "I as Josette's father," then both said, "We want to toast this new couple."

Both raised their glasses. Everyone stood up. Madame de Sèvres gave the toast.

"Best wishes to Josette and to Lucas for a long and happy life together, and for successful research and other endeavors that will give many victims of war and violence a chance at life."

Everyone mingled. Josette made sure she knew how to reach Private Vidal.

❧

Colonel Dubois talked to Captain Dufour. "Any plans to retire?"

"I'm thinking about it, sir."

"Keep in touch with me. My daughter is going to set up a new department in the Val de Grace, and the rehabilitation center of Maligny. She'll need someone who understands combat to supervise the soldiers who will undergo diagnostics and treatments as well as the therapists and doctors who will look after them. It's a brand new post and I'm not sure what the duties are going to be, but if the experiment is successful, there is no telling how important the job might become. If it's okay with you I'll talk to Josette when the time comes to fill the post."

"I'd love to find a position in life where I keep helping soldiers. Thank you, sir."

❧

Involved in Josette's trauma research, Doctor Tallec made a point of meeting Hana and was quite taken by the self-confidence she displayed in spite of the devastating recent events that had affected her in Algeria. He and Caroline talked for a long time. Eric Tallec told Caroline a Geneva hospital might be interested in hiring him.

"Make sure you let me know if you come to the city. I'll show you around," Caroline said.

"I will for sure. Thank you."

❧

Nicole took Lucas and Josette aside and told her, "Gilbert and I will be on our way to Lille after our wedding. We must try to stay in touch."

"We'll miss you. When does the new job start?" Josette asked.

"He will start next school year, the end of September."

"It's a great opportunity. Go for it," Josette said and hugged her.

Nicole hugged her back and did the same for Lucas. "You guys are special. I love you."

Eventually, everyone left in a mood of optimism for the future victims of trauma, especially children.

*

The next evening Josette got a call from her sister.

"Hi sis. What's up?"

"First, thank you for this uplifting wedding day. Your Lucas is a gem, and I was touched by all the fabulous guests, all dedicated to work for people and children who need help."

"It was a nice day, and as you saw, Lucas and I adore each other."

"It was obvious and heartwarming for all. Now, I also wanted to call you because something strange happened here. I found out from Sophie, Dad's half-sister, that her daughter Heidi, her son-in-law and his brother Helmut all died in an avalanche this weekend."

Josette gasped. "How tragic! Is Helmut your on-and-off boyfriend?"

"Yes, he is. It is so sad to see three vibrant young people dead at the beginning of their lives; but even more tragic is that the young couple's one-year-old twins are now orphans. It's the first time in my life I have been close to tragic events happening to children I knew. After your wedding, I now know that the two children have been traumatized, but unlike you, Lucas, and your guests, I have no idea what to do."

"I am sorry for your loss. It is too early to tell how the twins will be affected. Who will take care of them?"

"Sophie told me she is the only relative the children have, so she is in charge, but she is in her sixties."

"There's not much you can do, is there?" Josette thought out loud.

"I know," Caroline replied, "but Heidi, you, and I have a common grandmother, our granddad's first wife, so the twins are sort of family."

"We have to figure out how we could help, Caroline. Be strong, and call me any time you need to talk. I love you."

Chapter 26

Beaumes de Venise

June 5

One morning, a letter from Algeria addressed to Tom arrived unexpectedly at the winery. It came from Mustapha. He first apologized for his uneasy writing, and for addressing the letter to Tom while the message was mostly for Basira. The letter said:

"I know Basira cannot read this letter, so I'm imposing on you to share it with her. First, let me say that since the French troops left, shortly after your departure, things have settled down in sleepy El Boussaid, even in Mascara. Everything is quiet. All former French properties are occupied by responsible Algerian families, and there's no looting. I am enjoying living in your beautiful place.

"Basira's two boys are back in the village from their seven-week training camp. The older boy has been promoted to corporal and is stationed in a makeshift barrack on the edge of El Boussaid. He and his squad of boy-soldiers are in charge of maintaining order in the village. The younger son lives with me. He is on call in case needed. Both are healthy and would like their mom to come home. They miss her.

"Please Basira, do come back here. You can replace my second wife and live in Tom's house, the place where you lived when you were injured. I promise to take good care of you. You and Aisha will be safe and your family back together.

"Please let me know when your ship is due. I and your sons will pick you up (with Tom's old car) in Oran. Just give me the date and time. You can call me on the telephone at Tom's old number — It works some of the time — or you can ask Tom or Francine to write to me."

Tom shared the letter with Francine and asked her to come with him and read the letter to Basira.

"Basira, there's a letter for you from Mustapha," Francine said when she saw her sitting on one of the benches in front of the house.

"Really? Can you read it to me, please? I'm always embarrassed but I can't help it."

"Don't worry. I understand. Running a farm, tending to crops and to goats does require skills. Reading is not one of them."

Francine read the first few phrases that concerned her sons. Basira perked up. "I'm so relieved. I have been so worried about them. What else did he say?"

When Francine read to her about the offer to Basira to become his second wife, Basira blushed, and said, "I must talk with Aisha. Thank you for reading the letter. This is some news."

Basira went back into the house looking for her daughter.

She found her in Hana's room.

"Aisha, I need to talk to you." The two of them went to their bedroom and Aisha asked her what it was about.

Basira related to her the content of the letter. It pleased Aisha to learn about her brothers. But when she heard the offer from Mustapha, she immediately said, "Are you going to do it?"

"I would not mind going back. I'm not sure I want to live here, but I will if you want to stay and get a good education."

Aisha shook her head, and with a smile on her face, replied, "I don't care about education. People here don't like Algerians. They'll never accept me. Hana is going to be French and in a higher grade in school. I hate her. I'd rather go home."

"Let me think it over. Living as one of Mustapha's wives would be a big change for me. I'm not sure I'm ready for that. Also you need to have a couple of lessons. You might enjoy it and it would be good for you. Look at me, I can't read. You need to learn to have a decent life."

Aisha shrugged and turned her back to her mom.

ॐ

The next day when they both woke up in their room, Aisha asked eagerly, "Did you think it over?"

"I have thought about what to do."

Barely letting her mother finish her sentence, she asked, "What did you decide?"

Basira smiled at her daughter. "I think the only sensible thing to do is to know more. I need to know when we could sail back and how much it would cost. We need to know how you do with this wonderful teacher who is ready to help you; and most of all, I need to think through how my life would be back home."

Aisha pouted. "How long will all that take?"

"It won't take long."

Basira went to find Francine and told her she needed to find out potential schedule and costs of going back to Mascara to help her make a decision. She also told her, "I need to be sure it is the right thing for Aisha to go back. It'll take me some time."

"I'll get the information on the passage to Algeria," Francine replied. "Take your time; it would be a big change. I will respect whatever you decide and help you."

Francine shared the news with Tom who said, "I'm not surprised. I know Aisha is unhappy, but it would be a big change in Basira's life. I would hope she'll be happier whichever way she goes."

Chapter 27

Avignon

June 11

On June 10, Tom, Francine, and Hana went to pick up Josette and Lucas at the Avignon railroad station.

"How about Basira and Aisha? Are they all right?" Lucas asked.

Tom's face turned somber. "This is not a really happy story. Neither of them seemed to fit here. Basira is almost illiterate and Aisha has been struggling with her French. They just were offered an opportunity to go back to Mascara, which has quieted down now that the French troops have left. So, they might be leaving us. Basira has not decided yet. Aisha wants to go back to El Boussaid. The fascinating thing is that Basira would become one of Mustapha's wives, replacing the second one. We don't know what happened to the former second wife. Mustapha now lives on my ranch, familiar territory for Basira."

"Really?" Lucas asked. "That could be the best for Aisha and Basira now that the area has calmed down. They'd be safe and have a powerful protector, and she'll have her two sons back."

When they drove into the Segals' new winery and saw all the buildings, Josette and Lucas liked the new property, and enjoyed a tour of the grounds. They were to stay in one of the guest houses.

Every time Hana got out of the car in front of the house, Wolf ran to her. Josette took a look at him. "Who is this?" she asked Hana.

"His name is Wolf. He was a lost dog and he was here when we arrived. They gave him to me. We're best friends."

"It's good for you to have a friend like him. He's beautiful. I understand you also have a friend named Aisha."

Hana looked down at her feet, then up at Josette. "Not really. She's not happy here. She hates me." She shrugged. "She wants to go back to Algeria."

"Why would she hate you? You lived together two years at the farm."

"My French is better than hers, so is my reading and she resents that. It won't matter in her village."

"She wants to live in the same village you come from?"

Hana shivered and looked down. "Lieutenant Lucas got me out of it. I never went back after that day." She shook her head and almost whispered. "There are bad men there."

Josette got a firsthand look at Hana's trauma; though it did not seem that strong, clearly mentioning the village troubled her. "No need to think about bad times. You will have a new real family. Your French is excellent, and you have a bright future here."

Hana raised her head and smiled and said, "Do you want to see my room?"

"I sure do."

They went upstairs, escorted by Wolf. Hana showed Josette her desk and the new shelves that had been installed to hold her books.

"Did you read all these books?"

"Yes. I love reading." They talked about the school and the plans for the summer.

"I like you," Hana said.

"And I love you very much too, Hana." Josette put her arms around the little girl's shoulders.

When they came down to the living room, Aisha and Basira were there. Basira was genuinely happy to meet Josette, but Aisha remained the sulky little girl she had become lately.

✦

On the morning of June 11, Tom, Francine, Lucas, Josette, Basira, and Hana, in her blue dress of course, piled into the two cars and drove to Avignon. Aisha had decided she'd rather stay at the house. The adoption party got to the courthouse and asked for Judge Moran's courtroom.

They took the elevator to the third floor. Lucas and Josette met

Madame Tabris and everyone met Pierre Bellot, the civil records clerk of Montelimar, sitting with the lawyer. A few minutes later, a court official ushered them into the courtroom. Hana held Francine's hand. "I'm nervous," she whispered to Francine. Francine squeezed her hand and whispered back, "You'll do fine. Everyone in this room loves you."

A court official announced aloud the name of the hearing.

"This is the petition for the adoption of Hana Martin by Francine and Tom Segal. Please, all rise."

Judge Moran entered the room. He had a nice smile. "Welcome, everyone." He looked at Hana. "And especially welcome to you, little girl. I have heard about the difficult times that led you to my courtroom. Your troubles are just about to be over. Now I have to ask a few questions, because it is the law."

He looked at the people assembled in his courtroom. "Would the parents stand to the right of their daughter-to-be?"

Francine took Hana's hand and Tom stood next to Francine.

"Would the witnesses Lucas and Basira, please stand on Hana's left." Lucas took Hana's other hand.

The judge looked at Basira. "Basira Habib, I understand that you and your late husband Ahmed were Hana's guardians for over two years."

"Yes, Your Honor."

"Do you support the adoption of Hana Martin by Tom and Francine Segal?

"Yes, with all my heart, Your Honor."

The judge nodded and turned to Lucas.

"Lucas. I understand that, as a lieutenant in the French Army, you rescued little Hana, then an orphan abandoned by everyone in the village where she lived."

"Yes, Your Honor. I found out both her parents had died and no one in the village cared to adopt her, or even help her. My friend Ahmed offered to take her in, and I took Hana away from that village and brought her to Ahmed's farm. There, Basira agreed to take her in."

"Now let me ask you, do you support the adoption of Hana Martin by Tom and Francine Segal?"

"Yes, Your Honor, I do."

"Now I understand that we have a witness who can vouch for Hana's heritage."

Pierre stood up and talked about Frederic and Maurice Martin. He told the judge all he knew about the father's family. He told the judge that Hana's grandfather was killed in the first months of World War II, and that his wife passed way soon after. He asserted that nobody from the Martin family lived in Montelimar or anywhere else as far as he knew.

Judge Moran asked Tom and Francine if the adoption was their wish and was not forced onto them.

Both replied they wanted to adopt Hana more than anything else on earth.

The judge got up, and went down to take Hana's hands in his.

"Now I have to ask the most important person in this room." He gave Hana a big smile. "Hana. Do you want Tom and Francine Segal to become your legal mother and father?"

She smiled from ear to ear.

"Yes, yes, yes..." She paused, and then remembered to say, "Your Honor."

"Is everyone in this court in agreement?"

All said, "Yes, Your Honor."

The judge declared, "I rule that you are now Anna Segal."

He went back up to his seat and asked the witnesses to come next to the clerk who recorded the names and addresses of Basira and Lucas. Both added their signatures.

Judge Moran stood up and declared the court adjourned.

He told Anna, "Congratulations Anna. Come give me a hug."

Anna ran up the steps and gave him a big hug. "I thank you," she said.

"I'm happy for you," he replied.

Then Anna went back to kiss everyone including Pierre who looked pleased with the whole scene.

Anna shed some quiet and happy tears. Today was the end of the Algerian years of her young life, a difficult chapter as such.

Chapter 28

Paris

June 18

Josette would start her trauma research work in late July, a month from now, but she wanted to start on staffing her research projects as soon as possible. Her cadre of trauma specialists at Necker Hospital was well trained although not yet certified. The most competent were Doctors Tallec and Raynaud, both department heads. Their teams, however small, would be the nucleus she could draw on to train other trauma specialists. But Doctor Stanislas had called Josette to inform her that the Geneva teaching hospital had inquired about Doctor Tallec's availability to head a new trauma department they wanted to create.

"It's not going to help us if he leaves," Josette had told him.

"I know it's not going to help you but I have to let them interview Doctor Tallec because it is a great opportunity for him."

Josette had to agree with her boss. She could not deny Doctor Tallec a significant promotion. She sensed a renewed urgency to lock in her team, but the call for volunteers to join her team had just gone out and she had to let the process work.

When she mentioned her bad news to Lucas, he knew she would be working hard to put her team together. He thought he had better get busy also, instead of spending his time feeling sorry for himself, and decided he would start to look for a job. Madame la Comtesse had offered to help, Monsieur Boucheron had given him some advice, but although in no rush to choose a career, Lucas thought he could at least test the job market.

So one morning in mid-June, he went to the alumni association of his engineering school to find out about current opportunities. He met one of the lead advisers, Madame Fournier, who greeted him warmly and went to retrieve his school records. Lucas had graduated in the top third of his class, so they discussed his strengths and his interests. He stressed his leadership qualities which he had developed as a combat platoon leader, and also mentioned his uneasiness in re-entering the civilian world. He opened up about his resentment against the French government. "I'm not sure how to go about choosing a career," he told the adviser.

She smiled back at him. "You're probably still full of military memories, and you haven't been involved in the business world at all."

"Actually, I have been thinking about getting involved in helping returning soldiers who suffered from psychological wounds, but I don't know how. I have no background in medicine."

"Let me ask you a question," Madame Fournier said. "Is there any particular industry you're interested in? We have many positions in the automobile sector."

"Not really. I went to talk with the dean, Mr. Boucheron. I assume you know him."

She nodded.

"He asserted that the computer industry is the one with the most potential for growth. He also mentioned international companies with their French headquarters in Paris because of their worldwide outlook."

"We have some offers from companies working in that business." She showed him three different routes he could consider. The first was an American company, Computers Inc., which had a strong French division. It had two possible points of entry: a product-development laboratory in the south of France, in Nice, and a marketing technical support entry position in Paris; the second, a French manufacturing firm working on telephone equipment and trying to establish an alliance with an American business; the third, a French start-up in the computer industry which was linked to a German business specializing in printers, storage units and other peripheral equipment.

Very analytical and helpful, Madame Fournier knew her job and dismissed the start-up, arguing that his leadership qualities would not be a great asset for them. She recommended that he interview with the telephone equipment firm located in Paris and find out what their entry position would be, but she insisted, as the dean of the school had, that the computer industry in 1962 was in its infancy and would provide the most opportunities for growth in the next few years. She strongly suggested that, in addition to the phone company, he also interview with Computers, Inc., France. The man who ran the French division of the company had graduated from the same engineering school as Lucas, always an advantage in the French business world. She said she would try to have the vice president of personnel interview him and explore the two avenues she had mentioned in Nice and in Paris.

Lucas told her, "I just got married. My wife – it feels funny to say that – is a doctor doing important medical research work in Paris, so I'm not interested in a job in Nice."

"I understand, but you may want to interview in Nice to get a sense of the chemistry of the company, visiting product development departments, as well as product marketing and support employees."

"That makes sense," Lucas replied.

Lucas was thankful but felt a bit overwhelmed. All these possibilities were totally foreign to his military life, and almost made him dizzy. He closed his eyes for an instant and shook his head. Then he looked at her with a little smile and said, "I think I agree with your recommendation, but I have to admit, it is hard for me to grasp all that information. I got back from Algeria in early March, but I'm not all here yet. It's hard for me to keep focused; I'm sorry."

"I can see that, but you'll get back on your civilian feet soon. I'll help you through this process. Most graduates I see have had an easy time of the war, spending their time in assignments in France or in the big northern cities of Algeria. You served your country as a combat soldier. It obviously took a toll." She looked at him and added, "Let me do some work and schedule some interviews for you."

The adviser ended the meeting with that promise.

Lucas left that constructive meeting a bit disoriented. All of a sudden the life options in front of him proved to be totally different from his long months as a platoon leader. He did not really know how to reach a decision. Discussing the meeting with Josette when he got home, she suggested that he talk to Thierry's father.

"He runs a big division in his corporation. He can tell us what to look for and what are the key questions to ask when you have the interviews. I have to return Nicole's call. Let me ask her if she can arrange that."

Nicole was glad to hear from her. "Sure, Dad will help. Let me talk to him. You can come to dinner and get some guidance. I'll call you back."

She called within a few minutes. "Come for dinner tonight. I won't be there. I'll be with my fiancé. Our wedding is coming up soon."

That evening, Monsieur DuPont, Thierry's father shook Lucas's hand and Josette's. "Congratulations on your wedding. We wish you the best."

Once they were comfortably seated, Lucas thanked Thierry's mother for having them for dinner, then went straight to the point.

"These are confusing times for me. My reentry is a difficult challenge. That is why I wanted to get your guidance. I have to forget combat, forget living with a rifle in my hands. Josette is helping me with that, but I have to start my career, and I can use some help."

"Do you know which branch of industry you would prefer to work in?"

Lucas told him about the morning interview and about the suggestion from the woman at the school alumni association.

"But you see," he added, "I'm not sure how to decide."

"I understand exactly what your dilemma is, and what I would recommend is that you insist on personal interviews with every one of the potential avenues your advisor offered to you. Go to the labs, and the headquarters of the companies you're considering. Talk to managers and employees. Get a feel for the aura of the business. I would also try to get a feel for the requirements for overseas assignments. They can be important for advancement in international companies. Write down what they say, and if you are still confused or if you want to validate a decision, come back and see me, and we'll talk. If you are not satisfied with the choices you have, come and talk to me. My corporation has openings for smart guys and good leaders."

They sat down for a nice meal. Josette and Lucas talked about Nicole's upcoming wedding. Monsieur DuPont congratulated Josette for her grants. They talk about trauma without mentioning Lucas' issues with it. Being with friends ready to lend support was uplifting to Lucas.

At the end of the evening, Lucas thanked the mother for the nice meal and the father for his patience and his advice.

Chapter 29

South Devon, England

June 24

While the search for volunteers for Josette and the scheduling of interviews for Lucas were underway, the two of them decided to go to England for Josette to meet Ms. Rooth. They left Paris early on June 24, spent a night in London, and the next day a seven-hour train trip took them to Teignmouth.

Waiting in her usual place on the platform, Ms. Rooth welcomed the newlyweds.

"Josette," she said, hugging the young woman she had never met, "I have heard about you years ago, and it made me happy to hear you and Lucas had gotten together again."

She squeezed Lucas' cheeks between her two hands, and tenderly said, "Welcome to England, Lucas darling. I worried so much I'd never see you again. And here you are. You look fantastic — strong, healthy, and happy."

"It's so good to see you, Mother. You look good too."

"Let's get into the car. Mr. Rooth is dying to see you."

She drove to the hamlet of Bishopsteignton, some five miles west of Teignmouth.

Still sporting his mustache, although a little greyer than the last time Lucas saw him, the retired colonel of the British Indian army hugged Lucas firmly, and opened his arms to Josette.

"Welcome, both."

"It's a pleasure to meet you, sir." Josette said.

Mr. Rooth frowned, and then looked at Josette. "You have a British accent, Josette."

"Yes I do. I was born in Manchester, but moved away when I was two years old. My father was French, and my mother British. She passed away about three years ago."

They sat down for tea. Many a day when he spent the summer in Bishopsteignton, Ms. Rooth prepared cucumber sandwiches for tea. Again today, she made them for Lucas because they were his favorites. They talked about these old days, about Josette's grants and medical research, and of course about Lucas' years in Algeria and their effect on him.

They retired early, in need of a good night's sleep.

⁂

The following morning after breakfast, Ms. Rooth went to her room and came back with a stack of letters.

"Josette, you undoubtedly know that Lucas wrote to me regularly while he was in North Africa?"

"Yes, I do. Lucas told me how important your letters were to keep him sane."

"I'm glad to have helped. Now, there are two things that I need to share with you. The first one is that reading the letters from Lucas, I had a good idea of what was going on in his head. I could see that he would be traumatized when discharged. I suppose this is not news to you."

"I have known that the first day we met after his return."

"Good. The other thing that I want to tell you is important and might be significant for your research. When I spent all those years in India, I had the opportunity to meet and follow for years several officers and soldiers of the British army in India who were in my husband's regiment. I gained a good understanding of what went though their minds, and how combat affected their attitudes and their sanity. I saw the same pattern develop in almost all of them, and I must tell you that I saw that very sequence of emotional changes in Lucas' letters."

Josette sat up taller. "Really. Can you say more, please?"

"I treasured Lucas' letters, because I was afraid he might not make it. Fighting as an infantry lieutenant is one of the most dangerous jobs in the army. But he came back, and I have no more need for them, but I think you do, if it's okay with Lucas."

"That would be wonderful, but I don't want to rob you of your treasures."

"Here's what I think we can do. I have recorded what I learned over my India years about the evolution of a soldier's mind in fights not unlike the rebellion war Lucas experienced. I think I know where that paper is. I'll retrieve it and give it to you tomorrow morning. Then, after you have read it, we can go over Lucas' letters chronologically without dwelling on the details and psychoanalyzing them. I believe we'll be able to identify the phases I have defined in my paper in the letters from Lucas. Then we can decide what you can or want to do with them."

"That's perfect. You are so kind," Josette replied.

"I have seen too many soldiers affected with what generals and civilian doctors called battle fatigue to know that it is a branch of medicine that has been ignored. It is not fatigue. I am not a physician, but I think the condition many soldiers end up with is either a disease or a disorder. Not sure what the difference is, but I believe either warrants medical attention and professional treatment. I am glad to see a talented young doctor, like you Josette, tackling the problems of combat aftermath."

Lucas had been watching the conversation, and said to Josette, "May I add something to what Ms. Rooth told you?"

"Sure."

"There were several times when I was confused about what was going on in my mind throughout my war. Every time I felt strange about something, I would write to Ms. Rooth. Invariably the response would not only explain what happened in my mind and why, but also a prediction of what would happen next. She was always right."

"Do you still have these letters?"

"Of course."

"So I believe," Josette looked at Ms. Rooth. "I should take Lucas' letters to you, Ms. Rooth." Her eyes turned to Lucas, "And take her responses to you, Lucas. That would give me a solid base to start the military trauma diagnostic research."

Both Lucas and Ms. Rooth agreed to the plan.

Mr. Rooth came into the lively discussion and proposed to take advantage of the stupendous June weather in South Devon.

"Let's take a ride down to Teignmouth and go on to Dartmouth. We'll have lunch there. Josette, have you ever seen Agatha Christie's house?"

"No, it's my first time in southwest England. I would love to see it."

"We may be able to catch an excursion boat to Greenway gardens to look at the house," Ms. Rooth suggested.

"Right-ho," Mr. Rooth said.

"Tomorrow I'll share my knowledge of the phases of the soldiers at war," Ms. Rooth reassured Josette.

⁓

The next morning, Ms. Rooth told Josette that she had found the paper she had written on the phases of the soldiers confronted by a war.

"This is for wars like the one Lucas fought in North Africa, a war of rebellion or a guerilla war. I have no experience with world wars, intense battles with tanks, artillery, bombing, and so on." She gave her write-up to Josette. Lucas was also eager to read what she had written. It went like this:

The first phase of a soldier in his first skirmishes is bewilderment. He does not know where to look, what to do, even sometimes has trouble holding his weapon. He might be a sharp shooter, but he might not be capable of firing his weapon at first. This is a very short phase.

The second phase is shock. The soldier is fired at by the enemy. He is not hit, but he realizes the bullets were aimed at him. His mind has difficulty accepting that someone is trying to kill him. After a couple of incidents he returns fire. He is still highly inefficient, but he is no longer totally paralyzed. He goes through the motions, but is still not in full control of his actions. Depending on the level of activity, this phase can last from a few days to several weeks.

The third phase is uncertainty. The soldier becomes a full-time participant in the fight. He is a combat soldier, but he still has doubt about killing the adversaries. He is still hesitant at times to fire his weapons. His superiors still look at him as somewhat unpredictable. He does well if he's next to a buddy, but he has little initiative of his own. The soldier's superiors have him fight as part of a tightly knit team. Five guys and a corporal is ideal. The soldier is never left to his own devices. He's never given a task where his judgment is what decides his next actions. This phase lasts a few weeks, sometimes months, unless the combat activity is low, in which case the soldier might never gets out of that phase.

The fourth phase is an important one: a real soldier. One day, after a firefight with high casualties or a close friend of the soldier is killed or maimed, the soldier's mind totally changes. He has had it with the enemy. He loses his reluctance to fire at a human being. He hates his adversaries, and he wants to eliminate as many as he can. He wants to kill the enemy. He is angry and starts to hate the people he's fighting. This is a dangerous phase because he is not focused on his own or his buddies' safety. He might not take the precautions he should. This phase can be short or take a few weeks or months.

This phase four can but does not necessarily lead to a short phase five, which is depression. The killer-soldier is tired of the war, of the casualties, of the endless fights, He wants to go home and get away but he knows he cannot. The depression phase may end up in discharge, the famous battle fatigue being the official reason. But it is psychological trauma. The soldier cannot function as a combatant anymore.

The alternative to a phase five is the phase of the professional soldier. He is well trained and has become an efficient fighter, who knows what to do. He can lead other soldiers, and is reliable. In that phase, these soldiers make great point-men, patrol leaders, corporals, and sergeants. Combat is now a job, a dangerous job, a demanding job, some say a dirty job.

cℓℴ

When both Josette and Lucas had read the write-up, Josette asked Lucas what he thought of it.

"It's pretty much dead on. I remember going through all these phases, including the depression phase, following back-to-back battles where I lost half of my forty-five men, thirteen of them permanently. My senior sergeant told me I had become a professional infantry leader and that my platoon could not afford to have me feel sorry for myself. So my depression phase lasted less than a day, thanks to him."

"With this synopsis and with your and her letters, I have a sound basis to study soldiers' distress and to apply what I know about trauma on children to combat veterans," Josette said.

"Yes, you do, and you need to also find out if the phase in which a trauma-causing event happens makes a difference to the effect of the trauma. I'd guess it should," Lucas added.

While they were talking, Mr. Rooth interrupted them, and asked Lucas, "Are you game to take me out sailing in my sailboat? I still have it, but I can't handle it by myself. I remember you were a good sailor, we had a good time racing, I recall."

"That would be great. I'd love to."

Josette interjected, "Any outdoor activity which slows down the brain is good for Lucas. As his supervising doctor, I highly support that." She chuckled.

Ms. Rooth did not enjoy sailing, so Mr. Rooth drove Josette and Lucas down to the mooring. The boat, a thirty-two-foot sloop, looked to be in great shape. The two men prepared the sails, and Lucas motored out of the inlet into the channel. Once facing the wind, while Mr. Rooth stood at the wheel, Lucas raised the sails. He then trimmed the sails to suit the wind and they enjoyed a leisurely trip down to Torquay. Listening to the lapping of the sea against the bow of the boat was soothing.

"What a treat. I'm having a ball. This is beautiful. What about you, Josette?" Lucas asked.

"I'm loving it too. If this is therapy, I might prescribe it to myself when I'm stressed."

Mr. Rooth was happy too. Looking up at the sail, he told Lucas, "You do remember how to trim a sloop so it is properly balanced. It makes me feel good."

"I remember the Norwegian guest you had one summer. He taught me all I know about sailing."

"I remember him also. Leif was his name. He got us out of trouble when we were hit by that freak storm one evening."

After a restful afternoon, they sailed back into the mooring area.

That evening, Josette said to Lucas, "It might be my imagination, but I saw you as relaxed and at peace as when we were in the mountains."

"You're right. Mother Nature knows how to take care of me."

The next day Ms. Rooth, Josette, and Lucas went over the letters and ended the day at Mr. Rooth's favorite place, the local pub. Then Lucas and Josette had to start the long trip back to Paris.

"Write to me and tell me how you're doing with the letters," Ms. Rooth said to Josette. Then she looked at Lucas. "Lucas, you have a beautiful wife who has a compassionate heart and a sharp brain. Write to me now and then."

Chapter 30

Beaumes de Venise

July 2

Basira's head had been going back and forth on her decision to go back to El Boussaid. Today, Aisha was to have her first reading lesson with Mademoiselle Dumas. The two hours went fast, and Aisha did well. She felt comfortable with her teacher. The next day, as promised, Mademoiselle Dumas picked Aisha up and drove her to the school where she met the two village girls, Isabelle and Monique, who needed help to make it into second grade.

"This is Aisha," Mademoiselle Dumas said. "She needs a little boost like you do to qualify and to benefit from second grade."

Isabelle looked at Monique with a knowing smile, but did not say anything. The teacher went on to say, "Aisha lives at the winery and will attend our school next September."

"Where did she go last year?" Monique asked.

"Aisha lived in Mascara in Algeria. Both girls rolled their eyes "You have to make her feel welcome." Isabelle put her hand over her mouth to suppress a little chuckle.

Mademoiselle Dumas, of course, saw the antics, but she did not say anything.

"Isabelle, you start. Read the first two pages." She handed her a book opened at page one. Isabelle did reasonably well, having trouble only with three words. The teacher handed the same book to Monique. "Your turn. Start reading on page three." Monique had a bit more trouble than Isabelle, stumbling over about ten words. It was now Aisha's turn. She read very slowly, applying herself to enunciate every syllable so as not to show her accent. Unfortunately, although she had no more problem than Monique in her reading, she had trouble with pronouncing her Rs and mainly her CHs, tending to emit more guttural sounds than the classic French pronunciation demanded.

Mademoiselle Dumas said to her, "You did well. When I see you by yourself tomorrow, we'll work on these Rs and CHs."

But Isabelle and Monique snickered.

"This is not nice behavior, girls. You should be ashamed of yourselves. French is not her first language and she's doing very well with it."

In the car driving back to the winery, Aisha looked at her feet.

Mademoiselle Dumas said to her, "Don't be discouraged. These girls don't know anything outside of their village and their school. They'll learn to like you."

❧

Basira asked Aisha when she entered their room, "How did you do? Did you have fun?"

Aisha shrugged. "The French girls made fun of me. I'm not doing it again."

"Tomorrow, Mademoiselle Dumas comes here. You can talk to her."

Aisha pouted. "But if we go back to Algeria, I don't need to know how to read French."

"Aisha, the more you know, the better off you are. I wish I could read and write. If we stay here, I'll learn."

"You have not decided yet?"

"We have requested passages for us. I don't know when we can go over, and how much it will cost. I can't really decide until I have that information."

The next day, the teacher came to the winery to meet with Aisha.

Aside from helping Aisha with some difficult words, Mademoiselle Dumas started to help her with the CH sound which is easier to correct than the Rs.

When they were done, Basira came in and told the teacher what Aisha had said the previous day about not wanting to go back to the school with Isabelle and Monique.

The teacher faced Aisha. "I'm so sorry those girls misbehaved yesterday. I believe that as they get to know you and how sweet you are, they will become your friends. That will help you when the school year starts, and you have many more schoolmates."

"But why are they mean?" Aisha asked.

"It is called prejudice. It is something people of all ages use to feel superior when they don't understand why other people are different."

"But I'm not that different."

"No you are not, but you're not quite the same. They are ignorant of what made you that way, and they don't want to find out what it is. They don't want to have to work to learn your background, your culture, your religion, or your language. They have decided in their mind that because you are different, you are not their equal."

"I really don't understand that prejudice."

"I am sorry it is this way but honey, that's life. I hope things will change, but it'll take time. Please come tomorrow to the session we have planned at the school. It'll be easier."

"Okay. I'll try," Aisha responded.

"Thank you. I'll pick you up at nine-forty-five."

The next session turned out to be a little easier for Aisha. Mademoiselle Dumas had talked to Isabelle, Monique and to their mothers. She tried to convey how reprehensible it was to be mean to a young girl who had been terrorized by war, lost her father, and moved to a totally foreign environment with an uncertain future. Her lecture on prejudice led to some understanding.

Once at home, Basira asked Aisha how she made out. Aisha mumbled, without much conviction "I did okay."

Basira shrugged and said, "Let's go talk to Francine."

When they got together, Basira explained how Aisha fared with her first three days of remedial reading.

"Aisha wants to go back to Algeria. There is a part of me who wants to stay here, and find my way to help you as soon as my shoulder is one-hundred percent. It's a way to thank you for having taken care of us and brought us to safety. But there's another part of me who is looking at a life I know back in Algeria. A life that might not be ideal, but will be reasonably comfortable for me because of the many people I know in the village."

"Basira, I hope you know that you don't have to do anything to thank Tom and me. There was trouble, and when that happened, we all had to help each other. Now, do you have a date for when you can go back? Also, do you need to talk more to Tom and to me in order to decide?"

"I just received a passage booked for July 11, and I can afford it."

Aisha, who had not said a thing, whispered, "I want to go."

"Is that what you want?" Basira asked her. Aisha nodded. Basira looked at Francine and said, "I think I have decided. Would you please write to Mustapha and tell him? I'll give you the name of the ship and the time it will arrive on July 12."

"I sure will."

In the next few days, Anna and Francine helped Aisha and Basira select the belongings they could carry and pack the rest to be shipped separately. Now that she prepared to go back to Algeria, Aisha became noticeably more agreeable to conversations with Tom, Francine, and Anna. She had been thoroughly unhappy, and more scared of a future in Beaumes de Venise than she could imagine.

୬୬

On that Thursday morning, the eleventh of July, Tom, Francine, and Anna drove Aisha and Basira to Marseille and said a tearful goodbye.

"Come back if you feel unhappy or threatened. We love you," Francine said.

"Have Mustapha write to us to let us know you made it safely," Tom added.

A little teary, Anna thanked Basira for taking care of her on Ahmed's farm. "I will never forget that you and Aisha allowed me to have a safe life in your family."

Close to tears, Basira embraced her. "That was the only thing I could do. I could not say no to you. It makes me happy you have a chance at a good life."

A timid smile on her face, Anna tilted her head. "Say hi to the goats for me, they were good friends."

※

Francine had given Basira a copy of Anna's birth certificate once her new identity had been recorded in the French court. She had also given her a copy of the deed of the property that Anna's grandfather had purchased in Tiaret when he went there in 1938.

"When you're back in Algeria, would you ask Mustapha if he can find out more about Anna's father and her grandfather Frederic?" Francine asked Basira. "Also, what did Frederic Martin do in Tiaret? How did Maurice happen to end up in El Boussaid?"

"I will ask Mustapha," Basira replied. "He probably knows something about all that because he was in El Boussaid when Maurice Martin was killed. That was not so long ago."

"That would be great. It would end the mystery of Anna's early years."

Basira promised Mustapha would write if he knew or found out anything.

Tom, Francine, and Anna waited so they could wave goodbye when the ship eased away from the quay.

On the way back, Anna told her new parents, "It's too bad. They could have been happy here. People are nice. They didn't know us at first, but they're warming up to us. The teachers are really good. Aisha could have learned to speak French well. Maybe I didn't help Aisha enough."

"It's not your fault, Anna. France is a foreign country to them. They were intimidated, had limited ability to speak French, and they did not know our culture. To be back home will be more comfortable for them. I hope they find what they're looking for in El Boussaid."

Anna shivered. "I'm so grateful to you to have become my mom and dad. I'd have died there, if I had had to go with them."

"We love you, Anna," Tom said.

ᘓ

After a smooth passage this time, the ship docked in the port of Oran. It took a while for Basira and Aisha to disembark. When they went down the gangplank, they were spotted easily by the younger of Basira's two sons, who ran to greet his mother. Both had not seen each other since that fateful day when Ahmed was shot. That had happened about four months before, but much had changed since then. They hugged, and the boy grabbed his mom's luggage and carried it to Mustapha's car.

"Welcome, Basira. I'm glad you decided to come back." Mustapha greeted her with a warm smile. "When you left, things were disorganized and dangerous. Everything has calmed down. Your other son is the corporal in charge of policing the village. You'll see him tonight. "

"Thank you, Mustapha, for having me in your family."

"I have the best room for you and Aisha in the house you know well."

They did not talk much on the way to El Boussaid. The trip took close to six hours. It was July, and Aisha and Basira were reminded how hot the month of July can be in Algeria.

Basira closed her eyes, trying to imagine what her life would be like. But she had made her choice and she thought it was the right one for Aisha and for herself too.

ᘓ

One late afternoon, Mustapha and Basira were alone and talking. Basira asked him what he knew about Maurice Martin.

"I remember when, very young, maybe nineteen or twenty years old, he came to El Boussaid in 1954. He had signed up to be the schoolteacher because the current one at the time was getting too old. Maurice looked European, but dressed and spoke like a native Algerian. Be-

ing a teacher, he knew how to speak French and sounded very fluent
in that language. He came with his pretty young wife who also spoke
some French. She gave birth to Hana shortly afterward."

"Why was he killed?"

"I can't say for sure, but the men of the village did not like him."

"Why not?" asked Basira.

"Maurice did not look like an Algerian, for one thing, but the villagers got angry when Maurice tried to get girls as well as the boys from
the village, to come to school. For the villagers, education did not apply
to women. Also, Maurice and his wife spoke French to Hana, and the
villagers suspected he started to teach her how to read although she
was very young."

"That's why they killed him?" Basira said to herself. Then she asked
Mustapha, "Do you think you could find out about Maurice's father? I
have the deed of the property he bought when he came in 1938."

"I'll try. I would be curious to know something about him."

A week or so later, Mustapha told Basira, "I have found out a couple
of things about Maurice's father. His name was Frederic and he came
from France to Tiaret to be a teacher. His son Maurice was two or three
years old. Frederic found a wife and bought that little house which was
the one on the deed you gave me. They were apparently well liked.
Both spoke French, and Frederic and his son became fluent in Arabic."

"So Maurice could speak both Arabic and French?"

"Apparently so. But in the mid-1950s, Frederic contracted typhoid
and died. His wife followed a few months later. That is probably when
Maurice married and found a teaching position in El Boussaid."

"They killed him because he tried to teach girls?" Basira asked.

"Yes. A teacher came to replace him. He was Algerian and with his
brother moved into Maurice's house with Hana and her mother. The
rumor had it that strange things went on. Hana's mother died. Some
thought she was poisoned. Nobody knows for sure. I must add that
nobody cared. I did not get involved. I learned that Hana disappeared
for a few days, maybe one or two weeks. Some villagers thought she

had been killed like her mother. Nobody knew where she was until she reappeared and went to stand by Lieutenant Lucas' jeep."

"I'm sure Francine and Tom would like to know that story. Would you write it down and mail it to them?"

"Sure. I can do that."

Chapter 31

Beaumes de Venise

July 23

When Mustapha's letter found its way to Tom and Francine, many of the questions they had about Anna's early years were answered.

Francine told Tom, "It now makes sense that Hana, as she was called at the time, was so eager to learn how to read. Her dad had been dead for several months when she first came with Aisha for the French lesson. She did not remember him and did not recall him reading or speaking French to her. But in some place, hidden in her mind, these two special exposures to a foreign language and to books had left a mark. She had had a taste of French and a taste of reading."

Tom agreed, and added, "You also said she learned French so much faster than Aisha. She had heard it, and maybe the first words she learned to speak were French."

Francine nodded. "She comes from a tradition of teachers. Learning has to be in her blood. We must tell her what Mustapha wrote. I want her to be proud of her parents."

"You're right," Tom said. "They struggled, they fought back. But in the end they lost their battles against bigotry and hatred. When she was very young, Anna had to confront hostility too. She had to fend off aggression, and she was abandoned."

Francine added, "Yes. But Anna put up a good fight and won. She survived."

❧

Later that afternoon, they found Anna, reading in a chair out in the garden. Sitting next to her was Wolf.

"Anna, we heard from Mustapha. He dug up a few pieces of information about how your French father found his way to El Bous-said."

They told her the story they had just read.

"So my dad was a teacher?"

"Yes, sweetheart, he was, and so was your grandfather, a teacher in Tiaret."

"Was my mother French too?"

"Probably not, but your dad probably started to teach her how to read and how to speak French. Your grandmother was French. She had blue eyes like you do."

Anna thought for a moment. "So I can be proud of them. They were educated, at least dad, granddad, and my grandmother."

"Yes, they were, and your mom must have been smart too."

Anna looked up with a big smile. "Now, I won't let anybody put me down because I come from Algeria. I come from here. I did not get to go to school in the village, but you taught me," She smiled at Francine. "So I'm just as good as the kids in the school I will attend. And you know what, Mother?" She chuckled, and got up to hold Francine's hand. "I like to call you Mother."

"I like that too. What am I supposed to know?"

"What, is that I will be the best in my class. You'll see." She put her other hand on Wolf's head. "Hear that, Wolf?"

He wagged his tail and rubbed his nose against her leg. Then she jumped up and embraced Francine and then Tom.

The next day, Anna and Brigitte had a session with Mademoiselle Roger. The two young girls had gotten to be good friends. They both loved the creatures of nature and enjoyed their teacher's readings about the animals, wild and domestic. That particular morning, Anna told both Mademoiselle Roger and Brigitte what she had found out about her father and grandfather being teachers.

"Fantastic!" Mademoiselle Roger said, "That's why you are such a good student."

"What happened to him, Anna?" Brigitte asked.

Anna looked down and said, "They killed him because he wanted to teach girls and the villagers did not approve."

"That's crazy," Brigitte asserted.

"Also my new mom and dad told me that the villagers felt it was okay to do it because of the war. I think that's why my mom died too."

"You mean you lost both your parents? I feel sorry for you," Brigitte said.

"But I'm okay now. I have a new family, a new mother and father, and they love me. I have also a new friend: you. And, I'll go to school."

"You'll do great, Anna," Brigitte said, and Mademoiselle Roger agreed and added, "You'll make your teacher dad proud."

"Yes I will. I told my mom Francine I'd be the best in the class."

"I'll help you," Brigitte said.

The lesson started. Today was about domestic animals.

Mademoiselle Roger talked about cows, sheep and goats. "Sheep give people the wool that keeps us warm in the winter, and milk to make cheese. They're very useful and also gentle. Goats only give us milk, and tend to be less pleasant."

Anna's face reddened. She was flustered and said, "Why do you say that, Mademoiselle Roger? That is not true."

The vehemence with which Anna spoke surprised Mademoiselle Roger.

"I upset you, I see. Can you tell me why?"

Anna squirmed on her chair, looked down and blushed. Brigitte put her arm around Anna's shoulders. Anna started to cry. Neither Mademoiselle Roger nor Brigitte had any idea of what was on Anna's mind.

After a while, Anna stopped crying and looked at both of them.

"Can I tell you a secret?" she asked them.

"Yes, and we will never tell," Brigitte replied. Mademoiselle Roger nodded vigorously.

Anna almost whispered. "It is embarrassing, but after my mother died, I ran away from the bad men and I hid in the goats' shed for days. The only person who knew where I was hiding was a girl who saw me hide and brought me some food. She also milked some of the goats to complement the food she sneaked in for me."

"How long did you stay in the barn?" Mademoiselle Roger asked.

"I don't know. Maybe days, one week, two weeks? It seemed like a long time."

Anna went on. "One of the goats was my main supplier of milk and at night, I slept with my head on her to keep warm."

She paused and sighed.

"I loved them, and I think they knew I was in trouble. They gave me whatever help they could. I'll never forget that. They were nicer to me than the villagers."

"How did you get out?" Brigitte asked.

Anna explained the rescue by Lieutenant Lucas.

Mademoiselle Roger said, "We promised we'll never tell, but there's nothing wrong with what you did. You showed incredible resilience and will to live. I have so much admiration for you. I love you."

Brigitte had tears in her eyes. "Me too. I will be your friend forever."

Mademoiselle Roger took Anna's hands in hers. "It must have been very hard for you to tell us the story you have not told anyone. I also know that your friend Aisha who went back to Algeria was mocked by a couple of second-grade girls. I promise you that you won't have to go through anything like that."

"Would you like to see the goats we have here? I can show you they love me."

"Sure. Let's," Brigitte said.

The three of them went to the paddock and Anna talked to the goats in Arabic when she opened the gate. The animals ran to rub against her.

"That's amazing," Mademoiselle Roger said. "You're right. And I want to add, you have nothing to be ashamed of."

"I hope so," Anna said, not too convincingly.

"Listen, Anna, Brigitte and I will never betray your secret. You will be a new girl in third grade. Your story is simple. You came with your parents to Beaumes de Venise. Your dad and mom are running the winery, you love school, and you're good at it."

"What if someone knows about Algeria?"

"Say simply that you were orphaned in a tragedy of the French-Algerian war. Your French father, who was a teacher like his dad, was killed and your current parents adopted you. You don't remember anything else."

"You must be proud of the father you did not know or at least you do not remember," Brigitte said.

"Okay, girls, back to the animals," Mademoiselle Roger said. "I promise I won't say bad things about goats or any animal for that matter, without talking to Anna first."

Anna smiled, and Brigitte laughed.

Chapter 32

Paris

July 2

In the meantime, while Basira and Aisha were getting settled back in Algeria, upon his return from England, Lucas received a call from Madame Fournier, the woman at the alumni association.

"Could you come around eleven? I have set up some appointments for you."

"Yes ma'am. I'll be there. Thank you."

Lucas showed up at the alumni office promptly on time, wearing a dark-blue suit, a white shirt, and a rep tie.

"I see you're ready for interviews. Here is what I have been able to set up for you: I spoke to Madame de Graffe, the head of the personnel department at Computers, Inc. She agreed to meet with you tomorrow at nine, at the company headquarters, Place Vendome. If there is interest on both parts, she'll set up additional meetings."

"Thank you so much. That is perfect."

"That's not all. I also set you up to meet with the director of the department charged with establishing the relationship between the French telephone company and its American counterpart. This meeting is today at two in the afternoon, if that works for you."

"That's great. I will report to you the outcome of both meetings."

"I'd appreciate that. Just be yourself in these interviews. You have a lot to offer. They need talented candidates like you. Good luck."

Monsieur Nicolas welcomed Lucas at the telephone company head office in the 7th Arrondissement. He gave him a brief rundown on the company's business, size and goals.

"We are creating a team with employees from our company and from our American potential partner to study the feasibility of constructing a common worldwide strategy for product development, manufacturing, and marketing. I am staffing our side of it. That is where you come in. You would learn about our products and plans, and we would launch a six-month study when both sides are ready."

"Would the study be run here or in America?" I asked.

"Both places. If you are interested in being considered, you need to meet with my American counterpart. He will be here at the end of the week. I assume you are fluent in English."

"I am and I'd love to meet this person. But I have a question. What happens to the members of the study team once the strategy has been formulated and committed to?"

"They will be assigned jobs within their companies. I can't be more precise at this time."

"Would the assignments be in France or in the United States, and would I be able to choose where I am assigned?"

"Again, it's difficult to answer the question in abstract, but we certainly would do our best to assign people where they would be more comfortable."

Monsieur Nicolas said he would set up the appointment with the American and let Lucas know when it could be scheduled.

☙

That night, Josette attended a lecture, so Lucas relaxed at home and reflected on the afternoon interview. He did not feel any enthusiasm for the job outlined by Monsieur Nicolas. How could anyone contribute to the formulation of a worldwide strategy for a business he or she was new at? Lucas thought it might be useful to him to interview with the American fellow to observe how an American businessman worked, but he was not even sure he wanted to do that. He was not going to take that job no matter what.

The following morning, Lucas entered the Computers, Inc. headquarters on Place Vendome. The entrance lobby had spectacular high windows, green plants and modern furniture. The vice president, head of the human resources, Madame de Graffe, greeted Lucas and ushered him into her office.

"Welcome," she said. "My boss, Monsieur Duhamel, the president of the French division of Computers Inc., and I were pleased that you agreed to talk to us. Your academic records are great, but we were impressed from what we have been told of your military service."

"I am a hard worker. I did run my platoon for all that time and we became efficient, although not without casualties, and accomplished all our missions."

"That's good to hear. You expressed interest in a position in Paris. It would be in technical support for our customers. You might also want to consider our development laboratory located in Nice. It works on both software and hardware."

"I don't know anything about what I would be doing in either of these possibilities."

Madame de Graffe gave him a quick run-down on the French division and on the two openings and then added, "I can fly you to Nice for an interview. The product laboratory is active, and runs several projects."

"I just got married, and my wife is a physician doing important research on trauma. She'll be in Paris for the next two to three years. I believe Nice is out."

"I understand. The head of customer support is Madame Simon. Her office is in this building. Let me see if she can see you."

She called Madame Simon's office and stressed to her secretary that it was important that she see Lucas. The secretary said she expected her back momentarily and that Madame Simon could see Lucas as soon as she was back.

"Do you have any more questions for me?" Madame de Graffe asked.

"Are there many assignments in the United States, and are they mandatory?"

"People go for assignments overseas from the customer support department or from the labs. It is a learning experience and a growth opportunity for our employees."

৵

Madame Simon came back to her office, so Lucas went to see her. They talked for an hour. She explained how he would start in her department by going to several schools to learn the products and the company protocol. He would then be assigned to a project team to learn to use what he would have learned in his classes. After six months or so he'd be part of a regular support group. He told her that he thought he would be interested in talking to managers and employees in her product support division.

What an action-packed morning. Lucas felt the incredible energy that seemed to hang in the air around all the employees, and thought he could belong there.

⁂

That evening, he related Madame de Graffe's suggestions to Josette. They decided that Lucas did not have any interest in going to work in Nice, but that a visit to the lab might not be a bad idea. They recalled Mercantour Park, which was close to the lab. In the future, depending on where both their careers would lead, settling in that area might be a good solution. It did not cost anything to go find out about the place.

"So if you agree, as Thierry's father recommended, my next step is to go through a series of interviews in the product-support area. I'll get a good understanding of the work atmosphere," Lucas said.

"I agree," was Josette's response. "But, I don't hear a great deal of enthusiasm in your voice."

"You're right. I'm still confused. I want to do the right thing but I don't know what the right thing is. I guess I'm just testing the waters, but I liked the people I talked to."

Chapter 33

Paris

July 3

Josette had a few weeks before the facilities in the three research venues were to be ready, but she had to start on the staffing and study protocols.

She decided that although the Maligny location was already dedicated to rehabilitation of wounded military personnel, it needed new talent with background in combat trauma, or at least in traumatized victims. She would have to get a volunteer from Necker Hospital. She asked her father if he thought there would be a need to change the leadership because of the new specialty. The colonel said he recommended that Captain Dufour, who was about to retire, be the person to oversee the Val de Grace's new department, and added that the captain could also oversee the Maligny new department at least at the outset.

In Necker Hospital, Doctor Stanislas had asked for volunteers among the staff already working on children trauma to bring their knowledge and expertise to the two military recovery centers. A similar call for volunteers had gone out in the military hospital, but Josette believed that the staff there had little or no experience with psychological trauma. She had to meet with the person in charge of the Val De Grace to know the exact situation.

The doctor in charge of the Paris military hospital, Colonel Weimer, welcomed Josette in his office. He had been briefed by both Doctor Stanislas and by the senior military doctor he had sent to hear her presentation on the second day of her certification.

"I'm familiar with the talk you gave on your certification day and I read the excellent exposé you wrote to support your call for the grant.

Both were impressive. I believe that the time for focusing on the aftermath of trauma is overdue, and I want to help you succeed."

"I appreciate your confidence in my work," Josette replied. "What I need are doctors to learn the intricacies of what we know about children's trauma and are willing to do research to apply it to combat veterans. I have a retired captain, a seasoned veteran who understands the stress that soldiers go through in combat, who will help coordinate the effort at your hospital and in Maligny. The purpose of these studies is to catalogue the conditions the soldiers are dealing with, as well as diagnosing the extent of their struggles."

"I have a few interns who have some understanding of psychological matters," Colonel Weimer said. "They need guidance and training if there is any available."

"I have asked for volunteers at the hospital where I have been doing my studies on children's trauma," Josette replied, "They will be useful in guiding the process for the soldiers. They will also be the researchers who will work on identifying the key differences between the effect of catastrophic events on children and on adults. I will personally be leading and driving the study. The formulation of mitigation or treatment of the conditions will take place in a second phase."

"How many people are we talking about initially?"

"I will bring five or six of my people initially. I need the same number from you because I will pair them in teams of two."

"How would you like to proceed?" the colonel asked.

"I'll interview all volunteers in Necker Hospital personally. I understand you also put out a call for volunteers here. I will interview them also. Then, Doctor Stanislas, you and I will make the final call as to who are the ones we want to participate in the research."

"I like your plan. Your facilities are being prepared. You should review what we have for you around the beginning of August. We'll make the adjustments you need and you should be able to start work later that month."

"That is perfect, Doctor Weimer. I thank you for your support and I'm looking forward to working with you."

༜

A meeting with General de Vangarde was next on Josette's agenda. The general immediately asked Josette, "How can I help you?"

"You have created a working rehabilitation facility. We need to add a psychological diagnostic element to the facility. That new unit will have to be supplemented by a treatment team. My father recommended I use Captain Dufour as the head of the new trauma department in the Val de Grace hospital. He also said he could help coordinate the new focus at the Maligny facility. Do you agree with that?"

"I do indeed. I met Captain Dufour at your wedding, a fine soldier and an experienced infantry officer now retiring. I support your father's idea. I like using a combat veteran officer to run the new department. Once you get into combat trauma issues, I'd much prefer to have an experienced soldier guide the analysis of the patients' trauma background. The civilian who now runs the Maligny Center will probably retire in a year or two. When he's ready to do so, we will evaluate if the captain should replace him."

"Interesting idea. I will also go to Maligny and talk to the staff folks who have expressed interest in joining the new project. I know it'll be hard to find candidates in Paris who want to go into semi-isolation, but I'll find a few candidates. I don't need too many at the outset." Josette said to end the meeting.

"Nice to meet you again Josette. I will be in touch," The general said.

Josette interviewed Captain Dufour, who was delighted with the offer to work in the Val de Grace and also oversee Maligny. They agreed on a date for him to start on the job.

༜

On Saturday, Josette and Lucas attended Nicole's and Gilbert's wedding. It was a lot more elaborate than theirs, with many more people. At the end they said their good-byes to the newlyweds who were on their way to Lille.

Chapter 34

Paris

July 4

A few days later, Lucas received a call from Madame de Graff, the head of personnel at Computers, Inc. She asked him if he could come meet with her after lunch to talk about his plan. He agreed, and was in her office early afternoon.

"How was your trip to England?"

"It was very nice. Thank you. I have lots of memories there. It's always nice to be back in South Devon."

"I was wondering," Madame de Graffe said, "if you have thought about the interviews you had the last time you were here."

"I have indeed. I must say I was impressed by the tempo of the company. People ready to work, ready to help. It reminded me a bit of my company in Algeria. My platoon was always ready, ready to fight, ready to protect, ready to help."

"That is nice to hear. What would you like to do next?"

"Madame Simon, the head of Customer Support, suggested I talk to some of her department heads and managers. I would like to do that. Also, I would not mind visiting the laboratory near Nice. Although I think I might not want to move there now, I would still like to get the feeling of how a product development area works as opposed to a customer-oriented one."

"Let me arrange that. My secretary will schedule your visit to la Gaude, and I will talk to Madame Simon."

Late that afternoon, Madame de Graffe's secretary called and told Lucas she had scheduled a meeting with Madame Simon for nine the next morning, and a visit to Nice for the day after. He would leave early that day and return to Paris late afternoon. She told him he could pick up his ticket on his way to meeting Madame Simon, if that was convenient.

"This company does not procrastinate," Lucas told Josette at dinner that night.

"That's good, but what's your plan?"

"I'll go through the interviews tomorrow. I may go to Nice the day after, although I'm not sure yet."

"You're still wondering what you want to do, I see."

"I am, but I'll get there. I need more input from the company. I may need to talk to other outsiders too. And of course, I look to you for telling me what you think."

"That's great, but I'm not in your head. You have to be the one who is comfortable with whichever way you want to go."

"I guess I have to figure out who I want to be more than what I want to do."

The next day Lucas met with directors, managers, and workers of Madame Simon's division. He liked a lot of the men and women he met. He was impressed to see a company with young people in key positions. No one had been in that business for long. No such industry existed five years ago.

Lucas decided to go ahead with his trip south. There again he met young, enthusiastic engineers. All seemed sharp, knowledgeable about their work, and optimistic toward their future.

That night, after his visit to the lab, Josette asked him if he had made any progress.

"Yes I have. Remember when we went to talk to Thierry and Nicole's father a few weeks ago, and he encouraged me to come and talk to him once I had been through several interviews. I have had the meetings and I think I should take him up on his offer. What do you think?"

"I agree. Why don't you call him up?"

Lucas did and made a date for the next evening. Josette and Lucas were again invited for dinner.

❧

That evening, Lucas related to Thierry's father the process he had been through in the past couple of days.

"I see that you followed my advice and talked to many people in the company," he replied. "Now how do you want to proceed?"

"I'll be frank with you, Monsieur Dupont, I am still confused. I liked the people I met. I liked the energy and the enthusiasm I sensed in the company. But, for some reason I don't quite understand, I can't say I'm dying to start a career in a large corporation."

"Can you tell me why the reluctance?"

"It seems that it would be selfish on my part. I probably would be able to adjust, I might get ahead, but I'm asking myself how is that making the world a better place? How is that helping people? I fought hard in North Africa, and my soldiers did too. Some were hurt and some lost their lives. We did our job; we protected farmers and ranchers. It seems that nobody remembers the war, the human suffering on both sides of the conflict, the sacrifices of the soldiers, and the destruction of a beautiful country. Here in France, nobody seems to care. Well, I do!"

✧

Monsieur Dupont frowned. "I can see that."

"To some extent we were all traumatized by what we saw and what we did. I have not yet recovered from it. I still feel for all who were hurt, innocent children, unarmed men and women, armed combatants on both sides. I took care of my troops: most importantly, I helped many children, rescued and saved some, gave others some hope. I miss doing that."

Thierry's dad shook his head. "I see that the war still has a grip on your mind. I ache for you, but I cannot help you out of that. Your altruistic thoughts are world worthy, but…"

Lucas interrupted him. "My altruistic thoughts, as you called them, are not only my own. I came home to find Josette, who had redirected her career to help traumatized children. I feel I'd rather help her than anything else."

"But life has to be lived practically," Thierry's father replied. "You and Josette will have children and you will want to provide for them. How can you do that and not work in the corporate world? You worked hard to get an engineering degree. Why waste it?"

"The way I look at my degree is more as having acquired the wisdom to learn what tools I need to have to accomplish whatever my task is, tools to broaden my knowledge and my mind, tools to solve complicated problems. I worked just as hard, if not harder, at running an infantry platoon in a war than at earning a degree. I learned much more doing that than reading science and engineering manuals. That's my dilemma. I don't know who I am."

"Fair enough. But look. I can guide you to sort through the potential avenues you have in front of you in that computer corporation or another one. I'd say, go work for that Madame Simon. You will do well there. But I can't give you advice on how to define an occupation which will make you help people, and also earn a good living. I'm sorry."

"I thank you so much for your listening to my rambling. If I join this company, I will follow your advice and go work for the Customer Support division. If not, I may come to you to interview for one of your open positions. If I choose neither of these alternatives, I will be on my own. I will let you know which way I decide to go."

Thierry's dad nodded. "One last thing, Lucas. Your motives are admirable, but they are biased by the fact your mind is still traumatized. My last advice to you is: do not make hasty decisions, get healed first."

On the way home, Josette said, "I believe he is right. I see you're still hurting. I'm not sure how to help. I loved your words that you'd rather help me than doing anything else, but I'm not sure how to help you."

"Just standing by me is helping. I think I want to talk to Madame de Sèvres. She always gave me good advice."

"It's a good idea. Can I come with you?"

"Sure, Josette. This is our life. We need to both agree on the best route for you and for me. I'll call her."

❧

"My two favorite people in the world," The countess greeted them with these words. She nodded to General de Vangarde who sat in a chair next to her. "You remember the general, don't you?"

"Sure thing," Josette replied, nodding to the general.

"And you don't mind him listening to our conversation, do you?"

"Not at all, Madame. Let me tell you why we are here."

Josette told her she had started interviewing the candidates who wanted to participate in the research that had been funded by the grants, including the one from the countess. Lucas explained his job search and the interviews he had been through as well as the conversation with Thierry's father.

"I'm here because I love you and I trust your judgment. I need advice. I don't know what my next step ought to be."

Madame de Sèvres thought for a minute. "Let me ask you this: What makes you uncomfortable about a job in a corporation or in the computer industry?"

"It has little to do with the computer industry. I have been agonizing trying to answer the same question. Here's what I came up with: during the German occupation, even very young, I always made it my goal to support and do what I could for my classmates and the people I thought needed help. In the army, I rescued many children. I grieved for those who did not make it. I protected French and Algerian farmers and ranchers. I know my platoon killed insurgents. I feel guilty about that, believe it or not, but we were proud of the fact that we also took many prisoners. They're still alive. In other words, I think that in my young life, I did some good and helped people in need."

"And since you got back to France?" the countess asked.

"I found out that you were also involved in helping recovering soldiers. Josette had dedicated herself to treating traumatized children. Most of our wedding reception guests were involved or aware of the need for defining and delivering medical solutions to trauma for returning soldiers and for children. For me, to commit myself to a career that would essentially benefit only my family is not enough. It does not feel right to me."

Madame de Sèvres smiled. "I think I understand where your head is at. Let me also add that I have funded a small effort to help battered women. This endeavor is in its infancy, but I have been working to make it real and reach women hurt by men or by accidents of life."

Josette had been following this conversation and the one with Thierry's father with intensity, discovering a side of Lucas she had not known before and learning more about the effects of the trauma he suffered in Algeria. But she reacted to the countess' last statement.

"May I ask you, Madame, if the effort you are leading in sheltering women from predators is also identifying and treating the trauma they had been through?"

"I have no one working on the team who is qualified to address trauma."

Lucas became excited. "Today, there are facilities and teams of specialists researching and administering initial diagnoses and treatments for children. Josette has received grants to expand that work to traumatized combat veterans. You, Madame, have started to address the question of women traumatized in their relationships, or simply in their lives. Would it make sense to expand Josette's work and research to identifying the different types of trauma and their effects upon military personnel and children to include battered women too? And would it make sense to analyze the types of trauma and define the appropriate treatments regardless of whether the victims or the patients are soldiers, women, or children? Furthermore would it not make sense to have facilities that provide treatments for all traumas, and all affected people? The traumas can be caused by wars, of course, but by accidents, natural disasters, or raw violence. I think I have learned in the past couple of months that all traumas have many similarities and common consequences."

"How would you do that?" Josette asked.

"One would need a sort of trauma-focused organization." Lucas answered. "It'd be run by doctors, psychologists, nurses, and rehabilitation specialists. They would do diagnostics, prescribe treatments, and administer them. They would have a research department, a teaching department to train specialists. It'd be complemented by a team of people charged with delivering the treatments that would respond to the conditions of the patients in a dedicated facility. It would have international reach. That is, if someone would fund the venture."

Madame de Sèvres was enthusiastic. "I think this is a superb idea, Lucas. What do you think, General?"

The general sat up in his chair and cleared his throat. "If I look back at my life, I would be overwhelmed if I were asked to cite the instances of trauma I have witnessed. When I look around me at today's world, I feel surrounded by examples of psychological injuries. So, contemplating any attempt at designing a basic structure for an entity as the one you mentioned, Lucas, is too broad. You would need to limit the scope of its intent. There are millions of traumatized soldiers, children, women, and victims in the two-hundred or so countries around the world today, and no one is going to treat all these victims. "

Lucas wiggled uncomfortably in his chair. "When you put it clearly that way, I feel like Don Quixote. You are absolutely right, sir. It was only an idea."

"I didn't mean to put anybody down, but the first and basic question about any military operation is: What is the mission? Then, what are our resources? What is an achievable goal? What is the strategy most likely to achieve that goal? How do we recruit and train the actors who will be asked to execute the strategy? This is like a military operation. The enemy is trauma."

The countess crossed her fingers under her chin, looked at her lap and said, "Let me think, General."

After a few minutes, Lucas and Josette saw her lift her head and look at them.

"First, I must say that the general is absolutely right. But I think also that an enterprise of limited scope which builds upon the trauma research that Josette and her team are working on has merit. This enterprise would continue to do research, and as you said, Lucas, run a facility, or facilities that offer diagnostics and treatments to victims of traumatic events that affected children, combat veterans, and battered women. It would train diagnosticians and therapists, interact with other countries' research departments, interface with government agencies that cater to people hurt psychologically. The scope would have to be limited and controlled. Lucas, let me ask you a question. Would you want to run such a business?"

"I'd have to think about that. I don't have the experience to run such a far-reaching business, but I would like to be part of it, possibly running the enterprise interactions with government health-related entities, and international medical departments. Actually, I'd have to learn that aspect of the business, but I think I could do it. I would leave the management of the medical side of it to Josette and her crew."

The countess replied, "I could speak with Mr. Laforge about you. He is the man who replaced your uncle. I'm sure he knows you, because your uncle must have mentioned you to him."

"I may have met him once, I think. A tall, slim man with a receding hairline?"

"That's him for sure. I'd say the hairline has receded almost beyond visibility," the countess joked. "I'll ask him if he can hire you for a few months to give you some training in executive management."

"That'd be perfect."

"I need a few days to get my treatment set by Josette so I know its constraints on my time, then I'll be ready to meet him," Lucas said.

"That's a great idea, Madame," General de Vangarde said. "In the military, Lieutenant Lucas led by example. He needs to learn that in industry, executives do not have the time or the expertise to lead by example; neither can they just give orders. Therefore they have to define the goals precisely, let the experts find the best and most efficient way to achieve them. The executive asks questions of the experts, identifies the issues, and assesses the proposed solutions. Your main asset, Lucas, is that, as a good leader, you know how to listen."

The countess turned to Lucas. "I'll call Mr. Laforge, and let you know what he says."

"I don't know how to thank you, Madame, and General," Lucas said.

"On the contrary, I don't know how to thank you for sharing such a brilliant idea with me. And I find it admirable for you to think of potentially being willing to give your life to trauma victims of all kinds."

The general nodded and smiled. "Now, if I may, I'd like to make a suggestion. I would add a training effort to spread the results of the research to doctors and therapists, here and abroad." The general continued, "I would also suggest that you, Madame la Comtesse, be the one to oversee the whole enterprise. I would commit to help you do that."

Both Josette and Lucas nodded vigorously. "That is a fantastic suggestion, General."

The countess said. "It would be very rewarding to help this effort come to life."

"Let us all think about the idea and reconvene later to discuss it further," the general replied. "I need to think about developing a way to define the scope of what can be done by that enterprise."

⁂

On the way home, Josette told Lucas, "A few weeks ago, when you met my father, I discovered you were a hero and we decided to be married. Today I found out that, although still hurting from the war, your considerate, big-hearted, unselfish, and generous self is thinking of helping people who have also been hurt through no fault of their own. I admire you, I respect you and I love you so much. Maybe we will get to run such an enterprise."

"Possibly, but I have no experience in leading an international complex venture."

"But three years ago, you did not know much about running a platoon in a war of insurgency," Josette replied, "And you did not do too badly."

"That's right, but they were only forty-five guys; all spoke the same language and had a common goal." Lucas chuckled.

⟨✦⟩

The next day, Lucas went to call on Madame de Graffe. He explained to her what was on his mind. "If I may ask for your indulgence, I need probably a few weeks to assess whether my idea is workable. If I find it unfeasible, I would love to come back to you and apply for a job with Madame Simon."

"I understand your goal of helping victims of catastrophes, mainly of war. You are actually one yourself, and that is probably why you're still confused. Go find out if your enterprise idea can be done, and if you want to be part of it. If not, please come back. I'll be here, so will the business, and we would love to have you."

They both got up. She shook his hand. "Good luck to you. I hope you succeed. I have much respect for who you are."

Chapter 35

Paris

July 8

Retired Captain Dufour, now Alain Dufour, had accepted Josette's offer to run her Val de Grace hospital team and to supervise the soldiers being treated in Maligny in the experimental trauma ward. He started in his new civilian assignment by helping Josette interview the doctors and therapists interested in joining the trauma team.

There were ten doctors interested in learning how to diagnose the parameters of the psychological disorder that some soldiers suffered from in addition to their physical wounds. Josette and the ten candidates met with the soldiers in the Veterans Hospital. They were assisted by Alain Dufour, who could visualize and explain to the doctors the combat conditions that led to their trauma. After all the interviews, Josette asked the doctors the same question: "What would make you say that a patient might have mental trouble?" Most cited display of anger and depression.

Josette then went to talk to nine patients who were singled out for being depressed by several of the doctors. She agreed with the doctors' assessment, but also found out that one of the manifestations of the depression was the same for all of them. They told her that as soldiers, they had risked their lives to assist civilians being harassed, to help buddies in trouble during military operations, or to rescue children in state of despair. Now close to being back to civilian lives, being treated in a military hospital, but not in active duty, they did not have anyone to help, to save, or to fight for. They thought their lives had become useless and selfish.

Josette's ears perked up. She had heard the very same words before, coming out of Lucas' mouth. She called Private Vidal, whom she had met at the wedding, and said, "I'm sorry to bother you. I am putting together a program to address the anger and depression some soldiers brought back to France upon being discharged or in recovery from physical wounds. I have a couple of questions I would like to ask you if I may."

"Absolutely. Anything I can do to help."

"Were you depressed when you got back to France?"

"I must say that at first the physical pain took all my energy. I struggled with the surgeries, the reconstruction of the blood flow in my neck, and the reeducating of the muscles that had been affected by the bullet. But as soon as I got better, the depression started."

Josette jotted down a couple of sentences on her pad. "What were your dominant thoughts?"

"Mainly that I was having trouble picturing myself back in civilian life. Every civilian job seemed selfish to me and that caused me to be depressed."

"Did it last a long time? Are you still feeling that way?"

"It started to get better after my discharge from the hospital when I left my comrades who were also depressed. Today my remaining depression is mild, but my residual anger is still pretty strong."

"Thank you for your answers. I plan to have my department operational in a month or so. I will call you then and we can talk about what I can offer you. I may be able to help with your anger."

"Thank you, ma'am."

༺

Upon getting home that evening, Josette told Lucas, "We have to have a serious talk."

"Wow! Should I be scared?"

"This is not a joke, Luke."

"I'm sorry." Lucas smiled and kissed her."What is it about?"

"It's about your job, your career, that new enterprise you suggested to the countess."

"What about it?"

"Lucas, I know more about the effects of trauma on children than most doctors in the world, and I'm learning every day about your type of trauma. There are similarities between the manifestations of the traumatic experiences in children and soldiers. Depression is one of them. I have discovered today that depression in soldiers decreases over time, but the lessening of the condition happens much faster in any environment which is foreign to the one in which the trauma developed."

"How does that apply to my job?"

"I think you would agree that you are still affected by the time you spent in Algeria. We experienced the benefit of hiking the mountains of Mercantour Park and sailing Mr. Rooth's boat in the English Channel, both of which proved to mitigate your post-war condition to a certain but temporary extent, but it could not be enough to heal you. If you were to embark today in that admirable venture to create that all-encompassing trauma facility, you would be dealing with people coming from circumstances akin to the context in which you were traumatized. My professional opinion is that it would prolong your symptoms. I would like you to think about that, and share your reaction with me."

"I do have the utmost respect for your professional opinion. I remember Nicole's and Thierry's reactions when they first saw me after I got off the train back from Algeria. They saw that my mind was still in North Africa. Also, when I talked to Madame De Graffe about potential jobs, she observed that I was not out of the woods yet, to use her words. She told me to take my time to decide what I wanted to do. The dean of my school told me I needed professional help to heal. Similar words were Thierry's father's last advice. I must admit I have been thinking along the same lines. I love you; I saw the leaders of your profession applaud your presentation during your certification day. I trust your judgment. What do you recommend I do?"

"I need to do some work on that. The countess will hopefully talk to that Mr. Laforge. A period of time in a corporate environment to learn management would get you away from trauma victims for a while. That would help. I still believe your idea is great, but it's too early to get you thrown into it. It's time to act. We need to be proactive. You're right; Monsieur DuPont said that you need to heal. I'm sure you can be treated and move forward. I will talk with some of my crew at Necker Hospital, discuss the kind of treatment we think is best for you, and start the healing process. I'll decide who would be the best person to administer it to you. And it can't be me."

↭

Josette decided she needed to devise a comprehensive program to fully heal Lucas. She thought that Madame de Sèvres, who knew Lucas well, could help. The countess was surprised to hear Josette's voice when she picked up the phone.

"How nice to hear from you, but I guess this is not an idle call."

"You are right, Madame. This is about Lucas, and the work we talked about launching, the making of the trauma treatment enterprise."

"What about Lucas?"

Josette explained that in her professional judgment, Lucas still struggled with his memories of the war and that working on the trauma enterprise they had talked about instead of a corporate job would not improve his mental health. She added that continuous exposure to people or images that reminded him of his troubled past would not be good for him. "I'm also concerned about the long-term effect of not treating the stress he is fighting after his traumatic years. So it is time for a formal program to address his problem."

"I respect your judgment," the countess said. "What do you think we should do? How can I help?"

"I suggest Lucas and I come to see you, so we can come up with the best plan to get him back on his feet and ready for the next challenge. He is aware of his struggle, and he told me he wants me to help fix it. At the same time, I think his idea for the trauma enterprise is brilliant. Maybe the three of us can come up with a solution that is good for all."

"You're very wise, Josette. Let's do it. I'll have my secretary tell you when would be a good time for us to meet."

 ✑

A couple of days later, Josette and Lucas called on Madame de Sèvres who greeted them warmly.

"Welcome to you both. This is a working meeting. I'll defer to you, Josette, it is your show."

"Talking to some of the therapists and soldiers affected by trauma, I discovered that the longer the patient is confronted with images, people, or events that bring him back to the event of the trauma, the more difficult the recovery will be. My concern for Lucas is that if he dedicates his time to focus on this organization which will research trauma detection, diagnosis, and treatment, he will be dealing with issues that will do exactly that."

"That makes a lot of sense," the countess said. "What else have you found out?"

"I have not spent enough time to diagnose the type of trauma Lucas is fighting. It's my job to do that. I will ask one of my best diagnostic doctors to do the analysis as precisely as she or he can, and then we'll define the appropriate treatment. Finally, I'll have Lucas go through it."

"Do you have any idea how long the treatment will take?"

"No," Josette replied. "It could last several weeks or several months. I won't know until I have the diagnosis. But in the meantime, I think we should find a way to proceed with the definition of the enterprise we set out to build, because that is also most important, and will be a part of his healing."

Lucas had been quiet during that interchange, but he interrupted Josette. "I would also like to suggest that if I spend time preparing myself to build and to run the international and government interfaces, that would be a great help to my mental health. I hope to find an internship that would prepare me for it. I don't want to give up the idea of helping soldiers and children in their fight against the effect of the trauma."

The countess looked at Lucas. "I mentioned Mr. Laforge to you. I'm sorry I did not follow up on that. I'll make a point to talk to him this week."

"That would be great," Lucas replied.

Josette got up to leave. "I think we have a plan. We all have work to do."

Chapter 36

Beaumes de Venise

July 24

The day after the goat incident, Brigitte told Anna that her mom would hold an art afternoon on Friday.

"It's a lot of fun; I want you to come to it."

"Yes. I would love to, I'll ask my mother."

Later that evening when Anna asked Francine, she said, "I remember Brigitte's mother telling me about it. I forgot. Would you like to go?"

"Yes, please. It sounds like fun, and I would also meet other kids I'll go to school with."

"I'll drive you. Is the art class at the school?"

"Yes, it is. Thank you." She ran into Francine's arms. "It's nice to have a mother. And you are the best mom."

✦

Friday after lunch, Brigitte introduced Anna to five children her age: Sylvie, Chloé, Margot, Julien, and Olivier. All were pleased to meet her. Brigitte's mother gave each of her students drawing paper, a soft black pencil, an eraser and three color pencils: red, yellow, and blue. She talked briefly about the primary colors and how they could be mixed for making other hues.

"Now," she continued, "Natalie is going to have all of you draw a few complicated subjects to test your level of skills. Then I can give proper assignments you can enjoy and learn drawing without getting bored."

The young woman instructor took out of her bag a large picture of the head of a clown. "Now class, I want you to draw the clown's head, and try to apply some colors to it. Then we'll look at all of your drawings and learn from them. Remember, this is an art class, there is no failing. Be yourself."

Brigitte, Anna, and Olivier did pretty well. Anna had concentrated on the clown's orange hair, his yellow cheeks, and his red nose and mouth. The instructor pointed to Anna's drawing. "What I like about this, is the simplicity of the drawing. There are no details, and none are needed to make the clown look like who he is. The colors are fine." She showed what was good about each of the children's clown rendition.

"Now, let's try a more complicated subject. I'd like to know how far I can push you, and what to focus on to make you more comfortable with pencil and paper."

She took out the face of a horse.

"Take a stab at this," she said.

Both Brigitte and Anna did well. The horse's drawings they made were good.

"The two of you are talented," The instructor said. I particularly like the way Anna did the eyes of the animal."

Brigitte's mother said, "The two of them are taking a private course on animals. Maybe that's why."

Anna said, "I have also read a lot of books about animals. I looked at many pictures, and I like to copy them. I have done quite a few." She giggled a bit. "I love animals."

"Why is that?" Chloé asked her.

"Animals are nice. I have a dog, his name is Wolf. He follows me everywhere."

"What kind?" Julien was curious.

"He's a German shepherd."

The instructor was intrigued with Anna. She asked her, "Could you do a quick sketch of him from memory?"

Anna took her pencil, drew the two pointed ears, the long snout with the dark end, and drew the two eyes in approximately the right place. The instructor showed her where the eyes really belonged, but complimented her.

The other kids looked at her drawing and tried to copy it.

Chapter 37

Beaumes de Venise

July 28

On Friday morning, Eric Tallec, who was back from his interview in Geneva, shared with Josette how well his meeting with the heads of the teaching hospital had gone. He also told her about meeting her sister Caroline, and the orphan-twins he had gone to visit with her.

"Oh yes; the twins. My sister called me about them. What a tragedy."

"What is really puzzling is to try to figure out what if anything their less-than-a-year-old minds remember or had learned from their parents. They cannot talk, so their behavior is the only thing that can tell us if there is any indication of trauma from the tragic loss, or even simply any memory of it. I'm not sure how to tackle this problem."

"Let me call Francine, the friend of Lucas who adopted Anna, the girl he rescued from a village in Algeria," Josette said.

"I met them at your wedding. I remember the story. What about her?"

"She lost her father when she was very young and, from what Lucas told me, she has no memory of him. Her dad was French and Francine said she learned that language with ease and her pronunciation is faultless. It seems that her mind had been influenced by being with him for the first few years of her life although she may not have been conscious of it."

Josette called Francine who answered the phone. After the usual greeting, Josette asked, "How is Anna doing these days?"

"She is a darling. She is happy. She is studying with the teachers she will have in school next September, and doing very well. Also, we just found out in an art afternoon that she is a gifted artist, drawing animals with ease. I remember that, when I first taught her, she liked to copy the images in the books I gave her. There were many animals in those baby books."

Josette almost cut her off. "This is very interesting to me. Would you mind if I came and brought a child trauma expert with me? I would like to talk to Anna. We won't frighten her. We would just like to talk with her. Actually, if Lucas comes with us, she will be at ease."

"Great idea. Tom and I would be delighted to have you. Come this weekend if you can."

❧

Josette, Lucas, and Eric took the train to Avignon the next day on Saturday morning. Upon arriving at the station, they were greeted by Francine and Anna, who ran into Lucas' open arms. She also hugged Josette warmly.

Josette sat next to Anna for the short car ride to the winery.

"I understand you are enjoying learning about animals," Josette told her.

"Yes, I am, with my friend Brigitte. I'm also catching up on math and reading a lot."

"Wow! You're really busy, I see."

"Yes, and I love it. I also went to an art afternoon. That was fun."

"Did you draw?"

"Yes, a clown, and a horse's head. Then the teacher had me draw my dog Wolf's head from memory."

"How did you do?"

"The instructor said I had talent," she giggled. "I'm used to drawing animals because when I was in Algeria, I'd often draw the images from the book Francine gave me. It helped me pass the time."

"Josette said. "I'd love to see your drawings. Do you still have them?"

"Yes I do, the new ones and some of the old ones."

"I'd love to look at them too," Eric said.

So when they got to the house, Josette and Eric went to Anna's room to look at the drawings. Eric also talked with Anna about her love for animals.

"Did you always love animals?" He asked her.

Anna looked at him with a warm smile. "Yes. When I was little, I helped with taking care of the goats." She paused for a minute and said. "I felt safe with them. I felt they protected me."

"How is that?" Josette asked.

Anna shrugged, and with an enigmatic smile said, "When I ran away from the bad men, I spent a few days with the goats hiding in their barn. Then Lieutenant Lucas rescued me."

"How did the goats help you?"

"They kept me warm when I slept with them at night. Also, I think they knew I was hiding because they made a fuss any time they knew the women were coming to take care of them. So I had time to go hide in the hay."

"And you have been happy ever since?" Eric asked her.

She looked at him and shook her head, laughing at the same time. "Oh no! I was scared all the time at Ahmed's farm. I was afraid the bad men from the village would come and get me. That's why I stayed inside as much as I could. I drew pictures and read."

"What were you scared the bad men would do?" He asked.

"It's no longer important," she said. "I stopped being scared when I got here."

"And now you are happy," Eric asserted.

"Yes I am. I have a new mother and a new father. I love them and they love me. I also know that my first father who died was French and a teacher. So I am like the other kids here."

"What do you remember of your dad?" Eric asked.

"Not much. I was not yet four when they killed him. I remember my mom though."

"Nothing at all about your dad?"

"Maybe a warm feeling that he was a gentle man. But it might be what my mom told me about him. Francine thinks that he must have spoken to me in his native language. That's why I learned speaking and writing French fast."

"Your French is excellent. All that reading gave you a good vocabulary."

Eric continued to poke gently at her memory of her time with her father. So the three of them kept talking about her learning French and reading with Francine, and about Anna's time in Ahmed's farm. Eric also mentioned the orphan twins, saying he was not sure if they could remember their mother and father.

"I don't remember my dad," Anna said, "But Francine thinks he taught me French because I learned it so fast. So the twins may have learned something from their parents although they don't know they did."

"You are very smart, Anna."

༄

When they went back to talk to Francine, Eric asked her, "Is Gigondas close to here?"

"Yes it is, Very close as a matter of fact. Why are you asking?"

Embarrassed, Eric reddened. "I spent most of World War Two in Gigondas hiding in a convent or a school run by nuns. I was a Jewish kid and they hid me for over two years."

Josette looked at him her eyes wide opened. "Really? I didn't know that."

Francine told him, "There are still nuns there. It's more like a farm than a convent. There are a few nuns, and I believe they still take care of some children. Would you like to go there?"

"I don't want to impose, but I would love it. I have not been there since the war."

They all got in the car, and went to the old farmhouse. Eric rang the bell. A young nun opened the gate. "How can I help you?" She asked.

"My name is Eric Tallec. The nuns hid me in this very building for over two years during World War Two. The sisters saved my life. Are there any left from that era?"

"Our reverend mother, Mother Catherine, was here during that time I believe. Would you like to see her?"

"I would be so honored to be able to thank her again."

They all went into the yard, and entered the large building and were ushered into Mother Catherine's office. The young nun explained who Eric was.

Doctor Tallec, somewhat embarrassed pointed to Francine, Josette, Lucas, and Anna. "These are my friends."

"I am Francine Segal, a neighbor. I live at the winery in Beaumes de Venise, and this is my daughter Anna," Francine added.

The mother superior looked over her glasses and smiled.

"Thank the Lord, Eric. You are a man now. And you kept the name we gave you."

Eric was taken aback. "The name you gave me?"

"Yes, my child. Your name was Isaac Katz. A Mr. Tallec and his wife were killed in a nearby village. We gave you that name and the new identity of Eric Tallec, their son, because the Germans checked periodically on our children, looking for Jews. Isaac Katz would have been a dead give-away. Actually in the last months of the occupation when the Germans became nastier, we removed your name from our list and when there was a check, we hid you in a little hide-out in back of the barn. Its entrance, low to the ground, was hidden by the hay we kept for the few sheep we were allowed to have. The animals themselves were in the barn."

"I remember that," Eric exclaimed. "But I never knew I had another name. The distant relatives I went to live with after we found out my parents had been killed in a death camp never told me about my real name." Eric hesitated for an instant and asked, "Could I see my old hide-out?

"The barn is still there, but the cache does not exist any longer. Would you like to see the barn?"

"I'd love to."

They all went to the old structure, and when he opened the door, the familiar smell reminded him of the endless hours he spent in fear, hidden in the hay, dreading hearing the footsteps that would come to take him away. Eric, with tears in his eyes asked the head nun, "How can I thank you, Mother Catherine?"

"We did our best for the children we could help. That's what we do. Now can I ask you: what is your profession?"

"I am a doctor and I specialize in treating traumatized children."

Mother Catherine clapped her hands. "So we helped you, and now you help other children. God bless you."

Francine asked her. "Do you still take care of children?"

"We do. As a matter of fact, we have been asked if we could take care of orphans from Algeria; but we have not had to take care of any yet."

Francine put her arm around Anna. "We fled Algeria a few months ago with Anna who was an orphan. We have adopted her when we came here. She's now our daughter."

"I am so glad to have met you, and young Anna. God looks kindly on the ones who help children who are victims of wars. Come and visit now and then," the mother superior said, signaling the end of the meeting.

৵

On the way back to the winery, Anna told Eric, "Sheep protected you during your war, and goats protected me when I was in my village. That's funny. We are both orphans, and we were both saved by animals."

"Yes, we were and we're grateful to them."

Anna looked up at Eric and with her irresistible smile asked him, "Did you speak to the sheep?"

"I remember I spoke aloud to myself to cope with my fears. I'm sure they listened to the sound of my voice. Does that count?"

"I don't know. I spoke to the goats in Arabic. I think they understood me."

Eric chuckled. "Well, I could not speak anything but French, maybe the sheep were not fluent in the language."

Anna laughed. "Whether they understand what we say or not, I know that animals are nice to children."

Eric and Anna had become friends.

cﾟﾟ

On the way back to Paris, Eric could not stop thinking about this improbable reunion with the nuns who saved him years ago.

"Mother Catherine touched me deeply," he said. "So much courage! And she remembered me."

Then Josette said to Eric and Lucas, "Anna is really amazing. What I don't get is that she has done on her own and still does everything that a trauma expert would advise her to do."

"What do you mean?" Lucas asked.

"When the bad men, as she used to call them, went after her, she ran away and stayed in the goats' shed. An older girl who knew she was hiding there, and helped her with food told her to go stand next to your jeep in the plaza. She ran to you. That's when you rescued her. When she started French lessons with Francine, she asked her to teach her how to read and write, then she occupied her mind with books, and drawings. That's how she dealt with her fears. When she first got to the winery, she adopted a dog, etc."

"It is amazing," Eric chimed in. Then Lucas added, "Furthermore, she does not show any effect of the trauma she went through. She mentioned the village, did not cringe when she talked about the bad men. I remember that when she heard any mention of the village, she used to look at her feet, and mumble something about the bad men. She is totally relaxed now."

"I am so glad," Josette commented. "What a nice kid."

"Now, I have an idea I want to try on you," Eric said to Josette. "I think that something happened between Anna and her dad before he was killed. It left in her mind some thirst for the French language. Maybe her inner ear and her mind had gotten used to the sound, the rhythm, or the melody of the language. I also believe that because she had been happy in the first two years or so of her life, she had acquired a strong desire to live. Hence her healthy reactions to adversity."

"I'm sure you're right," Josette replied.

"And I wonder if there is an antithesis of trauma, like a positive trauma?" Eric added.

Josette nodded. "I think there's a psychological impact from the parents to their infants. I'm not sure if it is similar to traumas, but it is a one-way street. Events shape the mind of the youngster whether it is conscious or not."

"And it's what gave her the strength and the courage to deal with her fears?" Lucas asked.

"Most probably." Josette replied.

"So how do we apply that to any orphan or to the twins?" Eric asked.

"I need to think it through," Josette answered.

Still focused on Anna, Lucas asked Eric, "Can I assume that Anna is free of her fears of the village and the villagers?"

"Yes. I believe she has overcome that terror."

"I think so too," Josette said, "But I'm curious to know what made you say that," she asked Eric.

Without hesitation, Eric replied, "It's the way she said that when she found out her father was French. She knew then she was like the other kids in Beaumes De Venise. She is no longer part of that Algerian village; she belongs here with her new parents, her new school, and her new life."

"Agreed," Josette nodded.

స్తో

When he got home Eric found a letter from the Geneva hospital which contained an offer for the job of head of the new service, the Geneva trauma center. It outlined what had been discussed during the interviews. The compensation was generous, way over what he made in Paris, and it included all the perks that were mentioned to him.

The letter asked him to come to Geneva to sign the paperwork for the job itself, the perks, and the documents relating to his being a foreign national living in Switzerland. "Please come at your earliest convenience" was the last sentence.

Chapter 38

Paris

July 30

On Monday morning, Eric went to Josette's office and told her about the job offer he was about to accept.

"This is a great opportunity for you. You are very talented and you'll do a terrific job there. Who would you recommend to take over your job?"

"Mademoiselle Raynaud seems to me to be the best qualified. All the people I worked with are good, but she has the most experience and she's a great people manager."

"Wonderful. Can you stick around for a few days to pass the baton?"

"Yes, of course. I need to go to Geneva for a couple of days to sign papers, but I'll be back and stay until everything is comfortable for you."

"Are you going to follow up with the twins?"

"Yes, for sure. I'll see if they need help."

"May I ask why the interest in the little kids?"

"You know now that I was an orphan myself. I'm not sure what marks it left on me, but I feel obligated to help all orphans I am exposed to. I was lucky to overcome that trauma, and I want to give back."

"Thank you for sharing that. Are you going to see my sister?"

""Well I can't say much, and would ask you to be discreet, but the short answer is you bet."

Josette smiled. "Good luck on that front too. She's a terrific gal."

⁂

A couple of days later, the countess called for a meeting with Lucas and Josette. She addressed Lucas the minute they walked in.

"I have spoken with Mr. Laforge about you. He knew who you were because your uncle had mentioned you to him several times. He thinks he might have met you. I also told him about your outstanding record in the Algerian war, and the struggle you faced in reentering civilian life. I shared with him your idea for the trauma center, and your needs for acquiring the tools to run the relationship between the new enterprise and the French and foreign governments. He suggested he could hire you as a member of his personal staff. You would act as an assistant at first, learning all the facets of his job, then run his headquarters government liaison department. I can't say exactly what you would do, but he'll explain it to you. You could do that for a couple of years, or however long you think you need. How is that?"

"That's perfect. I think I need a few days to get my treatment set by Josette so I know its constraints on my time, then I'll be ready to meet him."

"That'll work. I will tell him. I'm sure he'll agree to that," the countess replied.

"Now," she looked at Josette. "Let's talk about the battered-women work I have initiated."

Josette nodded. "I'm anxious to get some study started on that, but I'm not sure how to approach it."

"The net finding of my conversations," the countess replied, "is that the problem or problems associated with battered women, I should add and battered children, have to do more with social workers and law enforcement officers than with doctors. Physical protection is a primary concern, redirection of their lives, and relocation in most cases are the next difficulties to be overcome. The people I talked to said they would welcome treatments that would help the women's heads get straight, but they would first have to be rescued and be safe from further assaults."

"I am not surprised, "Josette replied. "But from my medical point of view, it is clear to me that I need to understand the psychological impact of their plight before any idea of potential treatments might be formulated. So, in my own mind –and I have not shared this with Lucas yet — I need to find a way to do that work before we can think of how we could help these unfortunate women in the trauma center."

"I believe that's right. Maybe you and I can meet with the people I talked to," Madame de Sèvres agreed. "Together we will be able to find a way for you to get to analyze the raw impact of the battering on their psyche and identify the types of trauma they struggle with."

"I will put together a research team who will talk to several of these victims and understand their main issues. But I believe to incorporate the battered women in the program has to be a long way from today."

"Which says to me," Lucas added, "that I should not be thinking about that aspect of the trauma center for a while."

Both the countess and Josette agreed.

c→

On the way home, Josette said, "That was an important meeting. We made real progress. Now it's time to get your treatment set."

"Right. How do we start?"

"My thought is to have you talk with Mademoiselle Raynaud. She'll take over from Tallec. You'll have a few sessions with her; then the three of us will get together and nail down a plan."

Chapter 39

Beaumes de Venise

August 7

Madame Leroi had been requested by the mayor of Beaumes de Venise to attend a village meeting the next morning in the city hall conference room concerning arrival of children from Algeria. She immediately called the mayor's office to suggest to the mayor to invite Francine who had come from there a couple of months ago. Nobody called her back, so she was surprised to see Francine when she entered the mayor's conference room the next day. In addition to Francine, the mayor, and his lieutenant, the rest of the attendees included the head of social services, Mother Catherine, who was in charge of the farm and refuge run by the nuns, the head priest of the village parish, and the chief of police.

"Thank you all for coming." The mayor opened the meeting with these words. "I asked you to come this morning because I received a communication from the head of the Department of Vaucluse. Some of the townships under their jurisdiction have been alerted to get ready to accept a few refugees from North Africa. For those of you who don't know her, let me introduce Francine Segal who took over with her husband, Tom, what is now the Segal winery. She is here because she and her husband left Algeria a few months ago to settle here and she is fluent in Arabic.

"Evidently, the end of the war in Algeria has left many children, French as well as Algerians, without parents. They have been orphaned by parents who had been abducted, killed, or simply abandoned by families who had decided to go their own way. The French government social services have committed to accept some of these children in our country, and our village will receive a group of them. I have been given little information about the children who will come here. I don't know how many to expect, their ages, or where they're from. I have also no idea whether they are educated or not, if they speak any French, even if they are French or Algerian."

The nun asked the mayor, "Are we supposed to house them as an interim situation, or to place them in local families?"

"It is a permanent commitment," the mayor replied. "The answer is we need to find locals willing to take the kids. It would be better if we can keep the children of the same families together. I have asked you to come, Mother Catherine, because we need you to house some of them temporarily while we look for a family for them."

The head of social services said, "Let me do some canvassing. I know a lot of people in the village. All we need are a few local families to become foster parents and a plan to get them integrated into our village life."

Francine raised her hand, and looked at the mayor. "You mentioned that you did not know if the children spoke any French. Should we plan to have a French language program for the children if they only speak Arabic?"

"I think a formal program should be put in place if that is the case," the mayor replied, "even if they have some knowledge of French but it is not sufficient to attend school." He addressed Francine. "Would you help Madame Leroi? It would make it easier for the children to have a teacher who can communicate in their own tongue."

Francine answered, "I'd be glad to help. I'll work with Madame Leroi. Let me know when the children are expected. I'll make myself available."

When she got home, Francine thought for a moment and went to talk to Tom. She explained what she knew and asked him, "Should we be thinking of taking one of these kids?"

Tom replied, "We could, but I'd like to ask Anna what she would say if we did. I don't want her to feel uncomfortable. She is so happy the way it is now after all the terrible and scary years in El Boussaid."

"Okay, I'll talk to her. Anna is strong and she has a big heart. She knows what these children are going through."

Anna was reading, sitting in a chair in the orange orchard.

"Anna, I have a question for you." She explained the situation to Anna who smiled and said, "How can we say no? You can teach her French if he or she only speaks Arabic as you did for me, and Brigitte and I can help him or her be comfortable in the school and feel part of the village."

"You're so wonderful, little one," Francine said, and she went to embrace her.

Anna shook her head. "Lieutenant Lucas did not say no when he got me out of El Boussaid when I was scared, hungry, and did not know what to do, even who to ask for help. Basira did not say no when Ahmed asked her if she would take me in. You did not hesitate to bring me here when we had to leave Algeria because it became too dangerous to stay there. And now you are my mother." She sighed, took her mom's hand, smiled at her.

"I know how scary it felt when nobody wanted me in my village, and I know how wonderful it makes you feel when you are no longer alone or scared. It's my turn to be on the giving side."

Tom loved Anna's reaction, and Francine called Madame Leroi to tell her.

"Would you tell the social services person we would like to be there when the children come? We would like to meet them and maybe take one or two with us."

"I will. Will Anna be okay with that?"

"Anna is the one who wants to do it."

"Bless her" was Madame Leroi's answer.

☙

The following Monday, two groups of orphans from North Africa were escorted into the Beaumes de Venise city hall. The first group of six came from Arzew, a small town not far and east of Oran, on the

Mediterranean Sea. They were dressed in European children's clothes. Three of them, a boy and two girls, were from one family, two sisters in their teens from a different one, and a young girl by herself. It became clear right away that these six orphans were French. The nun in charge of the group explained that the six children had been orphaned. Some came to them a few months ago, others more recently. Their parents had perished in bomb attacks or other insurgency events. The children had been rescued by the Red Cross, and escorted by soldiers to the small nunnery, which also served as a civilian emergency health center. The little girl by herself was named Marie-Aisha. Her parents, who were schoolteachers, had added the Aisha name to Marie because most of her schoolmates were Algerian.

The second group had eight children, four girls and four boys between six and nine. They came from a little village west of Oran. They were from two families who ran farms. The parents were French sympathizers and had been abducted and killed. Francine and Anna went to meet them all and addressed them in Arabic. These children beamed to hear the language they could understand. Francine asked them if they spoke any French. The obvious answer came out that they only had a cursory knowledge of it.

Francine asked Anna what she thought.

Anna did not hesitate. "We could have another Aisha or Marie-Aisha in our home. I'm not sure I did all I could to help Basira's Aisha when we first arrived here. I was confused myself. I am sorry for that, but now, I can help this Aisha and I would like to do it. I know better what she'll have to go through than when I first got here."

The family of three went with the people who organized the bi-weekly open-air market for fruit, vegetables, and poultry. The bakers took the two sisters. The eight kids of the second group were to be taken by Mother Catherine and her nuns until they could be integrated in French families.

Francine made the arrangements with the social services person for taking Marie-Aisha. Papers were signed, and the person accompanying the children explained to Marie-Aisha that she would go with Francine and Anna. Francine told Madame Leroi that if the school could organize a class, she would be able to prepare the French children for their new environment, which would be a departure from their life in North Africa. She also said she would check with the nuns about the other group. She promised to help Madame Leroi put in place what the other Algerian children required.

Madame Leroi replied, "I'll take you up on the French group. I will test the children to assign them to the proper grade, and then you can teach them what they need if anything. We'll have to decide the best way to deal with the eight Algerian children when you know more."

"I have met Mother Catherine. I'll talk to her," Francine replied.

Anna went to take Marie-Aisha's hand and told her she would be coming to live in her home and that they were going to be sisters and friends. Marie-Aisha pointed her finger at Anna and chuckled. "Sadiqa?"

"Yes, friend," Anna replied. They both laughed.

Francine turned to Anna and said, "We're all set. Let's go." She turned to her new protégée and asked, "Is it all right if we call you simply Marie?"

The little girl whispered, "I would like that."

Tom and Wolf greeted the little girl warmly. Marie was six, quite a bit shorter than Anna. Her dark hair and dark eyes framed her light oval face. She was pretty but she tended to look down a lot. Marie felt intimidated and overwhelmed by the big house, the new family, and the sudden complete change in her life.

"We will make you happy," Anna told her, "And here, you are safe, and we won't send you back to Algeria."

Marie eyes and even bigger smile showed Anna that she had said the right thing. Anna remembered that although she had felt safe, and said so when she arrived at the winery, for a longer time than she would admit, she had felt anxious, afraid that something would go wrong and she would have to go back.

Francine asked Marie if she could read and write, and Marie showed her she could. She obviously had attended her parents' school in Algeria. Towns near the big cities of northern Algeria had schools managed by the French system, and girls were not prevented from attending. She should have no trouble fitting in first grade.

"Your French is good, Marie," Francine said. "Tomorrow we'll go to the school and make sure you'll fit in first grade. If you're not quite there, I'll teach you and bring you up to the level you need," Francine told her.

Anna asked Francine if the one bed in her room could be switched to two single beds so that she and Marie could share her bedroom. Francine agreed and asked Armand to move the beds. He also placed Wolf's pad between the two beds.

That afternoon, Anna told Brigitte and her teacher Mademoiselle Roger about Marie. Brigitte was thrilled. "She can be my friend too. We'll be able to help her in school. I have a neighbor who is starting first grade this year. We'll get them together so she will have a friend the first day of school. That's important."

Mademoiselle Roger added, "Bring her to our next session. I want to meet her too."

⚜

That afternoon, Francine received a call for help from Mother Catherine. So that evening, Francine, Anna, and Marie went to ring the bell at Mother Catherine's farmhouse. The young nun who had greeted them the first time said, "Oh it's so nice to see you again. I believe Mother Catherine will be glad you came. We need help."

They were brought to her office, and the Mother said, "God help us. These children speak almost no French."

"I can definitely help," Francine replied, "The three of us speak Arabic."

"Thank God. We need to tell them how they will live, where they'll sleep, what clothes they will wear. We have clothes for them, etc."

"Why don't you tell them in French what they need to know, and I will translate."

They went around the premises, rooms, dining room, playroom, classroom, and where to go on the property. The children, obviously scared, were grateful. They seemed to range in age from five to nine or ten.

Francine let Anna and Marie talk to the kids. Anna explained how good it was to live in Beaumes de Venise, with no threat and no fear. The Mother Superior and Francine discussed the next step. Obviously French language teaching was a priority. Francine started thinking about a special program of intensive teaching. She asked Anna if she had any idea who of the teachers she talked to in the school would be the best to help Francine with this project. Anna volunteered herself. "I can teach the three young ones to help you, Mother."

"That's very sweet of you, but you'll have your own studies."

"I know, but I can do it a few hours. I would like to. I am on the side of the helpers now, and my father and my grandfather were teachers."

Francine did get help from one of Madame Leroi's schoolteachers, but she enlisted Anna who did a good job. She had the patience and a good sense of what young children her age needed.

The arrangements were made for the teaching and the translating, and Anna took the lead in getting Marie comfortable in her new house with her new family. Wolf was considerate of the newcomer, and slowly the little girl relaxed. She had to get used to new food, new sleeping arrangements, and a brand new life. Anna got her to talk about the life she left in Arzew. Marie's parents were teachers and in the last days of the war had disappeared. She had been scared but neighbors took her in and called the Red Cross, which stepped in and brought her to the nuns. It took a few days to find out that the parents had died, and a few more weeks to get the six orphans on a ship to France, so like Anna, Marie had to go through much uncertainty, and therefore much apprehension. It had been difficult for her. Anna assured Marie she would enjoy the Segal family, the school, and mainly the feeling of safety. She praised Francine and Tom. Yet Anna sensed Marie still missed her parents. Anna talked about her own parents and promised her that things would get better.

Francine played the piano sometimes although she had much to do. When Marie saw the piano, she asked her who the pianist was. Francine sat on the bench and played one of her favorite pieces. When Marie heard her, her eyes moistened. Anna asked her what was wrong, and Marie replied, "My mother used to play. She had started teaching me."

"Would you like to play something, Marie?"

"She blushed and nodded. Then she sat on the piano bench and played a short piece."

Anna and Francine clapped. "That was lovely." Francine caressed Marie's hair tenderly and said, "I don't have the time or the talent to teach you, but I know that Mademoiselle Roger also plays the piano and has a couple of students. Would you like to take lessons?"

The young girl blushed again and with a timid smile said, "That would be wonderful."

"I'll talk to her. I'm sure she will be able to teach you."

✻

Francine spent quite a bit of her time teaching the French children so they would fit in their grades with remedial help from the teachers. She also helped force-feed the French language into the Algerian children's brains. Throughout that process, she became close to Madame Leroi.

One day, Madame Leroi told her, "I am impressed with your generosity, your energy, and your experience as a schoolteacher. In three months or so, you have become a leader in this village. That is admirable. I wonder if you would be interested in holding my job when I retire in a couple of years. The people of the village know you or know of you and your name is good here."

"I have never thought of that, but I am honored. If you think I could contribute to the village, I would certainly think about it."

"Why don't you? If you were to replace me, there are a few things you need to be trained on with regard to the running of the school and its relationship with the local education establishment. Let me know and over the next couple of years, I'll arrange for you to learn the system to prepare you for the duty of school principal."

☙

Francine reflected on the words from Madame Leroi and shared them with Tom.

"You have blossomed since you came here, "Tom said. "Obviously you enjoyed dealing with the school, but I think that Anna had a big influence on both of us. You helped that little girl, you built her confidence, but she helped us at the same time. The adoption changed not only her life, and her vision of her world, but also yours and mine."

"That's true. But what I think is that over two years ago, I fell in love with this needy and vulnerable little girl called Hana. I helped her become Anna, and I became her mother. Not because of the papers we signed, but because she entered my heart. Anna uplifted my spirits and my faith in the goodness of innocent children."

"You're definitely better suited to being a mom than to toting a rifle in an inhospitable environment," Tom told her.

"Do you remember how disappointed we were when we found out I could not bear children?" He nodded. "Now we have the precious Anna as our child. I am looking forward to raising her to become successful at being who she wants to be. Probably a teacher."

Tom nodded. "I also hope Marie will turn out like Anna. We might want to adopt her too," he added.

"I hope we will. We'll see," Francine replied. Then she added, "I think Anna will facilitate that. She will make Marie happy, and I believe she will respond positively. I think it depends on the circumstances of her becoming an orphan, but Anna can help with that, and we can always ask for help from Josette."

Later that day, Francine called Josette and shared the news of the new arrivals with her. "I'll let you know if I think they need trauma counseling."

The school year was about to start in a few weeks. The children of the village were anxious to return to the classroom. The influx of newcomers to the village would add a little spice to the usually laid-back atmosphere of Beaumes de Venise. The families of the village embraced their new civic duty, welcoming the new children with open arms. They dedicated themselves to making them accepted and happy. The same girls who had been nasty to Basira's Aisha seemed to have had a change of heart and did not set out to bully the new kids. The village was lucky to have Francine and Anna, who not only were fluent in Arabic but also familiar with their culture. They were able to smooth out many issues and made both the newcomers and their hosts more understanding of each other. Their enthusiasm was contagious. Francine felt good for helping children who had been traumatized, scared, and needed love and affection. Beaumes de Venise intended to do its part to mitigate the traumatic effects of the Algerian war on innocent children.

✥

Anna remembered how relieved she was when she arrived at the winery, but she also reminded herself that it was hard to get used to a different kind of life. She felt she could help Marie adapt faster. At first, Anna did not want her to stay isolated in her room and only read or draw like she did herself in Mascara. Armand had been helpful teaching Anna gardening, and having her help his wife with the chickens and him with the goats. Anna had Marie come with her and share these chores.

So Anna took Marie to feed the animals, and she brought her to her garden. They took care of Anna's little plot, planting flowers, weeding, and watering the little piece of soil Anna called hers. "I can ask Armand if he can prepare another plot next to mine for you, if you'd like."

"I would like that, but you'll have to show me what to do."

"Sure. Would you like to go to the top of the hill? There is a bench we can sit on and look at all the vines that belong to us. It's pretty."

"I'd love that, Anna."

So Wolf led the way and they walked up the steep slope.

When they were sitting on the bench, Anna said, "It's great that you have been accepted in first grade and you have met Antoinette, my friend Brigitte's neighbor."

"Yes, but how is the school going to be? Do you have any idea?"

"No. I'll be going into third grade, but I have never been in a school before. All I know is I'll be with Brigitte and a couple of other kids I met at art afternoon. And I know the teachers. They're really nice."

⁂

Mademoiselle Roger started to teach Marie on her piano. She was impressed by Marie's keyboard facility. She had done many scales and exercises in Algeria so her key-striking was crisp. She also had great notes memory, and a feel for the melodies she was playing. Over the summer, Marie became close to her piano teacher and developed into a good, advanced pianist for her age.

⁂

The first day of school came fast. Francine drove the two girls and left them at the school. Antoinette took Marie with her to the first grade classroom, and Anna followed Brigitte to the third-grade room. Chloé and Olivier whom she had met in the art afternoons were there and greeted her. The main teacher was Madame Roger who had tutored her during the summer. So it was comfortable for Anna who did not feel intimidated at all.

While her girls were in class, Francine went to sit in the room where the Algerian kids were learning French. It was a special class, and she sat there to help in case the teacher ran into a communication problem. She stayed there a couple of hours, but was not needed. The Algerian children were learning fast. They were eager to learn and helped one another.

When Francine picked up her girls, Marie shared her day with her and Anna. She had met two other nice girls and liked them.

"All the girls and boys are in school for the first time, so we're all learning being in school," Marie said. "It's exciting. Nobody made fun of anybody else, including me."

At the end of the week, it became clear that Brigitte and Anna were in a league of their own. But because they were generous with their helping their mates, they were not resented.

Chapter 40

Paris

August 8

Josette was bound for Maligny to assess the potential for research that could be done with Madame de Sèvres' grant. Before leaving for her meetings, she arranged for Lucas to meet Mademoiselle Raynaud and attended their first meeting. Michelle was her first name.

"Michelle, my husband spent three years in a fighting infantry unit in Algeria. He was decorated multiple times, but there are visible effects of the trauma he suffered during that time. I do not believe the damage to be deep and irreversible, but, observing him, I became convinced he needs professional treatment. My love for him can't do it by itself."

"I'll be happy to do that," Michelle agreed. "Why don't I have a couple of meetings with Lucas? I will determine what I think the trauma is, and select the best treatment for it. Then the three of us will meet and decide on the course of action. Would that work?"

"Definitely," Josette said.

During the consultations, Michelle asked Lucas about the problems that he could attribute to his time in the war.

"It's hard to pinpoint," Lucas replied. "There are the flashbacks and nightmares with terrible images and memories of explosions, screams, etc. There's also anger at times, although it's rather infrequent. There's also a general malaise, I'm not sure what I am supposed to do. I'm no longer a soldier, but I'm not yet a true civilian. There are the memories of the poor kids who were shot, maimed, or just terrorized. I'm not motivated to do anything at times and I tend to look at job opportunities as totally uninspiring and useless."

She then asked him to talk more about the combat memories that caused nightmares or flashbacks. Lucas described scenes that still made him angry, and he briefly recounted the most significant casualty-filled fights he led his platoon through.

"Do you think of these events often?" Michelle asked.

"When I see people who remind me of the images that are etched in my mind."

"Like what, for example?"

"Like seeing wounded soldiers, or recovering veterans struggling with re-entering normal life, whatever that is. But, the worst for me is to see children in trouble, orphaned or obviously depressed. It always brings me back to terrible crimes I can't seem to be able to forget."

Then Michelle asked him if there were atrocities he had been witness to that still bothered him. Lucas became uncomfortable. He described saving kids like Aisha and Hana. He mentioned the little shoeshine boy who was killed in Algiers when insurgents detonated a bomb, and the little boy who killed himself because he dropped a live grenade he had been asked to bring to Lucas. He stopped and squirmed on his chair.

"What else, Lucas?"

"I'm not sure there is more I should talk about."

Michelle's eyes drilled into his. "Lucas. You have to be open and honest. I can't help you if you don't level with me. I know you are not telling me the worst atrocity that still haunts you. What is it?"

Lucas looked down, shook his head, and whispered, "That would be hard for me to talk about."

"Yes, I know," Michelle replied gently. "That's why you need to tell me about it."

So Lucas described that fateful early morning when he and his platoon found their rancher friend, George, dead with multiple knife wounds, and his pregnant wife and his two sons, dead with their throats cut."

"Tell me more about what shocked you."

Lucas explained how he saw George's body after George had fought the attackers with his bare hands and died doing so and how he found the two boys on blood-soaked beds with their throats sliced.

"What about their mother?" Michelle asked.

"She was killed too."

"I know that. Tell me why it is so hard to talk about her."

Lucas started to sweat profusely. His face turned red, his lips quivered, and he shook his head. "I can't. I am the only person who saw how she was murdered. At that time, I promised her I'd never tell how she suffered. I swore to myself to keep that secret to respect the privacy of her last moments."

"You can tell me. I won't tell."

Lucas became angry. "I just told you why I can't tell you how Thérèse died."

Michelle put her hand on his. "I'm sorry. Lucas. I understand. Can you tell me what happens when your mind goes back to those traumatic events?"

"I feel depressed. In Algeria, I could get back at the rebels. I could not undo what they did, but I could prevent more atrocities, and minimize casualties. Now, back in France, I can't do any of that. I feel somewhat useless. My life has little purpose."

"How long does this sadness last?"

"Not necessarily very long. I am in love with Josette as you know, and my outlook for a long, happy life with her is uplifting. I'm happy when I think of my next job, my contribution to my future family. Revisiting bad memories is what brings me down. I guess when I get involved in my next job, it'll get better."

"What about when you think of George's family?"

"I don't."

"I see. Let me think about what you said. I'll do some reading, talk to a couple of people, and then we'll get back with Josette and come up with a plan."

"That is fine with me." Lucas agreed.

❧

At the end of the week, Josette returned from her visit to the rehabilitation center of Maligny where she spent time talking with the man in charge of the facility as well as the men and women in charge of the various services. Because the influx of recovering soldiers had slowed down substantially as no more casualties came back from Algeria, they had also discussed the further viability of the center and a potential redirection of its mission.

❧

While managing these initial projects, Josette was intent on providing all the support she could to Lucas. She, Michelle and Lucas got together late Friday.

Josette opened the meeting. "I'm anxious to hear your conclusions and recommendations. Go ahead, Michelle."

"Thank you, Josette. First, let me say that however real, Lucas' trauma impact is mostly not severe. I see absolutely no reason to look at any medication. I might not be able to totally eradicate his combat memories, but I know I can tone them down substantially. Not so for all civilian issues. There's one instance of atrocity that needs to be addressed." Michelle paused and looked at Josette.

"Go ahead, Michelle."

"Here is my recommendation, Josette," Michelle said opening her notebook. "I find that Lucas' anger at the enemy fighters, and at the injuries they inflicted on his troops, has faded considerably since the time of combat. But I also found that the atrocities committed on children and on civilians have not vanished from his mind. I might even say that some of the images of those horrifying scenes are still sharp. I found anger related to these incidents, but more than that, I detected sadness and depression. Depression, because they happened at all and he was not able to prevent them, but mostly that he can't do anything about it now. Lucas is still totally dedicated to helping the welfare of innocent kids."

"That is very helpful, Michelle. What do you recommend we do?"

"I propose to meet with Lucas twice a week for a couple of months, and then only once a week. What I would do is to execute trauma-focused psychotherapy directed mainly at the civilian-driven trauma."

"Are you okay with that, Lucas?" Josette asked.

Lucas smiled. "Yes. It sort of makes sense to me, although I don't know what trauma-focused psychotherapy is."

"It's a proven technique. You'll see. It works," Josette said, then she looked at Michelle. "Let's book it. And thank you Michelle for a sound study. One more question: Do you think a complete recovery is possible? And, if yes, how long will it take?"

"It's difficult to be certain, but my judgment is that complete recovery is likely, and that the time it will take will depend on the job Lucas chooses. I believe that some of his psychological wounds, mainly the ones related to the severe injuries to his soldiers, might not require much time. But I'm not sure about that one instance I just mentioned. I'll know more when I understand the details of the trauma after listening to Lucas. It might depend on whether his day-to-day life tends to bring these memories to the forefront. But I am certain Lucas will live a happy and normal life."

"You know, Michelle, that Lucas has had the idea of creating a trauma center, and is going to explore how to best create and manage such an endeavor. What do you think?"

Michelle looked at her notes. "Here is what I wrote to myself regarding Lucas' employment. Lucas should look for a leadership job in an industry far remote from war-related activities. An ideal business would be a growing field with substantial growth opportunity, in science or industry."

"In other words, you would nix the trauma idea?"

"Nix is a strong word. I may change my mind after the treatment when I see how it goes, but today, I would advise against it."

Josette looked at Lucas. "What's your reaction, Lucas?"

"I think Michelle has a point. For example, when I saw Aisha was still struggling with the loss of her dad and the disappearance of her brothers and learned she went back to Algeria, it made me sad, if not depressed. On the other hand, when we saw how vibrant Anna had become since her adoption by Tom and Francine, and how she dismissed any thought of being reminded of that village where she had a hard time, I felt so happy for her and for having given her that chance. The day of our wedding, it made me happy to see that Private Vidal had recovered well from his wounds, but seeing him brought me back to the moments he was hit. And that made me sad. Obviously, I'm still dealing with what happened."

"The plans for the trauma center are not for an immediate implementation. A lot needs to happen before we are ready for any kind of a launch. So we don't have to make any decision about it today," Josette said.

Michelle and Lucas both nodded, and Lucas added, "We have to wait two years anyway for your grant studies to be completed. We'll know more by then."

⁂

Josette had chosen a sizeable group of military doctors eager to upgrade their skills.

The selection of a staff ready to train and undertake the research at the Val de Grace facility did not take much time, and by the end of August, the selected volunteers had been identified by Josette and Mr. Weimer, the head of the military hospital.

Each of the military doctors she had was paired with a seasoned trauma specialist from Necker Hospital. Each team of two met with the soldiers were recovering in the Val de Grace hospital. The questionnaire had been constructed by Josette and Captain Dufour, using Ms. Rooth's paper and Lucas' and Ms. Rooth's letters, as well as from the base knowledge of the children's questioning methodology.

Josette had designed a precise training map to get the teams familiar with a series of queries they had to get the answers to. The question had to be asked her way to cause no additional disturbance in the minds of the soldiers. The goal was for the teams to comprehend all the relevant facts surrounding the event which troubled the patients without arousing their anger or making them defensive. A delicate balance. As the program progressed, each team suggested modifications and additions to the questionnaire for the veterans. The suggestions were to be reviewed periodically by Josette herself, and the list of questions updated after each review.

This was the plan for the first phase. The process would last until the end of 1963 because the data collected had to be solid. Then there would be a refining period. From that work, a training protocol, diagnostic tools, and a methodology for diagnosing the effects of the traumatic stress the soldiers had experienced would be put together.

Josette hoped to be able to create a classification of the different types of emotional distress that would have been identified in that first phase. Once classified, toward the end of 1964, the appropriate treatments to address each type of trauma could be developed.

༄

Michelle Raynaud and Lucas had a series of initial meetings where she asked him to relate to her in great detail the combat scenes he remembered most vividly, the ones that had affected him when they happened and still ate at him at present. She had him repeat his stories several times over the first meetings so that all the details of his memories came out clearly. Michelle also poked at some of the atrocities against civilians, but tended to stay away from that one scene she knew would be the hardest for Lucas to relive through.

Lucas told Michelle about his battles. In a sense he relived his war and told her how the inexperienced second lieutenant out of officer's school became the seasoned, a well-respected veteran first lieutenant. The therapy demanded that he tell his story over and over so that stories of battles became routine in his mind and not unusual events that stuck out in his psyche. The same was true of the atrocities he witnessed, but Michelle knew of George's wife's tender spot in Lucas' soul.

She had become convinced that George's family's story was key to his total recovery, so she waded slowly in these trouble waters.

"Lucas, you know you have to tell me the story of the murders of George and his family. I understand the promise you made and I respect that, but you need to talk about what happened; it is essential for your recovery."

"I know. Why don't you ask questions? I'll answer to the best of my ability."

"Start by describing how you discovered the tragedy."

Lucas proceeded to tell Michelle about the early-morning warning that something might have happened at George's ranch. He painted the scene of the farm building with its door ajar, not a good sign, and after entering with two of his soldiers. He told her they found George's body in the main room, then how he discovered the two boys with their throats slashed and the body of Thérèse. Michelle did not ask any questions about her.

Session after session, the same stories were told until Lucas seemed capable of casually telling the sequence of events in the battles, including the casualties and their evacuations. The atrocities to civilians followed the same pattern, however a bit slower. The account of George's family's murders was the toughest story to deaden. Over time Michelle got Lucas to describe the position of the body of the woman, and how the blood was splattered around her body.

One day at the end of three months of therapy, she said, "Lucas, now you're ready to tell me what happened to Thérèse. That will liberate you from that horrible picture in your mind. You trust me enough today to believe that I will never tell anyone, and you also must know that from wherever she is, Thérèse is looking at us. Be assured that she gives you permission to tell me her secret so that you can achieve peace of mind."

Lucas looked at her, lowered his head and told Michelle what the murderers did to her body and that of her unborn baby. He then put his head in his hands and started to cry. He lowered his head to the table and sobbed for a long time. Michelle let him be. She knew he was finally on his way to recovery.

"I'm sorry," Lucas told her.

"This was a big step, Lucas. You will repeat what you just told me in the next few sessions. When you can say it without crying, the images will become history like the memories of battles you told me about over and over."

"Will I be healed then?"

"You won't be haunted by the way Thérèse died. You probably won't think about the event but, if you do, it will not depress you."

"How does that happen?"

"Lucas, trauma is a wound in your psyche. A flesh wound festers and oozes body fluids to protect itself. Then over time and with repeated treatment, a scab is formed, soft at first, then it hardens. It's the last phase of healing; then eventually the scab falls off and a scar replaces it as a reminder of the flesh trauma. Oh, it's there all right. You can see it, but it does not hurt anymore. It is the same process that your psyche goes through. You won't see the scar in your soul, but it'll be there."

"Will I be cured, then?"

"I believe we could end the treatments at that time. We'll resume them if needed, but I don't think we will have to."

Chapter 41

Paris

August 13

Mr. Laforge's office called Lucas to propose a date for their first meeting. Lucas went to the familiar office area where he used to go often to talk to his uncle. The furniture and the aura of the office had not changed. Even the secretary remembered him and fussed a bit over seeing him again. "Welcome," Mr. Laforge said, his hand extended to greet him. "I must congratulate you on the decorations you earned in Algeria. You followed your uncle's example. I must add my thanks for your service and the courage you displayed during these times."

"I appreciate the nice words. One does not hear many compliments these days; the war seems to have been erased from the French people's mind, except for those who have fought there."

"Madame de Sèvres told me I could help you. Tell me how."

Lucas explained his idea of consolidating all trauma treatments regardless of the reason for the trauma, and the age and sex of the patients. He also hinted at creating or facilitating an international network of medical scientists specializing in that new branch of medicine to accelerate the progress badly needed in that new field. "It is ambitious. It may not be feasible, but I feel the need for international cooperation is essential in order to reach the many people in need of help around the world. It would give me a great sense of accomplishment to run such a venture. The trouble is that I don't have the experience needed for such a complicated job."

"Do you have a target date for the launching of the business?"

"Not really. My wife is conducting research programs recently put in place. That work needs to be done first. The estimate for that task to be completed is at least two years."

"I understand. What would you like me to do?"

"I understand from talking with my uncle that you essentially run the company, managing the finances, human resources people as well as the government relations, and international commerce while other executives are responsible to design, develop, produce, manufacture, sell, and service your products."

"That sums it up pretty well."

"Good," Lucas said. "What I visualize is that you essentially coordinate all the pieces of the business so they work together. I would like to comprehend how you actually approach your job with regard to government and international relations. I need to learn how you get the organization to function, and how you actually get these entities that do not report to you to work toward your goals. That's what I need to learn how to do."

"I can think about designing a job like that. I can have you run the part of my staff which negotiates contracts with national and international businesses and governments. What if you decide you do not want to run that trauma business anymore? Would you work for our company for good or look elsewhere?"

"I would expect to apply for a job in your company, but I don't know what your offer would be, and you would have to evaluate my capability."

"Fair enough. Let me think this through, talk to a couple of people in the company, and I'll get back to you. Your uncle did so much for the company; we all feel indebted to him and want to help you. It was a pleasure meeting you again. Your uncle thought the world of you, and I can see why."

❧

Mr. Laforge's secretary called Lucas to invite him to meet with Mr. Laforge again on the following Monday morning at seven-thirty.

When he came in, the secretary ushered him into Mr. Laforge' office who said, "I think we have a plan which will work for you, but before I get into the details, the brass wants to meet you: That is the president of the company and the heads of each of the divisions. They meet every Monday morning in the boardroom at eight. That's where we're going right now."

When they entered the posh conference room with its shiny, at least twenty-foot table and the twelve comfortable chairs, all the expected attendees were already seated except for the president. Everyone knew the position Lucas was to hold in the next few months. Mr. Laforge introduced Lucas, reminding the division heads that he was his uncle Raimond's nephew. They all shook his hand and welcomed him. When the president walked in, he went straight to Lucas.

"I am so glad to meet you. I understand that your military record as an infantry lieutenant even surpassed that of your uncle."

The meeting started with Mr. Laforge giving the sales and financial results of the previous week and the significant events anticipated for the incoming week. The head of the product development division gave an update on the new products expected to be available by the end of the year. After a short discussion of the new government regulations concerning financial reporting, the meeting adjourned.

Back in his office Mr. Laforge outlined his idea for Lucas' next two years.

"I have discussed your request with the president and a couple of division heads. What we suggest is that for the next six months, you be my assistant, run some meetings for me, and learn how our business works. Then, and that's the president's idea, you will spend a year in INSAD, one of the best business schools in the world. It's located in Paris. When you come back, you run the international relations department. By that time you might have a better understanding of what your future company will look like. Then either you stay with us or you go run the trauma business. How does that sound?"

"That sounds perfect, and very generous."

"Your uncle was a magician. He made the company strive the way it is today and we owe him. We trust that you are as brilliant as he was."

For the rest of the day, Lucas escorted Mr. Laforge to all his meetings, and started to get up to speed on the issues and challenges of the business. That was going to be Lucas' routine over the next few days while he learned how to help Mr. Laforge, and the dos and don'ts of business management. He focused on how to apply his leadership ability and experience to this new environment. He learned how to ask questions of the experts, dig up the issues, and assess solutions. The main questions had to be what is wrong and how we fix it, but not who did it. His learning curve was steep, but like any good leader, Lucas was a fast learner.

Chapter 42

Paris

Spring of 1963

After Josette had confirmed she expected her first child, both she and Lucas had celebrated the good news, but her involvement with the trauma enterprise had to slow down. The pregnancy conformed to the expected normal development and interfered little with her work. The trauma studies followed their course. Then at the beginning of May, after the end of the first phase of the research, the contractions started and Lucas brought Josette to Necker Hospital where her colleagues were waiting to take care of her.

Josette headed for the delivery room of Necker Hospital, the facility where she had one of the three thrusts of her research work going on. This time she went in as a happy patient about to give birth. Even for her, the rules were not to be ignored, so Lucas had to wait outside the delivery room.

He had been pacing for hours. It seemed to him he had waited much longer than normal, certainly longer than he expected. He had become conscious of being in a hospital as opposed to a workplace. The stark light was too bright, the white walls and stone floors too plain; the smell of antiseptic medicine added to the uncomfortably cold temperature and irritated him. No one had come out of the delivery room to keep him updated on what was going on. It got to be evening. His heart rate had increased, his pacing had accelerated, and his nervousness soared. Something was wrong!

He asked a nurse who passed by. "Can you go into the delivery room and ask someone to come out and tell me what's going on? I have been here for hours."

"I will, sir."

Finally a nurse came out of the room and said, "There's a problem. She..."

"She what?" Lucas asked, interrupting her.

"She has been bleeding a lot, but the doctors have it under control."

"What about the baby?" he asked.

"The baby is okay. She's just a little stressed."

"Thank God. Are they both going to be all right?"

"The doctors are doing their best."

Lucas shook his head. "Can I see her?"

"Not yet. The doctors will probably sedate her. Doctor Stanislas himself is looking after her. She's in the best hands. He'll be out in a few minutes.

Indeed, the doctor came out of the delivery room. "How are you doing, Lucas?"

"I'm worried. What's going on?"

She's being cleaned up. She had abnormal bleeding. We had to take care of it. The little baby girl was a bit stressed, but she's doing fine. Both need to rest."

"But how's Josette?" Lucas asked.

"She's okay. She's utterly exhausted. But she's okay."

"Can I see her?"

"You can glance at her. I had her sedated. Take a peek and come out. Don't talk to her."

"What about the baby?"

"She's in intensive care. Normal precaution. She's fine." The doctor looked at the worried face of Lucas, and said, "I tell you what. Why don't you go rest in Josette's research area? When I think you can see her, I'll send a nurse to get you."

Lucas thanked him and said, "I appreciate your help. Are you going to sit by her all night?"

"I'll stay as long as I have to until I'm satisfied she is out of the woods."

The doctor took another good look at Lucas and suggested, "You better take some rest. You look like you have gone through a combat mission."

Lucas smiled. "They were a lot less stressful than my last few hours."

ᴄᴙᴐ

He went into the research area. Everyone knew him there, and the staff was aware of their boss's problem. They showed him a bed and he closed his eyes.

At five the next morning, a nurse shook him awake. "Josette is awake and wants to see you. Here's a razor and a comb. You need to look the best you can for her and for your daughter."

Lucas got cleaned up in a jiffy and almost ran to the maternity area.

A nurse was waiting and took him to a private room where Josette had been moved.

She looked tired, her face a little pale, but she gave him a big smile.

"Hi, darling. How is my Josette?" Lucas said, so relieved to see she was okay.

"I'm fine. It has been a bit difficult. It was work, but the team kept at it and bailed me out. I'll be all right. It's over now. Doctor Stanislas stayed with me until an hour ago and declared I am back to normal."

Another nurse came in from the nursery, bringing the little baby girl. The bundle of joy was fast asleep, her eyes firmly closed, her tiny fingers moving at times.

"How beautiful," he exclaimed. He looked at Josette. "You said you would know what name to give her once you saw her, so...?"

"The answer is Claire Lucie. Claire for brightness, and Lucie for Lucas."

"How gorgeous she is. Can I kiss you?"

"Yes, yes. I need that, and I think I will try to nurse our little Claire, then I'll go back to sleep.

Lucas took the baby in his hands, and smiled at her. "She's beautiful like you," he told Josette tenderly. He kissed the little bundle delicately and deposited her in her mother's arms.

The attempt at feeding did not work. The nurse said to Lucas, "We need to have your wife sleep." So Lucas gave Josette a kiss on the forehead. "Rest and get well. I love you." But her eyes were closing. He came out and said to himself, *I guess her name is Claire.* They had narrowed the options to three names: Carmen, Lucie, and Claire. He was happy. He liked Claire and Lucie.

The nurse said, "Call this afternoon. I think you will be able to see her then."

Lucas went home and called the colonel. "Your daughter is fine and the little girl Claire too. I just left them. They're resting now."

"I've been checking on her with the hospital. It took hours. I bet she had a rough time."

"She did, but you know her she's a fighter. The nurses told me to call and ask if I could see her this afternoon. The nurse thought I could. Why don't you call them too?"

"I will. I might see you there."

Josette was discharged after a few days and Baby Claire went home with her. Lucas and Josette started to learn how to be parents. Like all new parents, they were challenged by their new responsibility but full of joy for their little girl. The only bad news was that the doctors told them that Josette could not have any more babies. They would have to confront that issue at a later date.

Chapter 43

Paris

Mid-1964

Lucas had finished his internship with Mr. Laforge and was attending classes at INSAD in Paris. He stayed close to home to keep an eye on Josette's recovery. She was doing fine, but Lucas made sure she felt no stress from the ongoing research. He advised her not to go to any of the hospitals but to stay home, resting and nursing Claire. From her home office, Josette had been monitoring the data gathering on the traumatic effects of combat on soldiers, and work had begun on the trauma suffered by the battered women but it still had a while to go.

Private Vidal had been diagnosed and a treatment had been going on for three months. Josette called him. "Do you feel you can talk to me about how the treatment is going or would you rather not?"

"Madame Josette, I had been meaning to call you, but the lieutenant got word to me not to disturb you. He said you had been through a difficult childbirth. By the way, congratulations on little Claire."

"I appreciate that. How do you feel?"

"It is amazing. I am no longer depressed. I have taken a position as an airline mechanic and I enjoy going to work every day. My anger is under control. I have a couple of weeks to go to conclude the therapy, but I am so thankful to you and to your people. They made me whole again."

"That is great. Make sure to share what you told me with your therapist. It'll be great input for my research."

꒰ꗃꗂ

Toward the end of the summer, fully recovered from the birth of her daughter, Josette and the heads of the trauma departments in Maligny, Val de Grace, and Necker spent a week reviewing the findings and recommendations from all the teams. The last day of that week, they analyzed what they knew and wanted to investigate further.

Josette summarized their findings.

"First, there are many similarities on the behavior resulting from trauma on children and on combat soldiers. That seems to validate Lucas's idea that there should be a single trauma focus with subcategories. But there are also differences.

"The emotional effects of trauma, whichever the source of it is, and whoever the patients are, seem to fall into a few categories, however many sub-categories there might be. They include anger, depression, guilt, and fear. Whether the patients are battered women, as far as we have been able to determine so far, wounded veterans, or traumatized children, the manifestations of the uncontrolled emotions are usually only two, at most three, for any patient. For the soldiers, it seems that the main traumas are: first, anger, with maybe hatred as an extreme facet of anger; second, depression which is sometimes tied to guilt; for the children, the main element is fear, the second is depression. It's too early to tell for the battered women, but it seems that although fear is definitely the dominant reaction, guilt amazingly appears to be sometimes part of the problem. Like most traumas, depression is strongly present.

"These main categories of trauma cause many different reactions that depend on the patient's state of mind at the time of the incident, at the time of the treatment, and on the age and social circumstances of the person being treated."

သာ

Her lieutenants agreed with the summary. Doctor Stanislas stated, "Depression is often part of the problem although, as you suggested, not all the time. But when present, it is the most dangerous because it is the one that might lead the patients, mainly the veterans, to take their own lives."

Doctor Stanislas added, "Mitigation for depression through medication has to entail a separate study. First, I doubt that any medication will be part of a treatment for children, except in rare cases, and I suspect that the medication requirements for battered women and veteran combat soldiers will be similar."

"I agree," Josette replied.

Josette concluded, "Let's take the next six months to refine these findings, then we'll document our data and write a report for the Journal of Medicine. The next phase of the study will have a solid foundation. The focus will switch to how to mitigate the different categories and sub-categories of trauma and patient's reactions. Because of what Doctor Stanislas pointed out, depression has to be at the top of our concern."

The schedule was designed so that a rigorous scientific approach to collecting and analyzing data would allow Josette to present her findings to her peers around the world and publish the detailed results of her research.

Chapter 44

Paris

Fall 1964

The countess and the general had been busy talking and consulting with the military and civilian leaders. In October 1964, they thought that some parallel work to Josette's research needed to be started immediately. When Lucas and Josette entered the parlor in the countess' residence, they found Madame de Sèvres talking with General de Vangarde and Colonel Benoit.

"What's your view of the Maligny center, Colonel?" The general asked.

The colonel had talked to the management team and came out of his review with questions about the long-term viability of the rehabilitation center.

"I see it as well organized, and functioning efficiently, but I doubt very much it can be financially justified anymore. Too few veterans seem to require that level of physical care and help, but that's the good news."

"What do you suggest we do?" The countess asked.

"I believe it will always be the best facility for those who need physical rehabilitation but we need to widen its target with patients beyond the military personnel if we want to keep it running. Also it is too remote and isolated for psychological trauma treatments which mostly last a couple of hours once or twice a week. But it is Madame la Comtesse's property, so I will defer to her."

Madame de Sèvres nodded. "Do you have any idea who the new patients could be, Colonel?"

"They could be victims of accidents who lost limbs, fingers, etc. and need to learn how to live with their new prostheses."

"In that case why should the military be in charge of running the facility?"

"They should not. I also believe that in addition to civilians hurt in accidents, some battered women could find safety and peace in this wonderful place, a haven as well as a rehab center. How would you feel about such a change? It is your place, Madame."

"It seems that the ministry of health should be interested in purchasing the well-outfitted place. A haven as, you call it." Madame de Sèvres said.

"If you accept the idea, I will investigate that possibility," the colonel said.

"Do you think we still need a trauma treatment center, but in a more suitable location?" the general asked Josette.

She replied, "Such a facility is needed and should be located in a city easy to travel to, and close to nature preserves to allow for a combination of psychological or psychiatric treatments with hikes in Mother Nature's domain, brain-slowing activities which are not central to the recovery of the patients, but can play a significant role in their healing."

"Should this new center be a military facility?"

The general answered, "I would suggest it be a trauma-focused private hospital or institution, one that Josette would run."

The countess stirred. "What I want you to do, Colonel, is to negotiate with the Ministry of Health and have them purchase the Maligny facility and research a suitable facility that we can acquire and equip to be a trauma research and treatment center."

"But the manor belongs in your family."

"It was in my husband's family. It is now mine, and I never had a warm feeling for it, so don't worry about that. Just sell it, and research a location for the new center."

The countess asked the general to talk about the studies he had been suggesting to her.

"The main asset we own is the research. I recommend," the general suggested, "to let Josette run her work which will refine itself as she progresses in her findings, and to begin two studies: first, to develop our ability to hire and train an expanded medical staff, and second, to acquire physical facilities that include the center the colonel has been charged to find and a training facility. That special school will educate doctors and therapists in trauma methodologies for our own center, and for trauma departments in hospitals in France and abroad."

Josette added, "As the scope is meant to be international, we need technical information exchange between teams from other countries, and consistent training protocols for trauma specialists wherever they are."

"So where do we go from here?" Lucas asked.

The countess took over. "I'd like to ask you, Colonel Benoit, to supervise the study on all the facilities."

Josette stepped in. "One of the judges on my certification day was a doctor from a hospital in Aix-en-Provence. I don't recall his name but we can find it. He was obviously interested in trauma but shared with me that his hospital did not see much activity. Maybe that should be on the list of the facilities to be considered."

Colonel Benoit said, "I'll look at it, thank you, Josette."

The countess continued, "Should Captain Dufour — I'm sorry, I mean Alain Dufour — run the study on training?"

The general nodded. "Absolutely, and this study will require training facilities and housing for the students. The captain will assist the colonel in his search because the trauma center and the training buildings should be within a short distance from one another."

They all concurred. The countess concluded the meeting by saying, "We will reconvene as soon as we have decisions to make on acquisitions of the potential facilities and on the hiring protocols for specialized doctors and therapists."

The colonel suggested, "Someone has to figure out how to work the financing."

"Let me worry about that," the countess replied. "Colonel, if I can sell Maligny, I can buy that private hospital or institution we need."

"That makes my search a lot easier."

"Fine," the countess concluded. "Those two studies have been commissioned so let's check hopefully in a couple of months for a checkpoint."

"I feel good about our progress," Lucas stated.

The general nodded. "There is a lot to do. Don't misunderstand me. I think this is a great idea with an incredible potential to save lives or at least make it better for many people worldwide. I just know we can't stumble out of the starting gate. We have to do it right."

"What time frame are we thinking of as far as launching the business?" Lucas asked.

"It's too early to put a firm date now, but let me say that the first half of 1966 should be the time frame to aim for," the general said.

Everyone agreed.

Chapter 45

Aix-en-Provence, near Avignon

November 1964

Alain Dufour and Colonel Benoit set out to go inspect the Aix-en-Provence hospital that Josette suggested might be in need of a new direction. They were met at the train station by the doctor who had been part of Josette's certification panel.

"I am Doctor Poisat. Welcome to both of you. I am so thankful to Josette Benoit for recommending your visiting my hospital."

The colonel introduced both the captain and himself and chuckled. "Josette is my daughter, so I appreciate the compliment."

Doctor Poisat proceeded to brief them on the status of the hospital on the drive from the station.

"Our financial situation is not good. We used to treat tuberculosis patients. Now that the disease has seriously abated, we have no specialty and there are several hospitals near ours which are more convenient for most patients. We have vast, beautiful grounds, close to the pre-Alps and Mount Ventoux. This was great for sanatorium residents, but it is of little interest to our current visitors and residents. I believe the trauma center will benefit from the peacefulness and the proximity of the wilderness. So the hospital management team, which includes me, is ready to explore a new mission that might revitalize the complex. I must add that I am personally interested in trauma treatment as you know."

"You need to understand," the colonel said, "that if we find the location suitable and the building adequate, we would expect to acquire ownership of it. Its mission would be to become the French national trauma center as you might have guessed."

"That would be perfectly fine with me. We have a strong staff of doctors, nurses, and medical technicians; most of them you could keep and retrain."

They reviewed the beautiful grounds and the several buildings which would offer ample room for the ambitious mission that Josette had envisioned. Doctor Poisat also mentioned a hotel that was not far from the hospital and also not faring very well because few patients meant few visitors. Alain Dufour was interested in it because he would have to find a training center not too far away, and he would need housing for its students.

When the visit was over, the doctor drove the colonel back to the station and the captain to a hotel in Avignon. The captain had to explore the area for a potentially suitable training building.

❦

Once settled in his room, Alain thought of calling Tom and Francine to pay them a visit. They were glad to hear from him, and Francine said she'd come and pick him up. When he arrived at the Segal winery, Anna welcomed him and introduced Marie to him.

"She has come from Algeria almost two years ago and now lives with us. She is my friend and she's now in second grade in my school. She is a musician and plays the piano."

"That's wonderful. Hello, Marie. My mother used to be a pianist too. I loved it when she played."

"My teacher is coming any minute for my lesson. You can listen if you want."

Mademoiselle Roger came in shortly afterward and he met her.

"I am Alain Dufour," he smiled.

"I'm Emma Roger. I have been teaching the piano to Marie since she came. She's very gifted. Would you like her to play for you?"

"I'd love that. It would be delightful," he replied with his signature engaging smile.

Marie did well in her playing lesson, and at the end Alain chatted with the teacher, complimenting her student for her skill and beautiful command of the keyboard. As it was close to dinner time, Tom came in and suggested that the captain stay for dinner.

"I don't want to impose on you. I need to get back to Avignon."

"Tell you what. If Emma Roger can, she can stay too and drive you back after the meal. She lives in Avignon."

"That would be perfect. I'd enjoy that," she said.

They had a nice evening and on the way to his hotel, Emma and Alain talked about the sweet, beautiful, and talented little Marie.

"Another orphan from that wretched war. What a shame," he said.

"Yes, but like Anna she is one of the lucky ones. She escaped with her life and found a nice family."

"You're right. They're the lucky ones. I have seen so many orphans who didn't survive or make it out of the country. There were so many who wanted to escape and never got a chance."

"You were in that war?"

"Yes. I ran an infantry company. One of my lieutenants was Lieutenant Lucas, who saved Anna."

He also explained to her what he was looking for in Avignon and she mentioned an old steno school which had some trouble staying afloat.

"Yes, it's on my list. I'll stop there tomorrow. Thank you."

When she left him at his hotel, she told him to look her up if he came back to Avignon.

He spent the day looking at the old school building, and made an appointment to come back the week after to meet with the owner of the school, who owned a few similar schools around the country.

❧

Before he got back to Avignon, he called Emma Roger. "Would you have dinner with me tomorrow night? I'm coming to meet people from that school."

"I'd be delighted. I'll pick you up at your hotel at six if that works. See you tomorrow night, Alain."

Emma had selected a quiet little place overlooking the Rhone River. During the course of the meal, she asked him about his military career.

"In 1938," he explained, "my father, who was a diplomat, was assigned to a post in London. So my mother and I followed him there. That's where we were at the outset of the war, so we had to spend the war in London. When I turned eighteen, I enlisted in the French Army, attached to the Allied forces which were preparing for the liberation of France. I went through the campaign from Normandy to Germany with the second armored division of General Patton's third army. Then I fought in Indochina. The last years of my military career were spent in Algeria, and here I am, retired after a twenty-year career."

"What dedication to your country. It's admirable." Emma was impressed.

"I was also lucky. I only was lightly wounded a couple of times."

"The young man I was engaged to was drafted in the Algerian conflict at the very beginning," Emma told him. "He did not survive two months."

"I'm so sorry to hear that."

"What are you going to do now that you are discharged?"

"I am going to work in that new enterprise dedicated to diagnose and treat psychological traumas coming from accidents, wars, and violence against women and children. I don't know if you have met Josette and Lucas, but they are the driving force, with the help of well-connected people who can generate funding and government support."

"Anna has spoken fondly to me of Josette and mainly of Lieutenant Lucas, who is the one who saved her."

"I know. Lucas worked for me. He was a most courageous soldier who had so much compassion for the children hurt by that war. After his discharge, he dedicated himself to that trauma cause. He and his wife asked me to join them. It's a chance for me to help veterans of combat and children who were victims of war. Josette is the pioneer doctor in this new branch of medicine. The center of the new enterprise will be in Aix-en-Provence and here in Avignon. We plan to launch it mid-1966."

"I may get to see more of you, I hope."

"You certainly will. I loved the way you talk about Marie and how you teach her to play the piano. I'd love to hear you play too."

"We'll arrange that when you come back."

Chapter 46

Paris

January 1965

Both Alain Dufour and the colonel were ready to report their findings to the countess and to General de Vangarde.

Madame de Sèvres opened the meeting. "General de Vangarde and I are quite anxious to hear your recommendations."

Colonel Dubois spoke first. "Let's talk about Maligny first. I would like to confirm my initial recommendation to change the mission of the Maligny facility to a rehabilitation focal point for adults and children who have suffered traumatic physical injuries. The ministry of health is doing a lot of those things today, but in a haphazard fashion which leaves out many who need help. The minister is quite interested in taking advantage of the Maligny facility and its people. I believe he is ready to purchase the property."

"Would they want to manage the facility or own it?" The countess asked.

"They would prefer to own it outright and deal with the agencies that would feed patients to them, including veterans."

"This sounds promising. Now, Colonel Dubois, any recommendation on a trauma-treating facility?"

"Yes, I have been looking for private hospitals easy to access, located in a region which offers nature recreational opportunities. I have looked at Grasse, twenty-five miles from Nice; Chambery, fifty-five miles from Geneva; and Aix-en-Provence twenty miles from Marseille. My recommendation is to purchase a former hospital sanitarium just northwest of Aix-en-Provence. Together with this, Dufour and I are recommending a building south of Avignon which would be the right size to satisfy our training needs. There's also a hotel located between the hospital complex and the training building which could house students and visitors. They're all within a few miles of each other."

"Captain Dufour — I can't stop calling you Captain — do all these facilities meet your needs?" the general asked.

"Yes they do. Actually, you can call me Captain as much as you like, sir. I have been called that for many years. I still respond to that although I'm now a full-time civilian."

"You'll always be Captain to me also," Lucas chuckled.

"Agreed." The countess replied and then addressed the colonel. "I am assuming that you have all the financial data I would need to sell Maligny and buy the Aix-en-Provence and Avignon locations."

"I do."

"Let's you and I discuss the finance transactions as I will be the owner of the trauma center and divest myself of Maligny.

"Does the schedule to take possession and to outfit the buildings fit our needs?" The countess went on. "If I recall our last meeting, we had a tentative target of 1966 for launching the International Trauma Center. Are we still on the same timeline?"

Josette replied, "The research projects will come to their conclusion in a few months, in early 1965. I need a year to validate and finalize the treatment recommendations."

The colonel reported, "We can reasonably hope to get ownership of the Aix-en-Provence hospital by June 1965 and refit it to our needs by early 1966. The Avignon building will be available within six months from today. So we will be able to train our staff in time for a 1966 opening."

"I think we can now proceed with the purchase of the buildings," the countess said. "And Captain Dufour, go ahead with the planning for the training facility."

"I'm ready to start. I'm planning to move to Avignon."

સ્જ

Over many trips, Alain Dufour had gotten to know Emma quite well. Marie, who adored her piano teacher, also loved the red-headed retired captain. After the last meeting with the countess, and the decision to go ahead, he was ready to look for a place to live in or near Avignon. He and Emma got along well together and over the weeks he grew quite fond of her. He hoped his feelings for Emma were echoed by hers. After years of globetrotting carrying a weapon, only thirty-eight, he was ready to settle down and start a family.

He did not think it was time yet to approach Emma on the possibility of a future together, but he decided to enlist her help in his house-hunting trip.

When he called Emma to tell her he was going to be in Avignon the next day, a Friday, she said joyfully, "You'll be here for the Saturday recital at two. My three students will play and I am also planning to share with the audience my love of Camille Saint Saens with his Concerto Number Two."

"I'm delighted. I would not miss it for the world. Can I take you and Marie out for tea and cakes afterward?"

"That would be great."

"Now I have news of my own. The enterprise will be launched next year right in Aix and Avignon. I have to prepare the buildings, so I'm moving to the area."

Emma was pleased, her heart started to beat faster, and she felt her cheeks redden. "I'm happy to be the first one to welcome you here. We need to talk about where you want to live."

"Yes we do. I was going to ask you to help me. You are familiar with the town, and I am not."

"What time do you come in tomorrow?"

"The train is due at four in the afternoon."

"I'll pick you up."

"Great. Thank you. See you then."

✿

At dinner in their favorite restaurant, Alain said to Emma, "I'm excited to start a new chapter in my life, dedicating myself to help victims of traumatic events, and planning to forget my years of military life. But the most heartwarming thing for me is that I'll hopefully get to know you better."

"Alain, since your phone call yesterday, I've been pleased to have you in my town, and looking forward to more time with you."

"We will find out what the future has in store for each of us. The past is only what brought us to today."

The next day, the recital was very successful. Marie was the youngest of the students, but her rendition of the Schubert piece she played was beautiful, full of emotion and technically perfect. Emma played her concerto with brio. Her heart was full of joy, and Alain could hear it in the enthusiasm with which she celebrated the classic masterpiece of Saint Saens. Marie, Emma, and Alain went to an old fashioned tearoom and had tea and sweets. It made Marie happy to learn that Alain was moving to Avignon.

With the innocence of an eight-year-old, she asked Emma, "Are you going to live together?"

Emma laughed, blushed, and said, "We'll have to wait to see what the future will be like."

Surprisingly, Marie jumped of her chair, went to hug both of them. "I love you both."

Chapter 47

Paris

December 1965

The Maligny facility now belonged to the Ministry of Health, and had been expanded to include battered women. The acquisition of the hospital in Aix-en-Provence was final, and the facility and its grounds were ready for the final adjustments necessary to accomplish the new trauma mission.

The construction and renovation required to accommodate the training requirements were close to being ready in the Avignon building. The hotel owners had decided they would retain control of their business and have the trauma center and the training facility as its sole clients. They would manage the reservations and run the hotel as they knew how.

Josette was satisfied with the data collected over the past year, and with the analysis which led to the classifications of the nuances of trauma-driven behaviors that were detected during her research. She decided it was time for her to share her findings with the medical world. She gathered a small team of her close associates to help put the final touches on the voluminous report she was about to publish in the Journal of Medicine to update the world on this important scientific milestone. Josette asked Michelle Raynaud to lead the writing effort.

Lucas was now virtually healed from his post-war issues and had completed his executive training, so Josette asked him to plan an international conference where over two days she would explain her findings to the medical research pioneers she had worked with over the years.

Lucas contacted the doctors who had been Josette's partners in the early days of the trauma awareness, and with his new experience from the INSAD school, established communications with Bethesda Naval Medical Center and Walter Reed Army Medical Center in Washington, D.C., from the Defence Medical Services in the United Kingdom, and from leading medical facilities in The Netherlands, Germany, and Switzerland.

He visited most of the leading hospitals and talked to many doctors, all eager to be brought up to date on Josette's findings. His fluency in English and German smoothed the way to amicable conversations. The enthusiastic response to the call for attending the conference warmed Lucas' heart.

Lucas decided to hold the international conference in the amphitheater of the Paris College of Medicine. Josette and her staff delivered a smashing performance. As a result, the response to a call for doctors and therapists to attend the four-week diagnostic class and the six-week treatment class was overwhelming. Josette had carefully selected the teachers among the specialists who had worked on the research program.

Alain Dufour, Lucas and two of the selected teachers who were fluent in English tailored the material to the English-speaking world. Classes in German were not planned initially. Alain Dufour created a schedule for the first months of 1966 and worked with the hotel management to have the required accommodations ready for the onslaught of students. His years in London had given him fluency in the English language which would enable him to communicate with the foreign students. The United States, now fully involved in the Vietnam War, was particularly interested and busy working on the trauma of their returning soldiers and sent a large contingent of their doctors. Lucas worked with them to facilitate an open exchange of scientific data with the Americans who had large resources to further the knowledge of the medical world with their voluminous data. Their contribution was anticipated to be significant, and their cooperation with Josette's team would further and speed up the research and add to the understanding of the new science.

CHAPTER 48

Aix-en-Provence

May 1966

About four years after Josette's certification in trauma treatment and the meeting that spawned the birth of the National Trauma Program, the countess' and Josette's team scheduled the inauguration of the Aix-en-Provence trauma facility.

The opening promised to be a medical event of large proportion. Innocent victims of harrowing events around the world were going to have a second chance at life. Doctors and medical science leaders from several countries crowded in the auditorium of the Anna Segal pavilion of the French National Trauma Center. The mood was electric.

∾

The French minister of health opened the ceremony by thanking the countess for her leadership of the enterprise. He continued by praising Josette's pioneering research and her published report to the medical world. He concluded his remarks by pledging the French government's support to the medical enterprise launched today.

∾

Madame de Sèvres thanked the minister and all the doctors and therapists who participated in the four-year research which led to a leap in medical science. She praised the soldiers who were the first to undergo the experimental diagnostic protocols and treatment. She thanked her team of General de Vangarde, Colonel Dubois, Alain Dufour, and Lucas, who managed the design and crafted the planning of all the elements of the new enterprise.

She had special praise for the dedication, energy, and leadership of

Josette, who single-handedly started her trauma research work about six years ago.

Then, she introduced Lucas. "You will now hear from former Lieutenant Lucas, who led his infantry platoon gallantly in the Algerian war, only to return home traumatized. Lucas was the one who conceived of the idea of this long overdue assault on the dirge of trauma and worked hard to bring it to life. He happens to also be the first success story of the trauma work that his wife Josette ran brilliantly and expertly."

ல்

Lucas got up and smiled at the audience and at the other speakers. "Today is a milestone in the science of medicine. Today is a new dawn for every doctor, therapist, nurse, and orderly who will work in this center and in trauma teams around the world. It is a new dawn for the people around the world who were psychologically hurt through no fault of their own. Today is a new dawn for my wife Josette and for me who can now dedicate our lives to heal children and soldiers who need help.

"What you need to know is that in North Africa, the main reason I kept my sanity and survived the stress of combat and the ferocity of the war was the inspiration and guidance I received from someone special. That someone managed by herself to mitigate the malicious effects of traumatic events on herself while she fought threat and prejudice, and dealt with her own terror. She made me believe that trauma could be healed. That also helped me convince the leaders of this new enterprise to expand my wife's research in pediatric trauma to that of soldiers and battered women. Most of you saw the name of Anna Segal on the façade of this beautiful pavilion and probably asked yourself who that was.

"Anna Segal is my inspiration and my guiding light, as she is to everyone she has touched in her young life."

Lucas told the audience about taking her out from the Algerian village of El Boussaid where she had become an orphan, isolated and ostracized by the local villagers, and how he brought her to Ahmed's farm.

"I had to admire the spirit and determination which allowed this young girl to survive the next difficult years. Witnessing her determination helped me in my own daily personal challenges of running an infantry platoon in a merciless war. She controlled her destiny. She escaped the dangers of the last months of the war, and minimized the impact of the war on her psyche. I learned from her example.

"She came to Beaumes de Venise with Tom and Francine Segal, who have now adopted her. In her new life, although having been deeply traumatized, Anna erased the dark images of her life in Algeria. She not only healed herself but started to heal others, working to help children who had escaped Algeria like she did.

"Going through my own trauma treatment proved to be difficult for me and at times stressful. The thought of Anna carried me through my struggle with my painful memories.

"She is only twelve years old. Here's Anna Segal."

⟊

Anna got to the microphone, which had to be lowered. She smiled at the audience. "I wrote you a message. I will read it to you." Then with a firm voice, the young girl read what she had written on a piece of paper:

"Lucas said I was the inspiration that led him to help create this direly needed enterprise."

She looked at him, then at the audience. "Lucas is a lot more than that to me. He's my savior, my protector, my hero, the man without whom I would never have survived, never come to France and never become part of a loving family.

"When the villagers who killed my father, and then a few months later my mother, were intent on doing me harm, I took refuge in a barn. The friendly goats who lived there did not say no to me when I went to hide in the straw inside their barn. On the contrary they kept me safe and warm.

"When Lieutenant Lucas got me out of the village, Ahmed's wife Basira did not say no when he asked her to take me into their family to live with them and their daughter Aisha. Tom and Francine opened their arms to me and took me into their house when the bad men in the village shot Ahmed and his wife. Furthermore they took me to France at the time the Algerian insurgents threatened all of us, and then they became my mother and father.

"Most people in this room today have gotten together to create a world where good people refuse to say no to children, to soldiers, to battered women who need help. They are the doctors, therapists, and nurses who will dedicate their lives to heal trauma.

"I believe that my friend, Doctor Eric Tallec, an orphan like me, saved by sheep, not by goats, like I was, and Josette's sister Caroline will adopt Pascal and Vivienne, the twins who lost both their parents in an avalanche. Marie, who was rescued in Arzew when her parents were shot to death, is now a happy child living in my family, and is a talented musician."

Anna let go of her paper, looked at Lucas and said. "Indeed this is a new dawn, Lucas, thanks to you and to the leaders of this new healing center."

Anna turned to Josette. "Lastly, Josette, thank you for having created a team ready to address all the traumas you have researched, a team that will change the lives of many." She smiled at Josette. "I trust that adoption is included in your treatments. If it were not, may I suggest that you consider adding it to your list. It works well for orphans. I know."

Anna bowed at Josette and went to sit down. The room exploded with applause.

❧

That evening, in their new home overlooking the slopes of Mount Ventoux, Josette told Lucas, "You said to me a long time ago that you wanted to have three children, and I agreed. Today Anna became my guiding light, like she did for you many years ago. I can't give birth anymore, but now I know there are two little children who need us somewhere in the world. We will find them. With Claire, they will complete our family. You and Anna inspired me. This is our new dawn."

Y.M. Masson

About the Author

As a young boy Y.M. Masson (Yves) struggled through four years of hardship under German occupation of Paris until he was liberated by the American Third Army. Twenty years later, after having served in the French army in North Africa during the French-Algerian war, he left France for New York City and became a United States citizen in the early seventies. After working as a marketing executive in corporate America, and then running his own consulting business, Yves turned to the arts. He is an accomplished portrait artist, and loves to share his life experiences with his readers. He knows what war does to people and especially to children. His ability to describe their daily fears, their devastating hunger, and the despair of deprivation draws his audience into their conflict.

When Paris Was Dark won third place in the Royal Palm Literary Awards from the Florida Writers Association 2018 competition. *The War Inside His Mind* won second place in the Royal Palm Literary Awards from the Florida Writers Association 2020 competition.

Other titles by Y.M. Masson:
When Paris Was Dark, ISBN 978-1-946886-09-5.
The War Inside His Mind, ISBN: 978-1-946886-13-2
Never Give Up, ISBN: 978-1-946886-14-9

Visit his website: https://www.ymmassonauthor.com

Made in the USA
Monee, IL
18 September 2021